Praise for Jim Crace's

THE PESTHOUSE

"Forceful. . . . [Crace's] prose carries the contours of a Donatello sculpture as [he] chisels gracefully flowing sentences with eloquence, precision, and the occasional cheeky hint of the impish."
—*San Francisco Chronicle*

"A dark envisioning. . . . The best part of this novel, perhaps for [its characters] as well as us, is the hauntingly rendered depiction of what is already gone."
—*The Boston Globe*

"Sly. . . . A sweet, screwball love story. . . . Crace lavishes his story with descriptions of nature and creates landscapes in crystalline detail."
—*The Plain Dealer*

"Subtly conveyed. . . . Crace manages to strike the right chord with clarity and precision."
—*London Review of Books*

"Refreshing in its scope and ambition. . . . A compelling adventure."
—*The Free Lance-Star* (Fredericksburg)

"Wonderful. . . . Crace is a writer of great gifts. . . . The poet of detail."
—*The Guardian* (London)

"Deft. . . . Crace's imagination is matched by his crystalline prose."
—*The Post and Courier* (Charleston)

JIM CRACE

THE PESTHOUSE

Jim Crace is the author of eight previous novels. *Being Dead* was shortlisted for the Whitbread Prize and won the prestigious National Book Critics Circle Award for Fiction in 2000. In 1997, *Quarantine* was named the Whitbread Novel of the Year and was shortlisted for the Booker Prize. Crace has also received the Whitbread First Novel Award, the E. M. Forster Award, and the Guardian Award. He lives in Birmingham, England.

www.jim-crace.com

the
pesthouse

the
pesthouse

A NOVEL

jim crace

Vintage Books
A Division of Random House, Inc.
New York

The Library of Congress has cataloged the Nan A. Talese edition as follows:
Crace, Jim.
The pesthouse / Jim Crace.—1st ed.
p. cm.
I. Title.
PR6053.R228P47 2007
823'.914—dc22 2006026555

Vintage ISBN: 978-0-307-27895-1

Book design by Caroline Cunningham
Title page photo courtesy of Caroline Cunningham

www.vintagebooks.com

Printed in the United States of America
10 9 8 7 6 5 4 3 2 1

For Tom and Lauren

the
pesthouse

Everybody died at night. Most were sleeping at the time, the lucky ones who were too tired or drunk or deaf or wrapped too tightly in their spreads to hear the hillside, destabilized by rain, collapse and slip beneath the waters of the lake. So these sleepers (six or seven hundred, at a guess; no one ever came to count or claim the dead) breathed their last in passive company, unwarned and unexpectedly, without any fear. Their final moments, dormant in America.

But there are always some awake in the small times of the morning—the lovemakers, for instance, the night workers, the ones with stone-hard beds or aching backs, the ones with nagging consciences or bladders, the sick. And animals, of course.

The first of that community to die were the horses and the mules, which the travelers had picketed and blanketed against the cold out in the tetherings, between the houses and the lake and beyond the human safety of stockades. They must have heard the landslide— they were so close and unprotected—though it was not especially bulky, not bulky enough, probably, to cause much damage on its own. In the time that it would take to draw a breath and yawn, there was a muted stony splash accompanied by a barometric pop, a lesser set of sounds than thunder but low and devious nevertheless, and worrying—for how could anyone not know by now how mischievous the world could be? The older horses, connoisseurs of one-night stands when everything was devious and worrying, were too weary after yet another day of heading dawnways, shifting carts, freight, and passengers, to do much more than tic their ears and flare their nostrils. Even when, a moment later, the displaced waters of the lake produced a sloshing set of boisterous waves where there had not been any waves before, the full-growns would not raise their heads. But the younger horses and the ever-childish mules tugged against their ropes, and one or two even broke free but hadn't the foresight to seek high ground in the brief time that remained.

What happened next was almost silent. The landslip had hit the deepest side of the lake and therefore took some moments to reach the bottom, ten man heights from the surface, and then it took some moments more for the avalanche of stone, earth, swarf, and ancient buried scrap to show how heavy it was and squeeze the life out of the gas-rich sediments, the volatile silt and compacted weeds, the soda pockets, which had settled on the bed through centuries and were now ready—almost eager—for this catalyst. Shaken up and shaken out in one great flatulence, the water fizzed and belched until all the gases were discharged, to form a heavy, deadly, surface-hugging cloud, not as high as the pines but higher, certainly, than animals. There wasn't any wind that night to thin the suffocating vapors and there was no longer any rain to wash the poison from the air, but there was gravity to direct them down, beyond the rapids and cascades, along the valley, past the tetherings, past the secret wooden bridge, past the metal fields, past the stone footings of the onetime shoe factory and tanning works, to seep between the palings of the pine stockades and settle on the town at the river's crossing point, where almost everyone was sleeping and dreaming of the ruined, rusty way ahead and all the paradise beyond.

Too near the lake and not sleeping was the boy called Nash, whose job that night was to protect the animals from cougars, wolves, or thieves—or bush fish such as rattlers, possibly—though there'd be nothing he could do but shout and draw attention to himself if any of these many perils did approach the tetherings. He'd been too cold and wet even to doze, but not as cold and wet as usual. He huddled over his stove stones—which, following the midnight downpour, produced more smoke than heat—in his new and somehow terrifying coat. He'd traded for it only that day (with a man half his height again and three times his weight), giving a good supply of dried fruit, some pork twists, and a leather water bag, hardly distinguishable from one another in taste or texture, and a flagon of apple juice that the giant, like a giant, had dispatched on the spot. So when the boy heard the landslip and the waves and stood to hear them better should they come again, his coat spread out around him on the ground like chieftain robes intended for display but—at least for anybody as short as he was—not ideal for walking.

Now Nash spotted the two loose mules and hurried out into the night to picket them again. He was not surprised when the coat snagged around his ankles and feet and brought him down. The coat had already toppled him several times that night. He didn't hurt himself—boys bounce—but he felt more winded than made sense, more dislocated than he should, and stayed on the ground for a few moments to catch his breath and find his balance. His coat of farmgoat skins and hair was as good as a bed and thick enough to keep the moisture out for a while. He'd have to shorten it, he thought. He'd have to cut off half a goat and turn the trimmings into belts or gloves, turn the trimmings into profit, actually. When he had time.

But for the moment, unaccountably, he was too comfortable to move. He had no time or energy for anything, not even sleep. He lost himself in the hairs and skins, forgot the nighttime and the mud. He did feel sleepy, finally, but not alarmed. Too lost to be alarmed. The air was weighty, and its smell was stupefying, somewhere between

the smell of mushrooms, eggs, and rotting, clamped potatoes. He'd
stand up in a moment, shuck off his dreams of belts and gloves,
remove the coat, and catch the mules. He'd be in trouble otherwise.
A mule was wealth. But though his dreams soon ended, he never
caught his breath and never caught the mules and never found out
what had happened at the lake. This wasn't sleep oppressing him. He
dimly recognized as much himself. He was the victim of magic, possibly, or fever—there was already fever in the town, he had heard—
or a curse, the sort that storytellers knew about, or else some dead air
from the grave, encouraged by the rain, had come to press its clammy
lips on his. He'd tasted it. His lungs were rigid suddenly. He was in
the gripping custody of hair and skins. He'd been a fool to trust a giant. It must have seemed the coat had always meant to smother him,
was trained to kill. This was a homing coat that now would flee, as
loyal and cunning as a dog, to rejoin the tall man who had traded it
and no doubt would trade it many times again, exchanging death for
apple juice.

Down in Ferrytown, not sleeping either, were two passengers
from ten days west, a beauty boy—no beard, not twenty yet—and his
slightly older wife. They'd found a berth in the loft of the dormitory,
against the guesthouse rules that naturally put the women behind
locked doors in different quarters from the men, but two-a-bed nevertheless. It was less comfy and colder than those first-floor beds
where his parents and his sisters were, but more private and consoling. These newlyweds didn't have to share their air with anyone. No
wonder they'd been making love, as usual. Moving on each day and
spending every night in some new space was oddly stimulating,
they'd found, as was having sex as quietly as they could in sleeping
company, against the rules. But now that lovemaking was concluded,
they were quarreling in whispers, despite the likelihood that everything they said could be heard by strangers. The consolations of lovemaking don't last long when you are fearful, regardless of the massive
hope beyond the fears. How many days would it be before they

reached the ocean and the ships? The beauty boy thought one more month. He'd not pretend that things were better than they were. The far side of the river was an odd, perplexing place, he'd heard, haunted, wrecked, and hard underfoot, with prairies of rubble where people had once lived in bastions and towers. The way ahead would be difficult beyond imagining. His wife did not believe such stories. She was uncompromisingly optimistic, hopeful beyond reason. The rain that night had been saltier than she'd expected. When the rain tastes like tears, the sea is close. She'd seen a white bird ("That's a sign"), and she'd heard another passenger say they'd reach the shore, the mighty river with one bank, in just three more days. Then the future could begin. So much for rubble, bastions, and towers. Her husband was too easily impressed. She drifted off to thoughts of boarding ship in three days' time, and no more quarreling . . .

Not sleeping and on the verge of calling out for the busy couple in the loft to keep quiet was a woman who had strained her back. She'd been too eager earlier in the day to help her horse negotiate the steep descent into the valley and had fallen awkwardly. She sat up in her cot and flexed her spine, hoping not to wake the woman at her side. The pain shot down the outside of her left leg and cramped her toes. She crossed her fingers, willing it to go, and in a while the pain disappeared . . .

Not sleeping was the ferryman, who, having heard the rain, knew that he would have to drag himself from bed too soon, call his four sons, and go down to the crossing to fasten the raft more securely and farther in to the shore before the water surge. Not sleeping were the baker and his daughter, who had just got up to start preparing flatbread, ash cake, and pea loaf for the morning, enough dough and cornmeal for at least one hundred and sixty passengers, who'd need to eat before they were ferried on the raft to the east bank of the river and yet another day of lugging to the coast . . .

Not sleeping was a woman who had been alarmed by travel and by travelers—all her life—and was not much liked by anyone she met, but who had been much more terrified of staying put where she was born while all her family and neighbors emigrated east, fired up by boredom, hope, and poverty. Now she was sick from too much way-side grain and drinking sullied water for more than a month. She'd rather breathe her last than gag anymore, she'd told her husband: "I should have stayed at home." He'd said, "You should have." She pulled her knees up to her chest and tried to belch the colic out . . .

Not sleeping was a tall man from the plains—not quite a giant, except to boys—who had to go out, barefooted, in the cold to the town palisade for the second time that night to urinate. He would have worn his goatskin coat if he'd not traded it that day. He was standing with his trousers down and pissing apple juice when what had come out of the lake with such a show just moments previously arrived without a sound and almost without a shape to overwhelm whomever it could find, the wakeful and the slumbering.

This used to be America, this river crossing in the ten-month stretch of land, this sea-to-sea. It used to be the safest place on earth.

❧ ONE ❧

Franklin Lopez had not been sleeping in Ferrytown, though he'd wanted to. He'd not been sleeping anywhere, in fact. Couldn't sleep. He'd weathered such pain the day before that he'd been forced to consider what anyone (other than his brother) who'd seen the wincing recoil in his limp or examined his inflamed leg had already told him, that he shouldn't walk another step. Certainly he shouldn't walk downhill on such a long and hazardous gradient, unless he wanted to damage his knee beyond repair and put paid to any hopes of getting to the coast and boarding ship before the worst of the fall storms. He and his brother, Jackson (named for their parents' small hometown on the plains), had left the journey rather late as it was. Too late, perhaps. The prairie tall-grass had already whitened and buckled. Apart from nuts and mushrooms, there was little free food to be gathered at the trackside. The first rains had arrived, and soon the winds and snow would get to work. Traveling would become more hazardous and then impossible. Only the ill-prepared, the ill-fated, and the ill-timed were still strung out thinly along the previously busy route,

hoping to make the final sailings before ice and squalls shut down the
sea, and anyway made shore-to-ship or ship-to-shore impossible. The
wayside going east was already littered with the melancholy camps
and the shallow graves—soon to be torn up by wolves—of those
whose bodies couldn't take the journey, those who had been fatally
chilled by wading through rivers, those who had starved and weakened, those who had been thrown by their horses or poisoned by their
suppers, those who had been crushed between the fears of going forward and the dread of going back.

Feet failed first; nothing could prepare the feet for this. Then the
stomach gave way, soured by ditch and pond water and the usual
makeshift meals of hardtack, jerked meat, pine nuts, and scrapple—
and, in the brothers' case on one occasion, a stew made from a hand-
caught rabbit too diseased to run away, with nettle tops as greens.
And if the stomach survived that, then the less sturdy travelers were
betrayed by bones and joints, starting at their knees and working upward, pain on pain, through hips, up spine, and into the shoulders
and the neck until there was nothing left to sour, fail, or be betrayed
except the soft pith of the head. Once summer turned and limped
away, its sack crammed full of leaves, the route was challenging.
Within a month, the weather would have mugged the final stragglers
and the roads and ways would be empty again, untrodden till spring.

So Franklin understood that he could not readily afford to waste
much time nursing such a slight injury. But neither could he afford
the purchase of a horse or passage on a wagon where he could rest his
leg. What should he do, then? Cut a stick and limp down to the
coast? "Just put up with the pain," as Jackson advised? Carry on regardless, let nature take its course? He'd tried the stick, the putting
up with pain; he'd trusted nature's course. His knee got worse. So finally he conceded. He'd have to find shelter and stay exactly where
he was, high in the ridges, to sit out the swelling. It was an exasper-
ating setback and something that he was slow to tell his brother. But
what other choice was there? His knee was too bloated to bend and

too painful to take any weight. The flesh between his ankle and his thigh was sausaging with every step he took. The skin was stretched and cloudy. One more afternoon of walking could lame him for a month. A day or two of rest might rescue him. Besides, this injury was not a failure that he should feel ashamed of, no matter what the stiff expression on his brother's face seemed to suggest. He'd done better than some to get so far—more than sixty testing days of walking from the battered, weather-poisoned village of his birth—without much damage beyond the usual aches and pains, the usual broken skin, and this damned knee, he told himself. He'd be a fool to take any chances now if he wanted to enjoy the undulating rewards of the sailboat deck, and then to put ashore this year in the other place, whatever that might be, with his pith intact enough to make a good start.

"It'd be crazy to take the risk, Jacko," he told his brother at last, coloring with self-consciousness as he spoke. He was still prone to being seized by sudden, girlish reddeners whenever he least wanted it.

"Only the crazy make it to the coast" was the older man's reply. Yes, that was the wisdom of the road: you had to be crazy enough to take the risks, because the risks were unavoidable. "Well, then, Franklin Lopez? You say."

"I've said."

"So say it again."

"Well, do what you want, if you're the crazy one. I'm staying here till it's good enough, my knee."

"How long's 'till'?"

"Three days, four days, I guess."

"I guess a month!"

Franklin knew better than to argue with his volcanic brother. He did not even shake his head. He watched Jackson mull over their problem for a few moments more, his eyes half closed, his lips moving, his fingers counting days. "That knee'll snare us here a month—if not a month, then half a month. Too long," Jackson added finally.

"By then the winter'll be on us like a pack of wolves. You hear me,
little brother?" Little brother? Less in everything. "You sit down
now, then that's the end of it. We're carrion."

This was their final argument, the last of many, with Franklin daring to protest that his "crazy" brother should press on to the coast
without him (but not meaning it—who'd want to be abandoned to
the winter and the woods, to be buried, along with the trail, beneath
layers of mud, leaves, and snow, even if it meant a few days free of
bullying and censure?) and Jackson insisting that he'd stick by his infuriating, timid, blushing sibling till the last if he really had to (but
resenting Franklin's physical weakness, his infuriating, girlish laugh
that seemed to buckle his whole body, his dreaminess, his hypochon-
dria, and saying so repeatedly—"That bitching knee's not half as bad
as you make out," and "Where'd we be if every time you got a touch
of charley horse you wanted three days' rest?"—until Franklin said,
"Ma's hearing every word you speak").

    The brothers should not have taken their ma's advice two months
before when they'd "embarked" so late in the season of migration.
"Carry nothing with you," she'd said, "then no one will pay you any
heed. And you can hurry on." So they had left the plains equipped with
just their boots, their knives, a double set of clothes rainproofed with
deer fat, a spark stone and some tinder in a pouch, a water bag and a
back sack each, full of nothing-worth-stealing or so they thought:
some cheese, dried fruit, salted pork, and a couple of ground tarps.

    To some extent their mother had been correct. They had moved
fast and no one had bothered them yet, while others among the emigrants who'd been rash enough to travel in the company of carts
and animals or had packed a year's supply of food and their prize possessions—best pots, jewelry, good cloth, good tools—paid a price
for their comfort. The more they had, the more cruelly they were
robbed, not by the other travelers but by the ones who wouldn't em-

igrate until they'd picked the carcass of America clean. But possibly two men like them—young, strong, and imposingly tall—would not be robbed even if they were walking naked with shards of polished silver in their beards. Jackson and Franklin Lopez, together, looked too capable of taking care of themselves to invite the attentions of thieves. And this had made them much valued as companions by other travelers, especially as their extra strength would always be prized by any wagoner, for example, who faced a hill or mud and would recompense them with a meal if only they would be his heavy horses for the afternoon.

No, Ma was right, wagons were slow and cumbersome. They might not have stomachs, feet, and knees to let their owners down, but their axles snapped if stressed too much and they were unsteady on gradients and hesitant at fords, with good reason. Rivers loved to test the strength of vehicles. A river's always pleased to have the opportunity to dismantle a wagon, to tear it into planks and carry it away in bits, together with its wagoner. Horses were less hesitant. They were fast and muscular. They didn't refuse the rivers or the gradients so long as there were sticks and sugar lumps to urge them on, but they were flesh and bones and prone to injury and sickness. Just like men and women. But just like men and women, horses' running costs were high, for oats and hay, board and lodging, tolls and tack.

Pack mules were the toughest of the lot. And cheap. More so than hinnies. A bucket of cottonwood bark or thistle and bitter water every night was all they needed. "If a rabbit can pass, a mule will pass," the mulemen boasted. But mules were stubborn, too. Both placid and stubborn. You could twitch the ropes in their lip rings or tug on their jerk lines until they bled, but still they wouldn't move unless it suited them. They had the patience to resist forever. The brothers had been wise, so far, to travel without animals or wheels.

But now, with their few possessions laid out around them at the top of the descent and the first indications that the coming night would be a wet and cold one, the brothers—Franklin especially—regretted that they had not equipped themselves better for such foreseeable emergencies. There were no cooking pots, they had no camping supplies, and except for a few scraps the store of food had been finished a month before. Their ma—she was far too old and metally at fifty-four, she'd said, to join them on their journey, too fat to go that far—was at that very moment most likely sitting on her stoop, rubbing her veins, and looking out across the now abandoned steads at the family cart and the three old roans for which she had no use. If Jackson and Franklin had only traveled with those horses and the cart, her sons would be at the river crossing by now and Franklin would not be limping. Or at least they'd have some warmth and free shelter for the night, up on the rapidly cooling hillside. But they had never been the sort to disoblige their ma. Big but biddable, they were, for her. Big and unprepared for what the world could do to them.

Now the brothers had to face the prospect of some nights apart—the very thing that Ma had said should not occur—while Jackson went ahead to sell his labor for a day or two and obtain some food. He'd leave his brother with their knives, the leaking water bag, the spark stone, the pair of tarps, their change of clothes, and make do trading with his strength and overcoat. That heavy, much-loved overcoat that his mother had stitched together from four farm goats would have to go, despite the colder days ahead. It was the one thing the brothers had that, though it had not quite been admired, had certainly been noticed by strangers. Being noticed might prove to be a handicap as they got closer to the lawless coast. So trading on the goats would be advisable. With any luck, Jackson would soon return with provisions and possibly the part share of an onward-going horse, or at least the purchase of a cart ride among the women, the children, and the old for his unmanly brother. Once in Ferrytown, if the worse came to the worst, they could pass the winter in relative safety. For the time being, though, Franklin would have an uncomfortable few nights on the mountainside; Jackson would have a proper bed. The best that Franklin could hope for was a mattress of pinecones.

Franklin might not be on his own entirely. Already he could hear the chirring of insects, the whistle of quails, and the barking of deer. And there was a boulder hut—evidently occupied, though possibly by lunatics or bandits, Jackson warned, amused to alarm his brother— on the edge of the tree line a hundred paces off, where a large but un- maintained bald had been burned clear by hunters. There was no movement from within, so far as they could tell, just smoke. "Keep your distance. That's best."

And Franklin would not be entirely out of touch with his brother and their shared hopes. Despite the pain in his knee, he had suc- ceeded in reaching the final woody swaggings in the sash of hills where there were almost uninterrupted views to the east. His hopes of getting free from America could be kept alive by a distant prospect of the lake, the town, and the longed-for river crossing, after which, they'd been told, the going was less hilly, though punishing in more unusual ways.

It was late afternoon when his elder, tougher, taller brother shook his hand and set off down the track, promising to come back to the swaggings within three days. The dusk was already pushing daylight back into the sun. Jackson would barely reach Ferrytown before dark. But he was fit and well, not injured yet, and unlike all the trav- elers still on the descent with their carts and sledges, their mules and wheelbarrows, he was unencumbered by anything other than his coat. Unlike the mule trains, with their whistle-nagging masters, and the packhorses, with their bridle bells foretelling all the merriments ahead, he descended silently down the twists of Butter Hill, as it was known locally. (A hill so tortuous and uneven, they claimed, that any milk carried up or down it would be jolted and churned into butter.) You could not miss him, though, even in that gloaming. He was so much taller than the rest and hurrying like a man who was counting on a hot supper, and walking even taller than himself, actually, cat-like and stretched (while Franklin walked shrinkingly, his shoulders bunched). The pinto patterns of the goatskins marked him out as someone of account, the sort of man who should be welcome and respected anywhere he went.

Franklin had not dared say so to his brother, but he was more than nervous of the nights ahead. It was not so much the unlikely prospects on such a busy route of cougars, bears, and snakes or the more certain prospect (on such a busy route) of human parasites that bothered him. Although he might not be as imposing as his brother—he was much lighter, easier in his skin, and so less dangerous—he was still big and strong enough to take good care of himself should he have no choice, even with Jackson by now far beyond his call. He had two knives. And there were rocks and branches with which to defend himself if any creature, beast or man, were ill-advised enough to take him on. But he was uneasy nevertheless, for no man's tall enough to fend off darkness, shadows, damp, and all the lonely terrors of the night.

Once he'd lost sight of his brother and the last few stragglers doing their best to negotiate the steep route through the rock chokes and the willow thickets down to the houses and a good sleep, Franklin made a cocoon of the two rolled tarps on a mattress of tinder-dry leaves and pinecones, and settled down for the night in a grassy bay with his back sack for a pillow. His knee was painful, but he was tired enough to sleep. He spoke the slumber verses to himself, to drive away regrets (the certainty that he would never see his ma again, would never walk their stead), and cleared his head of any thoughts of home or hungry animals or the comforts he was missing.

In what remained of the slanting light, Franklin Lopez tried to sleep while facing east, downhill. The closeness of Ferrytown was a comfort to him: from his high vantage point, he had seen the busy little lanes and yards and watched the ferry, its raft boards packed with the day's last emigrants and their suddenly weightless possessions, as it was let out on its fat ropes to drift downstream, never quite capsizing, until the four helmsmen dug in their great oars and poles to bring the craft ashore in the shallows of the deeply graveled landing beach. He had seen the emigrants unload with hardly a wet rim, foot, or hoof and set off on a boardwalk of tied logs, their burdens heavy again, across the flood meadows, steaming with mist. Soon the first of them reached the outer river bluff, and then, the last of the mountains safely at their backs, they began the long haul through what seemed to Franklin from his vantage point to be a green, oceanlike expanse of gently undulating flats and plains, stretching, swell upon swell, so far into the distance that his eyes ran out. He had then watched the ferry, unladen but now set against the river, being towed back upstream by a team of oxen on a winch and beached for the night at the mooring. He had seen the first lamps lit and heard what sounded like a song. Surely Franklin could not wish for a prospect more reassuring or more promising than this.

Once the moon came up above the leaden volumes of clouds, augmenting what was left of day, the lake in the valley, hidden up till then in mist, was like a silver pendant, with the river as its glinting chain. Franklin had not seen so much standing water before. Perhaps the sea would be like that, flat and safe and breathtaking.

❧ two ❧

The boulder hut on the far side of the bald, well out of danger's way, too high for that night's heavy vapors, was occupied by Margaret, the only shorn-headed person in the neighborhood. Red Margaret. Or the Apricot, as she was called by local men, attracted by her color—and her plumpness—in a land where nearly all the other heads were black, and then were gray or white. Her grandfather, as any parent would, had condemned her coppery tresses to the flames as soon as he had suspected that she was suffering from the flux. She'd vomited all day, she'd had diarrhea, she'd shivered like a snow fly but was hot and feverish to touch, she'd coughed as dryly as a jay, there were rashes on her face and arms, her neck was rigid and painful, and the onset of her problems had been cruelly swift, though not as swift as the news of her illness, which had raced around the houses as fast as sound—the sound of her mother weeping—and once again turned their compound of dwellings into a place to avoid. Once again, because only three months previously, in the high heat of the summer, her father had gone to bed healthy, sweet, a little overweight, red-haired, just as she had done the night before, and woken up soft, battered, and darkened. He'd died of flux, the first of seven townspeople to die and who knows how many unnameable travelers on their journeys to the boats who'd reached the far bank of the river and were out of sight and out of memory before they started shivering.

The flux was carried in and carried out by travelers, or by their goods, or by their animals, or in their bedding, or in their clothes. The illness was an intermittent visitor, unwelcome but well known. So what else could be afflicting Margaret except that selfsame flux, which must have hidden like a demon in their house since Pa had died, biding its time while choosing someone else's bed to share? And what choice had they but to carry out the rules and protect Ferrytown from her?

Her grandpa, repeating what he'd already done too recently for his son, her father, had shaved her skull, removing all the ginger drama from her head with a shell razor, and then called the closest women in the family, two sisters and her ma, to take off Margaret's body hair, snapping it down to the roots, the last of it wherever it might be— from her eyebrows and, most painfully, her lashes; from her nostrils, even; from her lightly ochered forearms and her legs; from elsewhere, the hidden hair—and massage her scalp with pine tallow until she was as shorn and shiny as a stone and smelling like a newly readied plank.

Everybody in the land must know what shaven baldness signified. No one could mistake her for a safe and healthy woman now. Not for some time. Not for a tress of time. She should not expect a welcome anywhere with that alarming head. But if she were that rarity, a sufferer who could defeat the flux, the regrowth of her hair, once it had reached her shoulders, anyway, would prove that she was truly safe again.

They burned her clippings on the outside fire, full thirty-one years of growth reduced in moments to a brittle tar. It smelled like a blacksmith's shop, like horses' hoofs, like carcasses, as you'd expect from such a pestilence. With any luck the venoms of the flux would now have been destroyed by fire and Margaret would survive her illness, as trees survive the winter if they shed their leaves. At least the flux could not be drawn back into her body through her hair now that she was almost bald. The signs were good, they told her, hoping to believe these baseless reassurances themselves. No bleeding yet, no body smell. Her father had bled from his mouth and nose. She'd be more fortunate than him. If there were any justice in the world, she'd have the good luck denied to Pa, her mother said.

But still, like him, she'd have to go up to the little boulder Pest-house above the valley for ten days or so, unattended and unvisited, to see if she recovered or was lost. There was no choice but to be hard-hearted. If any of the travelers were ill, they were thrown out of town at once. No bed or sustenance for them. But if the victim was a Ferry-towner, the Pesthouse was the only option. Margaret would have to take the westward route up Butter Hill, against the tide of history.

The women had already rid themselves of wool and fur and dressed in their safest waxed clothes—garments that were too slickly fibered, they hoped, to harbor any pestilence. They chewed tobacco as protection. Nevertheless, they were unwilling to resist this final risk and their last chance, probably, to make their farewells. They kissed Margaret on her cheek. And the men shook hands with her. Then, when she had gone to pack her bag with her three things and her brother had been sent to prepare the horse, they all washed their fingertips and lips in vinegar. You don't take chances with the flux.

Her grandpa led her on the horse up into the hills that same morning, three slow and ancient travelers, it would seem, the old man taking care with every step as if his bones were as fragile and as flaky as log ash, the woman slumped across the horse's neck, too weak to sit straight, the mare itself so displeased with the unrespon-sive weight and the loose stones on the butter-churning climb that it stopped and tried to turn whenever the leash was slackened.

Margaret had never been into the hills before. There'd been no need. It was unwise, and indeed against the community conventions, for a local woman to go beyond the palisades unless she was unwell.

Time was too precious for useful bodies to wander aimlessly in the neighborhoods. Margaret, like all the other women without husbands or children, was kept busy helping out in the guesthouse, where there were nearly always more than a hundred meals to serve each evening and beds and breakfasts to make next day.

Her grandpa hadn't been up into the hills very often either. Until the ascent with his ailing son three months previously, he hadn't been up to the summit of Butter Hill in many years, not since the travelers, drawn to the river's shallow crossing, had made his town rich. All the more ambitious huntsmen and fishermen had turned to making their fortunes out of farming for the table, ferrying, hospitality, and charging everyone for doing anything: crossing charges, passage fees, stabling costs, piloting, provisioning, protection tax, and levies just for wanting to go east.

It was astonishing how wealthy a little hospitality could make the locals. This fertile valley, of which it used to be boasted that you had only to flick a booger on the ground for a mushroom to grow overnight, was now fertile in even less demanding ways: stretch a rope across the road and travelers would pay you with their jewelry, their cloth, their inheritances just to be allowed to jump over it; toss a rag across a log, call it a bed, and they'd be lining up to sleep in it; shake a chicken's feather at a pot of boiling water and you could make your fortune out of soup.

The only problem was that travelers bring problems of their own and ones beyond control. Stockades and palisades could keep marauders at bay. The lockup beyond the tetherings with its no-bed and its no-light could hold and quiet down the troublemakers and those who couldn't settle bills in this stay-and-pay-or-on-your-way community. But illnesses, like bats and birds, were visible only too late, when the damage had been done. The toughest maladies have wings. There are no fees or charges high enough to deter the flux; no palisade is that tall.

· · ·

It was, as usual, busy on the road. Margaret and her grandpa stepped aside and hid from every descending emigrant they passed, every string of horses, every cart or barrow, every band of hopefuls that made its way downhill.

Her head was covered in a heavy blue scarf, so her shorn white scalp was out of sight. That would not draw any comment from strangers. Even at that time of the year, all travelers with any sense would protect themselves against the sun and midges with hats, headscarves, veils, or hair. The sun occasions modesty. It disapproves of flesh. But Margaret's face, if shown, would certainly betray the dangerous and appalling truth. What little of her skin wasn't raised and scarlet with rashes was gray with exhaustion.

It was uncomfortable—unbearable—to wear the heavy scarf around her hot and nagging head. She tried to lift it, push it back and off. But she could not allow herself to be seen, her grandpa told her—it would be too damaging for business if word got out that even just one person in the valley had the symptoms of the flux. A hundred meals, a hundred beds, would go to waste each day. Nobody would dare to spend the night with them. "Turn your head, Mags, if you can," he instructed her. "Pull your scarf across your face, let them mistake you for . . ." He couldn't think that she resembled anything, except a woman at death's door riding in the wrong direction with her back turned to the sea. He did his best to hide her from the stares and even from the necessary greetings. He pulled the horse into the thickets whenever he heard voices coming or the sound of carts and bridle bells. He made her duck into impasses of rock until the path was clear. And if anybody happened to get close to them or called wanting directions or news, he answered for the two of them, trying not to draw attention to himself by being either too unfriendly or too welcoming. If anybody asked, he'd claim his granddaughter was simple, not bright enough to speak. "Best let her float in her own company," he'd say.

So Margaret and her grandpa took half a day to reach the nearest woody swaggings in the sash of hills, where the rocky scrubland of the ascent relaxed into softer meadows and clearings of grass and highland reed, before the darkness of the woods and the distant, snowcapped mountain pates. The view was wasted on them. They hardly bothered to look back. The old man had to get home, while Margaret wanted nothing more than to sleep. She'd rather die than undertake another climb like that. So for her, the first sight of the Pesthouse at the edge of the hunter's bald was a relief.

Unlike the tree-trunk barns and cabins in the valley, the hillside hut had not been built for comfort. It was at core a woodsman's soddy, constructed out of sun-dried turfs, fireproof and wind-protected, much loved by mice, but easily collapsed. Indeed, it had collapsed from time to time, in those far regretted days when it had had little use, but since that healthy time, that time of remedies and cures, the Pesthouse had been strengthened by an outer wall of boulders, dry-built and sturdy. There was a sleeping bench inside, a hearth and chimney stack, a leather bucket and some pots.

Margaret hid in the undergrowth to empty her bowels—no blood, good luck—and then collapsed into the grass while her grandpa set to work. He swept out the soddy with snapped pine brooms, beat the stones with sticks in case any snakes had taken up residence, and set the fire in the stone grate with kindling and a striking stone. Provisions and a water bag were hung from roof branches above the fire, where they'd be marinated in wood fume and safe from little teeth. He gathered bracken and country corn for Margaret's bed. She rested her three lucky things—a silver necklace that was old enough to have been machined; a square of patterned, faded cloth too finely woven to have been the work of human hands; some coins from the best-forgotten days, all inside a cedar box on her chest—and lay down on the bed, with Grandpa's help. He placed an unfired pot of cough syrup made from onions mashed in sugar on the floor at the side of her bed: "Watch out for ants, Mags." He touched her forehead with his thumb, a finger kiss. "I'm ashamed to leave you here. I hope it grows. Thick and long." He wiped his hands again on a vinegary rag, then he and the horse were gone and she was sleeping.

When she woke, somewhat revived, it was already evening. The trees were menacing—they wheezed and cracked. Bats feasted on the early moths. The undergrowth was busy with its residents, and Margaret, Red Margaret, the Apricot, the drained and fragile woman in the hills, that applicant for unexpected death, felt shocked and lost, bewildered and unloved. Why had she been singled out? Why had the archer released his arrow into her? Such misfortune was too much to face alone—the pestilence, the pain, the degradation, and the restless meanness of the night, which she must spend on her own father's deathbed, breathing his last air. She coughed, a friendless cough, and had to listen to the trunks and branches coughing back, like wolves, too much like wolves for her to dare to sleep again. She'd never feared trees before. In daylight, trees had let her pass, ignored her almost, pretended not to notice her. But now that the moon was up, the forest seemed to be alert and mischievous.

The Pesthouse occupant took comfort from her talismans that night. She passed the necklace through her fingers, recognizing and remembering the contours of each engraved link; she rubbed and stroked her piece of cloth; she smelled the cedar in the little box. Finally she weighed the coins in her hands, the pennies and dimes and quarters that she had found among the pebbles on the river beach. She fingered all the images in the dark and tried to recognize the heads of people from the past, mostly short-haired men, one with a beard, "In God We Trust," one with a thickish ponytail bouncing on his neck, one heavy-chinned and satisfied. Was that the eagle she could feel? Where were the leafy sprigs and flaming torch? Was that the one-cent palace with the twelve great columns at the front? She dragged her nail across the disk to count every column and tried to find the tiny seated floating man within, the floating man who, storytellers said, was Abraham and would come back to help America one day with his enormous promises.

✥ tHRee ✤

Franklin had not expected so much rain. Anyone could tell from how brittle the landscape was that, in these parts at least, it had scarcely rained all season, and what clouds there'd been that day had been horizon clouds, passersby, or overtakers, actually, for they were heading eastward, too—but hardly any time had gone before the last light of the day threw out its washing water, splashing it as heavily as grit on the brittle undergrowth and setting free its long-stored smells, part hope and part decay. The rain was unforgiving in its weight. It meant to stay and do some damage and some good in equal parts. It meant to be noticed. It meant to run downhill until it found a river and then downstream until it found a sea. "If you're looking for the sailing boats, just follow the fallen rain" was the universal advice for inexperienced travelers.

Franklin couldn't sleep through this. He couldn't even sit out such a downpour. He'd have to find some better shelter. He shook out the leaves from his bedding, wrapped the two already damp tarps around himself, and limped as best he could onto a rocky knoll from which he could peer into the darkness and through the rain from a greater height. He hadn't noticed any caves or overhanging cliffs or any forest thick and broad-leafed enough to offer hope of staying dry for very long. This was the kind of rain that wouldn't rest until its job was done.

Now Franklin considered the little boulder hut on the fringe of the clearing, with its gray scarf of smoke. It was the sort of place where inexperienced or incautious robbers might make their den, well positioned for picking off stragglers even though anyone with any sense would give it a wide berth. But Franklin would take the risk—despite Jackson's warnings, but also because of his brother's stinging accusation earlier that day that "only the crazy make it to the coast"—and see if he could bargain any shelter there. He'd lost his bearings in the storm and in the darkness, though, and couldn't quite remember where he'd seen the hut. On the forest edge, for sure, but where exactly, how far off? What residue of light remained was not enough to spot its chimney. He sniffed for wood smoke but sniffed up only rain. He'd have to stumble in the dark and trust to luck, and still take good care not to wake any hostile residents, though the chances were it was just a woodsman's cabin or some hermitage, a no-choice place to rest his knee and stay dry for the night.

No matter where he stumbled, he could not see the outline of a roof, as he had hoped, or any light, but he was old enough to know where anyone would build a hut if there was free choice. Not entirely under trees, for a start, and not in earthy shallows where bogs might form. But half in, half out. Not too exposed to wind or passersby. But looking south and on flat ground, preferably face on to a clearing.

It was her coughing that led him to her, finally—the hacking, treble cough of foxes, but hardly wild enough for foxes. A woman's cough. So now Franklin knew the place, and where it stood in relation to the far too open spot where he had rolled his cocoon. He took his bearings from the coughing, waiting for it to break out, then subside, and then break out again, and from the heavy outlines of the woodlands and the hillside. He shuffled through the soaking grasses, taking care not to snap any sticks, listening for beasts below the clatter of the storm, until he could hear the telltale percussion of the rain striking something harder and less giving than the natural world, something flat and man-made. And now indeed he could hear and see the black roofline of a hut and a chimney stack. Then, between the timbers of its door—but for a moment only—he caught the reassuring and alarming flicker of a candle flame, just lit from the grate. He knew exactly what that meant: whoever was inside had heard him creeping up. They had been warned and would be ready.

Franklin hung his back sack on a branch, pulled off his tarps, and took out his knife, its blade still smelling of the meadow onions they had found and eaten raw earlier that day. The lighted candle meant that the occupant (or occupants) was nervous, too. So he grew more confident. Now he made as much noise as he could, trying to sound large and capable. He called out, "Shelter from the rain?" and then when there was silence, "I'm joining you if you'll allow." And finally, "No cause for fear, I promise you," though he was more than a little fearful himself when there were no replies. The boulder hut was big enough to house a gang of men in addition to the coughing woman, all armed, all dangerous. A man with a knife, no matter how tall he was, could not defend himself in the dark against missiles, or long pikes, or several men with cudgels. He tried again: "I'm a friend. Just say that you'll welcome me out of the storm, or I'll step away." A test of hospitality. Some coughing now, as if the cougher had to find a voice from far away, and then, "Come only to the door. Don't open it." The woman's voice. A youngish voice. Already he was blushing.

For a door, the hut had little more than a barricade of rough pine planks. Franklin said, "I'm here." He peered between the planks and could just make out the dark form of one person, resting on one elbow in a bed, backlit by a wood fire in a grate. Nothing to be frightened of. Nothing physical, at least. Some traveler, perhaps, who just like him was suffering from knees and needed shelter for a while.

"I'm going to drown unless I come inside," he said. She coughed at him. No *Stay away*, no *Come*.

Franklin pulled the door aside with his left hand, resting his right hand, with the knife, on the low lintel at his chin height. She held her candle out to get a better look at him, and in its sudden guttering of light they saw each other for the first time. Red Margaret was startled first by the size of him, two times the weight and size of her grandpa, she thought, and then by what she took to be a face of honesty, not quite a handsome face, not quite a beauty boy, but narrow, healthy, promising, a face to rescue her from fear if only he would dare. Franklin saw the bald, round head of someone very sick and beautiful. A shaven head was unambiguous. It meant the woman and the hut were dangerous. He stepped back and turned his head away to breathe the safer, rain-soaked air. He was no longer visible to her. The door frame reached only his throat. He put the door back into place and reconciled himself to getting very wet and cold that night. "A pesthouse, then," he said out loud, to show—politely—that he understood and that his curtailed friendliness was sensible. Too late to call his brother back, though calling out for Jackson was Franklin's first instinct, because if there was disease in the Pesthouse, there could well be disease down there, among the inhabitants of Ferrytown.

Now the woman was coughing once again. Her little hut was full of smoke, he'd noticed. And her lungs, no doubt, were heavy with pestilence, too. Dragging his tarps behind him, he crashed his way back through the clearing and undergrowth into the thickest of the trees, where the canopy would be his shelter. He had been cowardly, he knew. He had been sensible. Only a fool would socialize with death just to stay warm and dry for the night. He found a partly protected spot among the scrub oaks just at the top of Butter Hill, where he could erect a makeshift tent from his stretched tarps and protect himself a little. His decision to stay up in the hills to rest had clearly been a foolish one. Jackson had been right, as usual. A crazier, more reckless man would have faced the risks of pressing on, injury defied, and enjoyed the benefits of a warm bed, surely better for a limping emigrant than sharing a stormy night with bald disease, no matter how eye-catching it might be.

Franklin's knee had worsened in the rain and during his latest stumbles through the sodden undergrowth. Its throbbing tormented him. It almost ached out loud, the nagging of a roosting dove: *Can't cook, cook, cook.* Even when, in the early quarters of the night, the storm had passed and the moon, the stars, and the silver lake had reappeared, he could not sleep. Her face was haunting him, her face in candlelight (that celebrated flatterer) and the shorn scalp. He might have touched himself with her in mind, despite his pain, had not the valley raised its voice above the grumbling of his knee and the hastened beating of his newly captured heart. The dripping music of the woods was joined by lowland drums. There was the thud and clatter of slipping land, a sound he could not comprehend or recognize—he knew only that it was bad—and then the stony gust, the rumbling, the lesser set of sounds than thunder that agitated the younger horses and the ever-childish mules out in the safety of the tetherings.

On Butter Hill, above the river crossing where west was granted access to the east, Franklin Lopez sat alarmed, entirely unasleep, in his wet tarps, the only living witness when the silver pendant shook and blistered—a pot, a lake, coming to the boil.

❧ four ❧

Jackson had taken a liking to the modest town, with its smoke and smells and the clamor of voices, livestock and tools. Even though he had arrived at its boundary fences a little after dark, a few trading stalls were still set up, warmed and lit by braziers and lanterns, where he was greeted by dogs, his palms and tongue inspected for infection by gatekeepers, and told at once what the tariffs were—how much he'd have to pay to cross their land, the cost of food and shelter for the night, the onward ferry fee. He would be welcome as a guest if his face was free of rashes, if he wasn't seeking charity, if he didn't try to win the short-term favors of a local woman, and if he put any weapons—and any bad language—into their safekeeping until he traveled on. Weapons, rashes, charity, and short-term favors of any kind were "off the menu," he was told. But otherwise, they had good beds, fresh bread, sweet water, and easy passage to the other bank "for anyone prepared to keep the peace and pay the price." What had he to offer in return? He had only his coat to trade, he told them, and any labor that they might require of him during the few days that it would take his brother, Franklin, to recover from his exaggerated laming.

All the traders at the gates seemed interested in his piebald coat and gathered around him, admiring his mother's stitching and marveling at the immodest pattern. But their interest was mostly an excuse to question their oversized visitor and stare at him. None would purchase the coat, no matter how little he wanted in exchange. It was too grand for them. Nobody they knew was tall or outlandish enough for such a garment, they explained, and there was little likelihood that another man of such height and in need of protection against the cold and rain would pass through their community. Nevertheless, the traders were careful and flattering in their dealings with Jackson Lopez, as strangers always were, he'd found. His height and strength earned him promises of work in exchange for lodging: there were sacks of grain to stack and store for winter in the dry lofts, and as ever, there was wood to cut and sewage to be carted out, all familiar tasks. They even promised him a single bed. For once he wouldn't have to share his body space with Franklin.

Jackson need never sleep with his brother again. He was free to stop just one night in Ferrytown and then move on alone the next day, unencumbered. He was tempted to, or certainly he'd played out the idea as he'd come down the hill, still irritated by the unwelcome waste of time.

His brother had been a constraint even before his knee had let them down. Younger brothers often are. They're the sneaks who tell your parents who broke the bowl or lamed the mare or stole the fruit. They're the ones who hold you up, pleading caution, wanting home. They're the ones who'd choose to go roundabout Robert to avoid danger rather than to smell it out and face up boldly—and unblushingly, as Jackson always would—to the argument, the snake, the bear, the cliff face, or the enemy. And older brothers have no privacy, unlike older sisters, for whom privacy is considered fundamental. No, the firstborn males are expected to share their blankets with all the younger ones, and share the work, and entertain the others in the evenings with the light of just the single candle, and travel—even migrate!—in a pack, as if no future were possible except in the others' company. It certainly was dead right, that traditional warning to anyone with itchy feet, that there is no better way of getting to resent a friend, whether it's a brother or a neighbor, than by traveling with him.

"You take good care of him," his mother had instructed every time they'd left the farm buildings for a day of work, all the way through his childhood and adolescence. And those had been almost her final words to Jackson when her sons had set off toward the boats two months previously. "You take good care of him." She still saw Franklin as a boy who needed to be tied by ropes to someone bigger and more trustworthy. She hadn't said, "And you take good care of yourself." Perhaps he ought to start. Walking down the hill alone, at his own pace, had been an unexpected pleasure that he might happily prolong, on this side of the water and beyond. He'd sleep on it. He'd make up his mind once he'd tested the local hospitality and found someone to trade with him. No matter what he decided—return to Franklin and that maddening laugh of his (as seemed disheartening-ly inevitable) or hurry on (the thrilling fantasy)—he had to freshen his or their supplies of food.

As it happened, while Jackson was walking in past the tetherings toward the guesthouse, savoring his recent freedom and the prospect of his first good meal for many days, the boy called Nash was on his way to begin his night of caretaking with the local and passage ani-mals. He was wheeling a smoking barrow with a cargo of glowing stove stones from the family grate bedded in earth to keep him warm. He had pushed some sheets of thin cloth up the back of his shirt as well, but he still expected to be cold, especially in the period just before sunup, and on that night, at least, he expected to be wet. He could smell the coming rain, and the bats, always trustworthy forecasters of a storm, were out unusually early in search of rain-shy insects.

So when the immense man in the surprising coat asked him to point out the roof of the guesthouse and where the clothing broker lived, an opportunity was spotted and a deal was soon struck. Jackson parted with the coat, and Nash set aside his wheelbarrow and hurried briefly to his family yard to provide the dried fruit, the pork, the leather water bag, and the apple juice that he had traded with this astounding visitor, who seemed less astounding, shorter even, as soon as he pulled off his outerwear, kissed it farewell as if it were a friend, and draped it around the boy's narrow shoulders. Nash set off for the tetherings again, but slowly. The coat, twice too long, was a greater hindrance even than the heavy wheelbarrow full of earth and stones. Nevertheless, these were joyful moments for a ten-year-old—except that he felt anxious. He'd been overeager to win the good opinion of the giant and exchanged too many useful things for something inexplicable. Inexplicable to his parents and neighbors, at least. He'd been selfish, too. A coat serves only its owner (although in this rare instance, four small boys and their dogs could easily find shelter under it). Nash would have to spend the night perfecting his excuses. But for the moment he was glad of the opportunity, as the final strangers of the day passed by, to parade his new encumbrance.

Jackson felt the evening chill at once, but he was liberated, lighter in himself. He'd left his ma behind at last and distanced himself a little from his brother. The coat had been her manhood gift to him. In richer times. They'd feasted on four sibling goats with all the other families and she had scraped and tanned the hides to make his gift, which she said—too frequently—would last him a lifetime. It would outlast him. Jackson was certain that if she were to imagine him now and wonder how he and Franklin might have fared, the coat would be a sure part of it. Now he was beyond imagining, and glad of that.

The meal that night was not as grand as he had hoped, although the usual country protocols were followed closely before the food was served, raising expectations. Those eating had to wash their hands at the canteen door in water that, after passing through two hundred

hands dirtied by the journey, smelled of horsehair, sweat, and rope
and looked as brown as tea. And for at least the second time that day
(for news of Margaret's illness had made the Ferrytowners vigilant
and fussy) they were all inspected for rashes or livid spots before they
were allowed to take their places. The women had the best benches,
on the wall side of the tables. The men sat in the central gangway,
with nothing to support their backs. Their children and any adoles-
cent boy too young to grow a beard gathered on their haunches, on
mats to the side of the fires, and were forbidden to move or speak
above a whisper. No dogs. Hats off. And sleeves rolled up, in optimistic readiness.

Jackson was given a low stool at the head of the shorter table so
that he could stretch his legs and use his elbows without fear of brain-
ing a neighbor. It suited him to take this mostly practical and cautious placement as a mark of respect not only for his size but also for
his bearing, which he considered dignified. The candlelight made all
the faces seem rudely healthy and animated, and soon new friends
were being introduced and stories told. Jackson, though, stayed
mostly silent, partly because he had no direct eye contact across the
table, partly because his immediate neighbors were too old and tired
to draw his attention, but largely because he was taciturn by nature,
prepared to express a short opinion but not eager or even able to prat-
tle. Besides, his head was full of awkward possibilities.

When the food was served, it was clear that the hosts had gone to
no expense. It was hog and hominy with corn bread, they said
(though it was later claimed by one of the travelers—possibly a
joke—that he'd pulled a yellowish raccoon hair from between his
teeth. "I've never seen a ring-tailed hog before!"). Hardly anybody
failed to clear his plate, however. Anything was better than the travel
pantry that had provided yesterday's meals.

The meat was followed by oatmeal and molasses, offered without
the benefit of silverware, so eating it by hand was a noisy, self-
conscious business. The adults felt obliged to extend their little fingers

respectfully as they ate, using their fores and indexes as spoons and re-
serving the pinkie for dipping into the dishes of salt and for scooping
pine-nut mash onto their molasses. Such good manners seemed exces-
sive for that quality of food but necessary in the company and under
the scrutiny of strangers.

Nobody was truly satisfied. This was not the meal that they'd
been dreaming of on the journey, when they'd been making do, at
best, with brushjack stew and feasting on the skeletal corpses of pack
horses and mules, or on carrion. A chicken's egg, some milk, some recent, cultivated fruit, true bread and mutton, would have served
them better.

Despite the quality of food, however, Jackson could have eaten
twice as much again. At least his stomach was half full for once, and
sweet. And eating in the company of so many other emigrants had
been a kind of nourishment as well, even though he had not spoken
yet. But when the elderly woman to his right offered him her unfin-
ished oatmeal and some untouched quarters of bread, he felt required, once he had cleared his board, to set aside his dignity, provide
his name, and say a word or two about his journey east. He had listened to the travel tales of his fellow diners with little interest. So
much disaster and regret should be not be spoken of when it was
over, Jackson thought. What was done was dust, as far as he was concerned. Such rapes and robberies and injuries and deaths, so many
bolting horses, snapped axles, wagon fires, and sudden floods, did not
fit his experience. His account would tell of uneventful days marked
out by boredom and hardship and livened only when the weather or
the landscape played its trick of exposing travelers to mud or drought
or, when the route had not been notched or blazed on tree trunks by
preceding travelers, luring them into valleys that had no exit at their
farthest ends. He told his story in a sentence, one that did not mention his brother.

"We could use a pair of shoulders like yours," an old man said,
nodding at his wife for her approval. "Our cart's too heavy and we've

lost a horse. We're moving out tomorrow, if you'd appreciate the ride. Pay your fare with your muscles, when the going's poor."

Jackson nodded. Yes, he'd sleep on it and let them know. He'd be sleeping on a lot of things that night. His single bed would be crowded with temptations.

In fact, it was not at first easy for anyone to sleep that night. What they'd eaten crept around inside their guts, foraging with its nocturnal snout. And then the storm arrived, beating against the rest-house walls, keeping them all awake to wonder what state the route ahead would be in and whether they should rest up in the town for another day, allowing the mud some time to crust. The men called out in the deafening darkness from their shared beds, exchanging advice and providing their versions of the likely route ahead. No two versions were the same. The liars and the teasers could exaggerate as much as they wanted to. The worriers could share their greatest fears without shaming themselves. They were only faceless voices in the night. And they could safely list their various adversities—the beatings and the robberies, the time that they were stoned by bears, the five nights drifting on a lake, the treachery of so-called friends, the toil and drudgery, the hunger and the thirst, the murderous temperatures that they'd survived—from between warm coverings and underneath a decent roof.

The optimists among them believed that once the river had been crossed, something of the old America would be discovered, the country their grandpas and grandmas had talked about, a land of profusion, safe from human predators, snake-free, and welcoming beyond the hog and hominy of this raw place; a country described by so many of their grandparents in words they'd learned from *their* grandparents, where the encouragements held out to strangers were a good climate, fertile soil, wholesome air and water, plenty of provisions, good pay for labor, kind neighbors, good laws, a free government, and a hearty welcome. A plain and simple ambition, surely.

Here were men who'd come from places with flat and functional names like Half-Day Bridge, Boundary Wood, Center Island, and, yes, Ferrytown, but within a day or two they expected to travel on the Dreaming Highway, which led, so they believed, through Give-Your-Word Valley to Achievement Hill and a prospect of the Last Farewell, with its long views from the far shore of America. On the journey the country would be flat, they'd heard, with surfaced tracks as hard as fired clay. "Not flat," someone corrected them, "but down-hill all the way, sloping to the sea. The wheels do all the work. That's why it's called the Dreaming Highway. The country lets you sleep." The journey to the boats, he said, would be an easy and a speedy one. "A hog could roll there in a sack."

But there were doubters in the darkness, too, men who'd heard less comforting reports. Rivers too wide and wild to cross. Forests so impenetrable and gloomy that nothing grew at ground level except funguses and little moved except wood ants and blind lizards, both as white as snow, and rats that hunted for their prey by smell alone and so had noses longer than their tails. Great, dusty, waterless plains. Ridges sharper than a knife, that tore your clothes. Others spoke of brackish swamps that could be crossed—in twenty days, if you were strong and lucky—only by travelers who dared to leave their horses and their carts behind and drag themselves across the mire on wooden rafts.

And were there any people, beyond the river crossing? A multi-tude, yes. Everyone who'd ever headed east to catch the boats. There were no boats. Or else it was a land where no one lived and there'd be not a soul to provide, once in a while, a good dry bed or any hog and hominy. "You'd be glad to dine on raccoon then." Or otherwise the people were all unwelcoming, or they were naked cannibals, or they were dwarfs "smaller than a prairie dog, but uglier."

"But furrier!"

"And very tasty on a slice of bread!"

By now the laughter in the room was louder than the rain. In-deed, the rain had relented somewhat, as had their indigestion. Now they could fall asleep more easily, apprehensive but amused. "Watch out," one of the men whispered, wanting to be the final voice, after all his companions had fallen quiet. "There's folk out there, one day ahead of Ferrytown, who are as handy with their toes as with their fingers. They can wipe their butts, scratch their noses, poke your eyes out, and pick your pockets, all at the one time."

But still another man was simmering to speak. "From what I've heard tonight," said Jackson from his single bed at the far end of the hall, too softly to be heard by many of his fellows, "there's at least a hundred different lands beyond the river. And none of them strike me as likely. Maybe all of us should only wait and see what we'll find when we've planted our feet on the actual earth ahead of us." He wanted to say out loud what he was hoping for within—that if he advanced his shoulders to the couple with the heavy cart and left his brother to take care of himself, then he could square it with his conscience only if the way ahead for Franklin would prove to be an easy and a kindly one. He fell silent for a little time, judging his words and wondering, too, whether he could ignore the pressure in his bladder from the flagon of apple juice he had traded and drunk, before adding, "I'll tell you something. For free. This afternoon, I walked down the very same hill as all of you and I looked ahead and used my eyes. I saw the view. Nobody missed the view, I'm sure. And what I saw ahead of me was land and sky just like the land and sky we've always known. Tomorrow you can see it for yourselves." Tomorrow, he was thinking as he fell asleep, will be like yesterday.

❧ five ❧

The dawn seemed tired and hesitant at first, hardly capable of shaking off the clouds and pushing out into the day. The sun, rising for its daily journey to the west, was veiled by that night's retreating storm, which, like everything else, including the slight wind, was—typically for this season of migration and withdrawal—resolute in going east, unlike the light. The last stars lingered on, just happy to be visible beyond their time. But once the breeze stood up, the storm was cleared entirely. No cloud at all, and only gray-white mist and yesterday's smoke in the hollows of the valley, hiding Ferrytown.

When Franklin, drenched and stiffer than a log, finally emerged from underneath his bedding and dragged the tarps into the clearing where they would drain and dry, it was unusually warm and bright on Butter Hill. The undergrowth was steaming, and the air was fragrant with pine and earth, and faintly sulfurous. A henhouse smell. He stood for a while in the sunshine, hoping to recover quickly, and indeed, he soon felt well enough to walk around a little. The rest had benefited his leg, but not sufficiently to pledge a day of walking. He washed in standing water and cleaned his teeth with a snapped branch, which smelled of nuts but left his gums bleeding. He would be sensible and put his feet up for one more day, he thought, flexing his knee. Less swelling, yes, though no less pain when he put any pressure on it. He would not be surprised if his brother returned that afternoon with food or some transport. But actually the prospect of another day free from Jackson's nagging temper was not unwelcome.

Part of Franklin was uneasy and just a touch alarmed. He sensed that there was death about. He'd felt it in his bones the moment that he'd tried to stand. He recognized it in the fragile colors of the morning. On days such as this the sky is so thinly blue and hollowed out that death's great hand can at any time reach through to harvest anyone it wants, to pick off lives like berries from a bush. And he could smell it on the air, beyond the pine, that faintly eggy smell, the chemicals of hell, the madman's belch. Was this the smell of pestilence? He hardly wanted to check. He did not want to exchange the memory of the young woman alive in candlelight with the reality of her perished in the night, borne off on death's enormous wing.

Franklin chose a good stick for support and made his way across the clearing to the Pesthouse, hoping not to waken her or frighten her, if she was still alive, but also ready to defend himself if there were any devils at her bed. But looking through the Pesthouse cracks and the smoke-heavy fume of the little chamber, he found her well, still breathing in her house of turfs and boulders, still palely beautiful. He was far too thankful now, too teetering, to wonder or to care whose death he'd heard during that long night of rain and sleeplessness in the forest-frowning, eastward-looking hills.

It would be a pity not to be of service to the woman in the Pesthouse, he decided, straining to see her face and shaven head more clearly, hoping to see more—a naked leg flung out of bed, perhaps, a breast. He wanted an excuse to help her, rescue her. Not just to enjoy the true heat of her wood fire or to share her provisions. Not just to do his duty for the sick, either, obeying what his people called the

Golden Obligation. He simply wanted her close company. If he was careful and wrapped his face, he would be protected from infectious air; then surely he could dare to sit beside her in the hut, not too near, but near enough to see her fully and to study her more easily. Oh, don't let Jackson ruin it by coming back too soon.

Franklin pulled aside the wooden door of the Pesthouse to let in fresh air. A corridor of sunlight fell across her bed and hands. "Pish, pish," he whispered, a gentle call that he had learned from Ma, a greeting that had allowed him many times to walk up to a horse or among cattle without distressing them.

Margaret did not wake, even when Franklin stooped into the Pesthouse. She was dreaming of her father, as she was bound to in that place. She was dreaming of a death like his. She could not forget how red his eyes had been, his sneezing and his hoarseness, or the black and livid spots across his face, and how his body, especially his neck and thighs and arms, had erupted overnight with boils as solid and large as goose eggs.

Margaret twisted on her bed, beset by recollections that she had learned to push away when she was conscious but that in sleep she could not shift—how, early on, he had bled from the nose and laughed it off as "picking it too hard"; how then his tongue and throat had swollen so that he could barely speak; how later, in his delirium, he had tried, and failed, to stand; how they had carried him, as weightless and boneless as a discarded coat, to his cot, where he'd convulsed with hickeye, dry-heaving into his bedclothes and producing nothing but thick and ropy sputum, that harbinger of death; how finally, once he had dropped into a daze, the further end of sleep, they'd sent him up Butter Hill to the Pesthouse on the same horse as they had Margaret, stenching and insensible, with no farewells from anyone, no touch of lips, no vinegar.

Franklin pulled his coat and collar up around his mouth, stepped farther into the Pesthouse, and—his first touch—pressed his hand on her forehead, her exposed arm, and then—he dared, but not without blushing—he felt her shoulders. She was warm and damp, but nevertheless she should stay wrapped, he judged, or she would take a chill on top of everything. Yet when he pulled the coverlet over her, she soon pushed it off again, still unwilling to bear the weight of cloth, even in her sleep. Her scalp, though, was cold. He imagined he could feel the first growth of her hair under his palm, more like the underbelly of a pup than like a peach skin. He turned the fire, banked the ashes, added fresh wood, and held his hands above the smoke in case his touch had picked up her infection. It seemed too like a fairy tale: the sleeping woman, troubled evidently by her dreams, unaware that she was visited, unconscious of the stranger who would come to save her with his . . . friendliness. What could he do to help her now? What magic could he summon that would drive her fever out and take away the rashes and the heat? What must he do, so that he could touch her without fear?

Encouraged by a day of sun and by the full sling of nuts that he had foraged as a gift, Franklin found the courage in the afternoon to go back to the Pesthouse. Margaret was still barely awake and could manage only a faint "Yes?" to let him in when he pish-pished.

"Are you well?" he asked, the common greeting between strangers but heavily appropriate on this occasion.

"I'm tired," she said. But not dead, apparently. Instinctively she felt her armpits to check for any goose eggs. She could hardly check for buboes in her groin with Franklin watching her. She took comfort from the fading of the blotches on her arms and from the absence of any dried blood around her nose or mouth and, indeed, of what would have been a certain sign of approaching death, three pock-shaped black marks on her hands, or, worse, the clot of blood—a present from the Devil—that corpses were said to clutch in their palms to pay their entrance fee to Hell. Perhaps she would not die after all. Perhaps she'd have the good luck denied to Pa, as her mother had promised. Margaret even chanced a smile toward the stranger at the door. "What color are my eyes?" she asked the man.

"I haven't seen your eyes," he said. "It's dark in here." He blushed, of course.

"Not red, not bloody red?"

"I'll see. Can I come close?" Her eyes looked clear enough. "No blood," he said.

"No blood is good." She closed her eyes again.

"You ought to eat." He showed her the heavy sling of cloth and chose the plumpest nut for her.

"Can't chew." Her jaw and throat felt stiff and timbery.

"Maybe I could make a soup . . . from . . . the woods are full of things." From leaves, from nuts, from roots, from birds. From mushrooms, possibly.

"Nothing, no."

"What can I do for you?"

She shook her head. There's nothing to be done, she thought, except to sleep and hope for the best. The last thing that she needed in her state was a mouthful of dry nuts or a stomachload of soup from the woods. She felt both half awake and dreaming. Deeply conscious, in a way, but inebriated, too, by the toxins that accumulate when hunger, fever, and exhaustion are confederates. "What color are my eyes?" she asked again, almost sleeping now.

"Do you know where you are? Do you know who I am?" asked Franklin, not wishing to bully her with questions but worried that she might be slipping into unconsciousness rather than slumber.

She raised her head just high enough to see him for an instant. A silhouette. No expression on her face. It didn't matter who he was. "I don't know you." But she managed to lift her head again and study him for a moment longer. "What do they want?"

"Who do you mean when you say *they*? Your family? Are *they* the people in the town?"

"I don't know who they are."

He had to let her sleep again. He left her to it and went out into the clearing to check the hill for any sign of Jackson and to bring his two dried tarps and his possessions into the Pesthouse. He had persuaded himself—too readily—that he would be safer, drier, warmer with the feverish woman than he would be outside for another night. More useful, too. The Pesthouse smoke would protect him from her contagion. He sat down at the far end of her bed, his back warmed by the fire, looking out through the open door across the clearing as the light lifted and receded once again and the cold returned. The last few of that day's travelers led their carts and horses to the lip of the hill and disappeared from sight, leaving just their voices and their bells to briefly dent the quiet.

That evening, emboldened by the darkness and keen to wake her lest she slip too far, Franklin sat and spoke about himself, as strangers should. Occasionally he could tell by her breathing or by some note of interest or sympathy that she was listening in between her bouts of sleep. He gave his name, his age; he told her about his father's death, the family farm, their animals, the mocking sets of storms and droughts that had destroyed their crops and fields, the famine and lawlessness, the day that he and Jackson had begun their journey to the ships and how his mother had busied herself indoors rather than witness their first steps of departure. He described their hardships on the road, the damage to his knee, how Jackson had volunteered to go down the hill to Ferrytown to replenish their supplies.

Her voice at last, less small than it had been. "They'll take good care of him," she said, glad to hear the mention of her home.

And then he told her what they hoped to find on ship: "those tiny rooms, just made of wood," and great white birds among the sails, to show the way. He could not imagine exactly what awaited them when they set foot abroad, what type of people they might be, what language they might speak. But he was sure that life would be more prosperous. How could it not be better there? Safer, too. With *opportunity*, a word he'd come to love.

"And when we're there," he said, hoping to restore her with his optimism, "they say that there is land enough for everyone, and buildings made of decorated stone, and palaces and courts and gardens planted for their beauty, not for food. Because there is abundance in those places. Their harvests never fail. Three crops a year! Three meals a day!"

"They'll all be fat."

"They *are* all fat. Like barn hogs."

That night he slept beside her bed, his feet below her head kept warm by the fire and his head by the Pesthouse door, where he could be on guard against any animals or visitors and breathe the colder but untainted air. Margaret was restless, though she seemed to sleep. She turned around in her bed, gasping for breath, disturbed by nightmares, troubled by the sore skin on her torso, legs, and arms. Not one of her bones seemed in its normal place.

Franklin did not remember how it happened, but when he woke in the early light, he found that Margaret was sleeping on her back and that she had shot her legs out of her bed coverings and that he had been sleeping holding a foot between his two hands, restraining it, perhaps, or keeping it warm. He knew at once, shivering, how risky that had been. Diseases depart from the body through the soles of the feet. That's why, when pigeons were so plentiful and decent meat was served at every meal, the people of his parents' generation had strapped a living pigeon to a sick child's feet. He'd experienced this remedy himself. When he'd been eight or nine years old, he'd caught a tick disease that had paralyzed his body for a day or two, until his brother had been sent out with nets to trap a bird and his aunt had tied it to his feet, pinioning its wings and back against his insteps. "Stay there, don't move until the illness passes into the pigeon," she had instructed. She had remained with him, making sure he kept still, helping him to urinate and defecate into an earth jar, feeding him by spoon, until, after two more days of feeling its warm and beating heart against his insteps, the pigeon stopped protesting and went cold and silent. It had done the trick as well. His illness had passed, and he had been able to walk up with his father to the bone-yard and bury the bird and his disease under a stone. He could see that stone still in his mind's eye, a gray, dismaying slab that had haunted him ever since. When the harder times had come and pi-geon meat, even at feasts, was often all they had to eat, Franklin had preferred to go without. The flesh was tainted in his view: the bird was hazardous. Jackson always ate his share.

Now, with Margaret's cold and clammy feet in his hands, Franklin felt unwell himself. His body ached. His throat was dry. His shoulders and neck seemed fixed. His eyes were watering. His hands were tingling. But he chose to hold on to her feet and massage them, exactly as his mother had massaged his feet when he was young. He pressed his thumbs against each toe, he pushed against the hollows of her ankles, he worked his knuckles against the soles, he stroked each nail. She seemed to push her legs against his hands, as if she knew what he was drawing out of her. He did not want to let her go, not even when he heard the first arrivals of the day begin to come out of the woods and make their way down Butter Hill to reach the longed-for welcome at a town just blocked from sight, as usual at that time of the day, by mist.

❧ SIX ❧

Perhaps she would have gotten better anyway, but as usual nature's undramatic remedies would remain unrewarded. Margaret was bound to credit her rescue to Franklin's busy hands. At first she had been startled by the pressure of his thumbs on her soles and heels and by his shocking, intimate invasion of the gaps between her toes. No one had played with Margaret's feet since she'd been a child. Certainly since she had been ten years old or so, she had been taught how precious her body would be in securing a husband but how untouchable it should remain until that man had revealed and committed himself with an exchange of labor or of goods. The phrase "The virgin pulls the plow" did not mean that in Ferrytown the young unmarried women were put to work in the fields, but that a pure girl would be worth a pair of horses or a team of oxen in a marriage contract. You wouldn't get a brace of rabbits for a girl who'd drifted.

When she'd been younger, Margaret had hardly dared even to touch herself for fear of losing value, but lately, as time and opportunity elapsed and it seemed less likely that any man in Ferrytown would volunteer to embrace a wife whose lovely, tempting copper hair was such an ancient omen of disaster and such a sign of waywardness, she had broken that taboo. She was, at thirty-one, she had admitted to herself, a woman who might be a daughter and a sister and an aunt, but never a wife or mother. Her body would retain its value and remain unshared.

But she'd been approached many times by the strangers who had traveled through her town and who evidently did not share her neighbors' wariness of redheads. She'd had her rear slapped more than once. She'd had her fingers kissed. And one fine-mannered man, her father's age, had proposed a midnight meeting place beyond the palisades where they might talk and hold each other's hands. She'd often wondered what might have happened had she done what he'd suggested, where she might have ended up, if she hadn't opted instead to seek Ma's advice, with the result that it was her brothers and her father who went out at midnight with their sticks to honor his proposal.

So this caressing of the feet was something both alarming and overdue. She had been tempted to protest. To kick this stranger, even. To judge his touch as cheapening. But who doesn't like their feet caressed? Who isn't weakened and disarmed by such discreet attention? It helped that Franklin spoke to her while he was working on her feet, making less of a stranger of himself. He recounted how his mother had tipped him on his back and "loved his feet" when he was very small, and even not so small, a teenager. He talked about his patient aunt and the pigeon that had cured him when he was young. If this was something that a mother and an aunt might do, then surely it was innocent.

Except it could not feel entirely innocent. Margaret found it hard to tell if this narrow fever that encompassed her, this breathlessness, this pounding of her heart, this fresh disorder that seemed to want to shake and flex her by the spine, was something else new that could be blamed on her flux. Or was it something that she owed to Franklin's thumbs and knuckles? She drifted in and out of it. She even dreamed that he brought shame on her by venturing beyond her feet along her hairless leg to press his thumbs and knuckles where only she had pressed before.

The first thing Margaret noticed when she woke was how quiet it was. She had to remind herself that she was no longer at home, waking in the family house, with just moments left before the call to work. She could lie back and let the shapes absorb the light. But she knew at once that something had changed, both within her and beyond. Her body ached. Her mouth was still so dry and bitter that she could barely swallow. But she was feeling partially restored, not sinking now and fearful, but strengthening. Her feet and lower legs felt supple and alive. Her head was clear. Her scalp was bristling. She did not have to struggle to remember what had happened in the night. She could recall every movement of the young man's hands. He was responsible.

Margaret raised herself quite easily onto her elbows and peered through the thinning gloom at the body slumped at the side of her bed, a silent silhouette as still and heavy as a sack of grain. Was he alive? He hardly seemed alive. She dared to push his shoulder with her foot. No sign from him. She'd not detected any body heat. Her panic was short-lived, but strong enough to make her cry out loud. What had he said? The pigeon drew the toxins out through the soles of the feet. The illness was defeated but the pigeon died. Its warm and beating heart would stop protesting and its body would be cold and silent. She stretched her leg again, pushed her toes against his chest, and waited for a heartbeat. Yes, Franklin was still warm, but even so she was not sure. She pressed again. A kick, in fact. An ill-judged kick. The sort of kick to wake a dog or mule.

Once Margaret had washed herself and drunk a little water, and was, she said, "now clean enough to show my face to the day," Franklin helped her to her feet. It would do her good to sit and recover in fresh

air with views from the sunlit hillside down into the still-shaded valley of her home. This was the first time she had stood since her abandonment at the Pesthouse. He had to steady and support her for the
few steps to the wooden door, and the more difficult fifty steps beyond to the fallen tree trunk that he had partly covered with one of
his tarps, but he was glad of that, and glad as well to see her face in
open light. Her eyes, without the distraction or the competition of
any hair, were huge and thrilling.

"Your color's good," he said, something that she'd never heard
when she had heavy auburn curls.

Margaret could see at once that something odd had happened in
Ferrytown. There was hardly any hearth smoke, for a start. And at
that time of day, too early in the town for the sun to make a difference, she would have expected to see the flames of braziers and courtyard lanterns, not yet doused in households lucky enough not to have
to start work "on the nose" at first cock.

Everything was indistinct in those murkier moments of morning.
Perhaps she was mistaken and nothing was unusual, except her own
state of mind—and her eyesight. Her eyes were good enough when
she was face-to-face with work or conversation. Anything beyond a
hundred paces was blurred. But later, once the sun had directed its
angles above the treetops on the far side of the river and into the valley, Margaret could see her home in slightly less blurred detail. By
now there should be fifty fires or more, she thought. The lanes and
roads should be busy as animals were led out of the tetherings and
neighbors went about their tasks. The ferryman's raft should be taking its first plunge across the river with its paying cargo of animals,
carts, and emigrants. There should be at least some movement near
the guesthouse.

"What do you see?" she asked Franklin. "Can you see something
moving?"

He looked with her, although he didn't know what she expected
him to see. "Nothing," he said, meaning *Nothing to worry about.*

"I can't see anything either," Margaret said. "Maybe there's something moving by the ferry beach. Is that a cart?"

Indeed, it was a cart. But by the evening the cart would still be there at the river's edge, with its bewildered owners and some others newly arrived that day, yet no one living, no one able, no one in attendance to take their crossing fees and set them safely on the far bank.

Franklin had not wanted to abandon the Pesthouse so soon. He had started to take pleasure in its intimate darkness. He'd argued that Margaret ought to allow more time for her recovery; she was too weak to walk, even if it was downhill all the way. The flux was unpredictable and might return. Her shaven head would frighten people off. He was not fit enough to walk himself, as his knee was still troublesome. Besides, his brother, Jackson, had promised to return within a day or two, and if anything had gone wrong down there in Ferrytown, Jackson would certainly have come back to Franklin at once. That was his way. "He's mightier than me."

Margaret's immediate apprehension had been that everybody in Ferrytown had come down with the flux. And that made sense. It would explain the almost empty roads, the stillness, and the absence of smoke. Everyone would be confined to bed, too weak to move or light a fire, too battered to be visible. Her fear of such overwhelming pestilence was not illogical, or unprecedented, even though, according to her report, since the deaths of her father and the six other Ferrytowners three months before, there had not been any disease among her neighbors, other than her own. She'd been the only victim of this outbreak, as far as she knew, and now look at her, starting to recover after only a day or two and nothing lost except some weight and a lifetime's worth of hair.

So Franklin was not unduly worried. If it was illness that had stifled Ferrytown, then it was a weak and passing visitor. But in his view, he and Margaret would still be wise to stay up on the hill, at least until the fires were lit again, if not until Margaret's hair had reached a respectable length, as was normally required.

"Let's wait to hear what my mighty brother has to say," he suggested.

"What if he doesn't come?"

" 'Mighty Jackson, but Jackson mighty not.' " He laughed like a boy. Immediately he felt embarrassed to have been so childish in her presence, and blushed again. Blushed like a redhead might. "That was our joke," he explained, feeling half her age and suddenly recognizing with a further blushing shudder how foolish and immature and unreasonable he was to be so smitten by this woman, this sick and older woman who would regard him, surely, as a silly youth. "That's what we always used to joke about my brother," he repeated. "I only meant to say, let's wait at least a day or two, until you're well enough to walk, and see if he comes up for me."

His brother's failure to return so far had bothered Franklin. Jackson was mighty, but he was impetuous and unpredictable as well—"mighty not," indeed—the sort of man to take off on his own for days on end. That also had been his way, since he'd been able to walk. The world was not a dangerous place to him, and so he could never understand why people worried about his absences. Besides, he had a thirst. If there was liquor in Ferrytown, Jackson would sniff it out and knock it back in quantity. And he'd have to sleep it off in quantity as well. So two, three days? Inconsiderate, perhaps, but not unusual.

Franklin had that morning left Margaret sitting on her tree-trunk bench and hobbled as best he could into the clearing at the top of the trail where he and Jackson had parted. Was there any sign of his brother? she'd asked. Nothing yet, so far as he could tell. Nobody coming up. Just stragglers going down, the usual travelers in family groups, alone, with horses, carts, or nothing but their legs for company, a little string of refugees from Hardship House picking their way down the track for a night in bed and a country breakfast. Sea dreamers. Everything as normal, then. He tried to challenge her fears. Ferrytown, from his high vantage point, had simply looked quiet and uneventful, he said, hardly a scarf of smoke to be seen, perhaps without the usual bustle at the crossing point, no casual sound maybe, but it still seemed flourishing to him, a sleepy habitation, blessed to be exactly where it was, staying rich at nature's bottleneck.

No casual sound? His phrase was like a slap. Margaret could hear perfectly, even if her eyes might let her down. She knew too well the way the community was ordained, how if every single mortal there were lying down in bed, unable to lift a finger for himself, at least you could expect, even at this distance, the dogs to be complaining and—suddenly it occurred to her—the cocks to carry out their duties for the day, proclaiming their raucous intentions to the hens as soon as the sun came up and maintaining their vanities until sundown.

She pricked her ears and concentrated. Ferrytown was not providing any noise. Again she did her best to focus on open ground, on the dark shapes of the mules and horses in the tetherings, but nothing moved, so far as she could tell, nothing was impatient for the trail or its harnesses. Indeed, it seemed that every living thing was lying down like cattle expecting rain. The only movement Margaret could now discern, other than the few recently arrived carts and people who were gathering in increasing though unusually small numbers on the river's edge, was that of the ferry raft itself, which was neglected and had worked itself free of its mooring posts. It was swinging in the middle stream on its securing ropes, in a river still bloated from the rains of two nights previously.

In the end Franklin did what he was asked. Well before midday, he quickly gathered up their few possessions—her few clothes, his travel kit—and combined them into one pack, which he wore forward on his chest. He threw earth on the Pesthouse fire. He cut two sticks, one for himself to support his leg, an extra wooden limb, and a spare for Margaret. There was no point in pretending that she would have the strength to walk more than a few paces and certainly not down Butter Hill, with its harsh gradient and its unpredictable gravel. The days of vomiting, diarrhea, and fever had weakened her. So he wrapped the two tarps around her shoulders and stooped to let her climb onto his back, and then he tied the corner ears as tightly as he could around his waist and chest so that his warm burden was pressed tightly to his upper spine and shoulders. Finally he slipped the spare stick behind her knees and through the lower tarp knots at his waist, so that she was sitting in a kind of wood-and-canvas rescue chair and her legs could not dangle.

Margaret did not weigh much, scarcely more than the chest pack, it seemed. Despite the stiffness in his knee and the increased pain, Franklin could stand with the help of his stick and move easily at first. He'd carried deer carcasses in much the same way before, and on one occasion an injured ewe that had struggled all the way back to the stead. Margaret was a more compliant burden, and actually, if only he could put aside his lasting fear of her dry and bitter breath, and his embarrassment, she was a welcome one, the softest and the warmest pack he'd ever portered. Giddyup, he told himself, and began the slow and painful walk from the little Pesthouse that he'd grown to like so much across the clearing to the start of the descent. They were an alarming and a comic couple all at once: the oversized limping man, not quite a giant, the emaciated, recently scalped woman, with her bone head—now almost imperceptibly fuzzed orange—warning everyone and anyone who wasn't blind to avoid her at all costs.

Margaret had refused to wear her blue scarf again. The heat and weight were still too much for her. But covering her head would have made little difference to her pestilent appearance. She had no eyebrows; they had hardly begun to regrow. And even her expression seemed scalped and ominous. But for the time being, she and Franklin were happy anyway to be together on Butter Hill and amused to be playing piggyback, despite the fear of what they might find below. Were they in love? Well, no, not yet. He was too young and inexperienced; she was too old and inexperienced. They were, though, getting there with every step. And they were as intimate as lovers. How could they not be, with her legs pushed open, wrapped around his back, her breath and lips against his nape, her arms embracing him, clasped across his breastbone, so that, she thought illogically, she could help him bear her own weight and share the weight of worrying? Franklin gripped her knee with his spare hand, spreading his thumb onto the clothing of her upper leg. How weak and newly thin she was.

Margaret and Franklin did not attempt to catch up with the family that was negotiating the decline with a string of pack mules ahead of them. Rather, they hung back. Margaret did not wish to chance upon a Ferrytowner or a stranger who might pass on the word to her family and neighbors of how this virgin had been wrapped around a young man's back, or how personal he seemed with her. She'd be devalued all at once. Then what? It would be better if she'd joined her pa. She was almost thankful that her shaven head gave her and Franklin the excuse they needed to keep only their own company. Besides, you would not welcome any other company if you were with a person who at the very least (in Margaret's view) had drawn the flux out of your feet or who (in Franklin's view) had allowed such arousing intimacies.

Franklin concentrated on his balance and on the tribulations of the path, measuring his steps and rationing his breaths. He was determined not to show any weakness or tiredness. Here was his chance to prove to her how useful he might be and how mature. What luck had put this woman on his back? His damaged knee had proved to be an unexpected blessing.

Once they had sorted out the problem in Ferrytown, whatever it might be, thought Franklin, he could consider more fully what he ought to do about Margaret. He would not want to part from her at once. He'd not be happy to proceed without knowing her better. But what would Jackson say if his selfish, blushing brother insisted on delaying their departure from Ferrytown or if he made a decision on his own behalf for a change and chose to stay on there at least

through the winter, at least until Margaret had recovered and could
be persuaded, perhaps, to join them in their emigration east? What
would he say if Franklin was determined to settle his future in Ferrytown and court this woman—what, six years older than himself? To
take her as his wife?

Yes, this matter of their ages was an impediment. Franklin could
not avoid admitting that to himself, whatever his brother might say.
She was so much older. As old as his youngest aunt, in fact. But his
size made up for that, surely. Her time on earth equaled the volume
of his presence. Possibly, in his view, she was all the more enticing because of the age difference. Even with her illness and her shaven
head, Margaret had struck him as being irresistibly adult.

Margaret herself was too drained and fearful to think much of the
future. Certainly her personal porter was an agreeable young man,
kindly-featured if not exactly handsome, sweet-smelling, biddable—
and strong. She could not forget the patience and the tenderness he
had lavished on her feet nor the mixed sensations it had given her, a
breathless nausea together with a heat that was separate from the
fever. It did not seem possible that he could carry her for such a
length of time, down steep and difficult terrain, without stopping to
rest once in a while or demanding that she at least try to walk the last
part on her own two feet. She clung to his shoulders, exuberated by
the closeness of his company yet also exhausted by his efforts, because
each step he took shook every bone in her body. But she was not
making any place for him in her life. He'd just be another one of
those missed opportunities, another passerby whom she would miss
for a day or two and then forget. All that mattered for the moment
was the state of Ferrytown and her impatience for the sound of dogs
and cocks.

What first disquieted them, when they emerged below the hill
from the thicket of junipers, laurels, and scrub oaks that flourished
on the lower slopes, was the smell—sour milk and mushrooms,
earthy, reasty, and metallic. It was an unfamiliar smell that they rec-

ognized but could not name. It was as if this new experience were one that life itself had stored for them. The next thing that they spotted from the access path—alarming and unambiguous—was the mules and horses in the tetherings, not resting and expecting rain as Margaret had imagined, or at least hoped, but spread out and gaping, dead as stones and seemingly untouched, no wounds except the fresh ones inflicted by the crows and jays and turkey vultures that had already abandoned the hills to gather on their bodies. Dead animals, still picketed.

But their alarm was manageable until Franklin spotted what he did not mistake for long as dead piebald goats. Jackson's coat was spread out in the middle of the tetherings beside a dead mule. There was no confusing its color and its length and who its owner was. No two mothers in the world could stitch together such a piece. The body underneath seemed small, but Franklin was sure, as he stumbled forward with Margaret bouncing on his back, that he'd discover no one else but his brother, dead drunk, he hoped, and not just dead. But the body rolled too readily as he pulled at the coat. Too light, too small. A boy. He tumbled out of the goatskins as easily and weightlessly as a dog might be rolled out of its blanket. Franklin was relieved and horrified, all at once. "Who's this?"

Margaret had not seen, at first, what had induced such panic in her porter. She could barely see over his shoulder and had to stretch her neck to discover what had caused his sudden stumbling and his cry of alarm. She saw the puzzling coat in Franklin's hand. She was puzzled even more when he began to shake its creases out and smell the fabric. "It's Jackson's coat," he said. The brother's name. Then Margaret spotted the body at Franklin's feet and was in shock herself. This bundle was a neighbor's son, the nightwatch boy called Nash, a boy she'd known very well since he'd been a baby and she, barely out of her teens, had been his little nurse. "What's happened? Let me see him."

She was too firmly trapped at Franklin's back to release quickly,

so he kneeled down by the side of the body, twisting so that she could
see it clearly. Already it was smelling a little, like cured bacon. There
wasn't any blood on the earth or on the coat. No wounds. No sign of
blows or bruises.

"There's not a mark on him," Franklin said. "Just look at those."
He lifted his chin to indicate the carcasses of mules, horses, and donkeys. There was as well a single dog. Franklin closed the boy's eyes,
then cleaned his fingers in the soil. "There's not a mark on him," he
said again.

"There's something else," said Margaret. She had to concentrate
to hit upon the oddity. She was not familiar with human corpses. But
still it came to her, a chilling absence. "No flies. These tetherings are
always full of flies. They love the horses. But there's not a single one.
Can you see one?" Both she and Franklin put their hands across their
mouths and stepped away. They held their breath. No flies.

So Margaret's premonition had been correct: here was pestilence,
or flux of some new sort, that did not care if you were man or fly or
horse or mule or (now that they were hurrying into Ferrytown and
discovering more beastly cadavers at every step) chicken, hog or dog
or rabbit. The ground outside the stockade was scattered with animals. Even before they found the second human victim, Margaret
had begun to blame herself. Who else? She'd been the first to host
this current flux, so maybe she had passed it on to her grandpa and
he'd brought it back into the town once he had left her safely in the
Pesthouse. And without the benefit of barbering and pigeons to protect them, every beating heart in the village had been stilled. Yes,
every beating heart. She guessed exactly what she and Franklin
would discover if they dared to go beyond the stockade and the palisades. Not a single fly. No living creatures, other than the few travelers and the birds that had arrived since death had done its work.
No welcome from her family.

❧ SEVEN ❧

What should Franklin and Margaret do, other than flee the valley as quickly as their bodies would allow? They dare not squander any time on shock or lamentation. Any thought that Franklin might have had of settling or tarrying in Ferrytown could come to nothing now. This was the habitation of the dead. The living had to turn their backs on it and speed away.

They'd entered through the western gate, the usual threshold for emigrants, and walked a good distance from Nash's body before discovering another human form, or indeed any greater signs of widespread disaster. At the outer palisade, they'd passed within a few paces of where Jackson had gone out, barefooted, in the middle of the night to urinate for the last time and where his mighty body was still lying, coatless, doubled up, and finally incapable of defending itself against even the beak of a crow. But Jackson was not discovered. In fact, Franklin never found his brother's body. He found only the coat and later, possibly, his shoes. So one slim hope was allowed to take root and cling to life during the months ahead, the not uncomplicated hope that somehow Jackson had survived and might return, as big as ever, to reoccupy his piebald skins.

There could be no such hope for Margaret's family, however. The second human corpse they found was in her compound. Her younger brother, less than Franklin's age, was still in bed, his eyes wide open, staring at infinity from his wood cot on the screened veranda.

They persevered. Franklin held her legs. Margaret wrapped herself more tightly round his back. They went into the house. Her grandpa was in bed as well. So was her elder sister. So was her ma, her hair spread out across the pillows that all too recently she'd shared with Margaret's pa but now shared with the little serving niece called Carmena. The second brother, with Jefferson, the family rat-catcher, curled up at his side, the dog's ears still perked as if his hearing had outlasted death, was in the parlor, by the grate. Only Margaret's room and bed were empty. No corpses there. Her luck was inconceivable.

Across the courtyard, in the annex house, Margaret's younger, married sister, Tessie, her husband, Glendon Fields, and their boy, Matt, were almost hidden by their quilts but unmistakable—a balding man and the tops of two brown heads with just the slightest hint of red. All the hens were dead, their feathers still as beautiful and soft as the day Margaret had gone up Butter Hill. The other dog, the little terrier Becky, had deserted from her usual guard duties at the rear door, but there was no yapping from anywhere else. The compound seemed so quiet and ordered that it was easy to imagine that at any moment this merely inert, suspended world could spring alive again, that this was only sleep and that the compound's residents were simply resting late, untroubled by the light or by the summons of their usual daily duties. Death usually expressed itself more forcibly. But here it seemed that everyone had merely tumbled into a longer, deeper dormancy than usual. The one truly ugly sight was a neighbor's dove, which must have ventured out at night and died in flight, only to tumble into Margaret's yard and strike its head against a water pot. Its neck was broken, and there was blood, dried almost black, around its beak and underneath a wing.

It was Franklin who broke the silence. "We mustn't stay. You see how dangerous it is? Just smell the air." But first, before she could even consider her departure, Margaret wanted at least to feel and suffer the family earth beneath her feet, so Franklin released her from her mobile chair on his back, equipped her with a walking stick, and let her lean on him while she went around and paid her brief attention to the members of her family. "Try not to touch," he said, but did nothing to stop her folding their arms, closing their mouths, covering their faces with their blankets, pressing a fingertip kiss onto her mother's cheek. It was a numb experience. No weeping. Margaret's body, drained already by her illness, had shut down many of its functions, concentrating on the most urgent, which was the impulse to be dutiful quickly and then escape. Weeping was not urgent. There would be time for that. Besides, Margaret was too overwhelmed to feel much more than guilt. This slaughter surely was her fault.

There did not seem to be much evidence of flux on her family or on any of the many nonhuman bodies they had passed—no traces of vomiting or diarrhea, no rashes or blood. But what explanation could there be other than that her illness of a few days, perhaps released by her to go about its mischief the moment that she had broken its murderous grip, had passed through her feet, through Franklin's hands, and started its own descent down Butter Hill, had somehow strengthened while it had dined off her and ended up so strong that it had been able to sweep away these many lives with hardly more than a bruise and a single bloody beak to signify its cruelty?

There could be no funerals. Margaret, on her knees at the porch, between the herb pots and the little chair that her father had made for his children but that now was the resting place for their dead cat, merely said the simple words of the burial lament to herself, too dry-mouthed and appalled to sing them. All of the rhyme words—*done, alone, fade, gone, bone, shade*—seemed to fall like dead weights from her mouth, whereas whenever she'd sung or recited them before, at neighborhood funerals, the lament had always been comforting and measured and perfectly sufficient.

Franklin and Margaret did their best to avoid encountering any more bodies too closely as he carried her through the Ferrytown lanes toward the river. That wasn't hard. There were hardly any bodies in the public spaces. So far as they could tell from what could be seen when they dared to peer through open gates into the compounds and through windows into rooms, nearly everyone—not just her own family—had died while sleeping. That was an oddity, surely, because a pestilence will always take the weakest first and the strongest last, so that normally the deaths would be spread throughout the day or even spread throughout a month.

The only bodies that they did discover, dressed but fallen at the steps of their oven house, were those of the baker and his daughter, both on their backs and looking more startled though no more ashen than usual. Franklin was praying not to find the body of his brother, even though he was expecting to. Margaret was fearful of discovering the body of Becky, the missing family terrier. If only Becky had survived, she thought, there'd be something left to love. The thought of Becky still alive was enough to make Margaret call out her name and for Franklin to join in, except that once he understood that Becky was a dog, he called out, "Anyone?" "Someone?" "Is there anybody there?" And once or twice he called out Jackson's name. It must be possible that someone had survived, they reasoned, that at least one breathing body was still sick in bed and might be strong enough to tell them what had come to pass in Ferrytown.

They fell quiet again, both exhausted, as they reached the last few houses in the town and started on the flood-smoothed slopes above the river. Here, eighty paces away, there was finally some welcome evidence of life: people, horses, mules, livestock tied to the backs of carts, some ducks and chickens in baskets, even one or two dogs, on leashes to stop them running off to tuck into the corpses.

A group of lucky latecomers to Ferrytown, fewer than forty adults, had gathered at the river's edge, uncertain what to do. They knew exactly what they wanted. They wanted some kind of godly hand to bring the raft ashore from the midstream shingle where it had irretrievably grounded itself and ferry them to safety. The adults had gathered around to exchange ideas on how they could rescue the lost raft, how they could manage it if they succeeded. Was it possible to cross with carts, or were the rapids too strong and the channel too deep for wheels and horses? There was a smaller barge, strong enough only for human passengers, in one of the lofthouses just fifty paces away, as Margaret well knew. She would have told them, certainly. She would have told them, too, about another route, a dry one, that would allow them all, though not their carts, to reach the eastern side safely and quickly. But she was not allowed to help. Once her shaven head had been remarked and it was seen—further evidence of her sickness—that she was being carried, the travelers shouted out at her to keep her distance; and then, when she and Franklin continued to approach, hoping to explain themselves and join the group, the men began to pelt the pair with stones and even draw their bows and exercise their staves. A man ran forward and a slingshot of shingle struck Margaret's back and the side of Franklin's head as they turned to make their escape. His ear was cut.

Margaret jockeyed Franklin to a path that headed upstream on the river's bank, until, at the back of a group of boathouses, they reached a dry, rocky ledge surrounded by planted fruit trees where someone had built a wooden bench and a fishing platform. Beyond the ledge the river narrowed into cascades and was no longer navigable, except to trout. Franklin could carry her no farther, and she could ride no more. It had been a heavy day. Margaret could rest. But he had duties to perform. He would have to leave her there alone for the afternoon. She took the knife he offered, though she was in no state to protect herself if she was discovered by any of the living emigrants, or any ghosts.

Franklin, wrapped up in his brother's coat, his mouth and nostrils stuffed with wads of cloth, had agreed to Margaret's shamefaced proposition—why hadn't she thought of it while they were there?—that he should take the risk of going back into the village and to her home to make the best of their chances in the voyages ahead. As soon as he arrived in the compound, he should wash his hands and face, and the cut on his ear, in fresh vinegar, she warned him. There was a pot of it outside her family house. Then he should begin the job of salvaging. Should he salvage other people's property? he asked. "It can't be theft, to take things from the dead." No, it wasn't theft, perhaps, she agreed, but it wasn't seemly either.

Franklin went first to the second-largest boathouse, as she'd suggested, and found the open-keeled barrow that was used to wheel the one-man skiffs down to the fishing pools. He spread one of his tarps across the baseboards and tied the corners to the uprights of the frame with creel ropes, so that his barrow had a strong, sagging basket for carrying their spoils. The vehicle was long and clumsy in his hands at first, but Franklin was strong enough, despite his nagging back and still troublesome knee, to push it on his own. He soon got used to it, the trick of trading weight with balance, allowing the one to take care of the other. He was glad of having something useful to do, as otherwise his head would have been overcome with fear, doubt, grief, dismay—too much gloom to quantify. At least he had a purpose now and, he anticipated, a companion for the future, who might be as dependent on him as he had been on Jackson. A new experience. His world had never been shaped that way before.

He and Margaret hadn't settled on a plan, exactly, but no matter. A plan might not be any value in a world where everything had already been bludgeoned out of shape. They'd simply have to proceed instinctively, like children trying to walk a tightrope. There were no choices to be made on a tightrope, just the one and only step ahead, and then the next.

His first step now was to load the barrow with provisions. Taking fresh food would not be sensible, she'd said. An illness always settles on the food. But it might be sensible, if not entirely safe, to bring as much sealed food as he could find. She told him where the family larders were, where Ma had stored her honey and flagons of juice, where he might secure a good supply of salted meat and taffies as bright and hard as flint, which Margaret had made herself. She told him what clothes she wanted from her box, where blankets were that had not been tainted yet by the occupancy of death.

It was an odd experience, opening her box of clothes and other possessions. The smell was intimate for the few moments that it resisted the stronger odor of the dead from rooms that, thankfully, Franklin did not have to visit again. He could see how careful she had been with her possessions, packing everything tenderly in matching folds. He found the woolen pants that she'd described, the cloak, the green-and-orange woven top, the hat and scarves, the undershirts. He added the cleanest of her combs and a stiff hairbrush, with tangled copper evidence of her ownership. Her hair would grow again, to be as long as the strands caught between the brush's teeth—and he would see it growing. How many years would that take?

What would his mother have said if she could have witnessed what he did next? He opened chests and cupboards, uninvited, the looter, looking for valuables, some jewels or decorations they might trade, or anything to benefit their journey. But finally the stench of death and his fear of it was too much for him, and he fled the compound with nothing more except for some nicely carved ceremonial platters, a heavy silver cup that surely must be valuable, a hunting bow and a wrap of as yet unbloodied arrows. Already men had drawn their bows at him that day and loosed their slings, so he would be prepared next time. Jackson would be proud of him.

The family yard provided more: two extra water bags; some cattle skins, scraped but not yet completely cured; a coil of decent rope; a pair of wading boots; and a weighted fishing net. Finally he damped his face and neck with vinegar and poured what remained over his hands.

The boat barrow was not overloaded, but it was heavy, though slightly easier to maneuver now that it was weighted down with spoils. He added one more thing, a lover's touch. He lifted the clay pot of kitchen mint that was growing on the porch beside the cat and chair and wedged it safely at the center of the barrowload, so that the leaves would not be damaged. He hoped that this one living thing from Ferrytown might bring Margaret some comfort, though the plant itself was gasping for water after its almost three dry days of neglect and no rain. Surely she'd be grateful for his gifts, though *gifts* was not perhaps the right word for property that was either already hers (the comb and brush) or her unexpected inheritance (the family platters that she would have eaten off on feast days and at funerals, the mint that would have flavored so much of her summer food, the silver cup whose purpose, probably, was just to be valuable).

Franklin could have—should have, almost certainly—abandoned Margaret at this point, now that he was so well equipped and so en-riched. Any sensible man would have. Any person truly set on get-ting to the coast would not have stripped his chances to a sliver by traveling with a plague-ridden stranger who had to be carried. There were companions at the ferry point whom he might join, if he dis-guised himself by taking off his coat. He could trade his strength for their camaraderie and for their meals. He could save himself from many of the troubles ahead by being level-headed now. But then, what had his brother said? Only the crazy make it to the coast.

It had taken Franklin Lopez half the afternoon to equip himself from the pickings of Margaret's compound for their journey, and only half a moment, once he was certain that there was nothing else of irresistible benefit, to set a flame to Margaret's family home, as she had requested, and do her folks the honor of cremation. He was more than fifty paces away, still negotiating the rutted lane with his long barrow, before he heard the roof straw whoosh and the timbers crack. And he was a hundred paces away before the smell of fire re-placed the stench of bodies and he began to feel the heat himself. The wind pressed smoke on him, but he was glad of that, glad to have his lungs filled up with something other than the heavy odor of death, glad, too, to have the corpses of those two early risers who had fallen on the steps of their oven house far from their beds hidden from him by the smoke. The wind also helped to spread the fire, carrying the burning chaff from Margaret's roof across the alleyways first to the family outhouses and then into the yards and compounds of other houses, the timbers screeching and the flames leaping from thatch to thatch like nightmare cats.

Franklin hastened forward with his load to reach the outskirts of the village before the fire caught up with him. His size and strength mattered now. He could not afford to rest or be distracted by his problems. Living flesh burns just as well as dead. But when he reached the large guesthouse with its adjacent dormitories in a wide lane that he had not walked down before, he knew at once where his brother must have spent his night in Ferrytown. The first dormitory that he entered was where the women migrants slept. It took him only moments to recognize what kind of clothes were hanging over the bed ends—too voluminous and colorful for men—and to retreat outside into the deafening air.

Franklin found the men inside the second rest-house hall. The first room had the boys in it. The larger dormitory was still dark inside. The odor of decay mixed a little with smoke was striking and immediate. But it took a while for Franklin's sight to adjust. He moved forward slowly between the three lines of beds, all pushed close together, head to toe, checking on the bodies there through squinting eyes: two dead men in every bed, their clothes and best possessions scattered on the floor. He did not expect to recognize a face. The light was too gloomy. Too many heads were turned and buried in the pillows. Too many men had curled up underneath the bedclothes and were only shapes. No, Franklin was looking for a very bulky corpse, one that would deserve the nickname Mighty. But there wasn't a single body nearly large enough. Nobody's feet protruded from the bed end.

Oddly, at the very tip of the dormitory, one bed, set sideways to the others, was empty, the clothes pushed back tidily. A pair of huge shoes was turned upside down and fitted over the wooden bed knobs. They looked a lot like Jackson's. And certainly that had been Jackson's habit, too, to leave his shoes upturned on his bed head. "Ready for the fray," he used to say, whenever Ma asked him to remove them and leave them "where they belonged," under his bed "like anybody else's."

Franklin moved toward the bed, his heart tight in his chest, his throat suddenly so dry and papery that it felt as if it might tear if he dared to swallow. But he had only a moment to wonder if the shoes he seemed to recognize were really Jackson's. The far end of the dormitory, around the door, ruptured into flames and then began to produce spurts of smoke from both the rafters and the floorboards. The heat was brutal, ruthless, and swift. It gobbled up dry wood. Franklin left the shoes to burn. He found the nearest shutter, pulled it open, dropped into the smoky lane, and—none the wiser, and even a little less certain than before that Jackson was already dead—ran along the outside of the flame-licked dormitory to save his barrow from the fire.

Most of the little group of emigrants were at the ferry point, still debating what to do about their crossing, when the first smoke reached them, burned wood and roasted meat. The stink put them into a fresh swivet. Now what? What else could go wrong? How on earth would they escape a choking without a ferry and a ferryman? The river was too wide and swollen. What could they do? Wait for the winter to ice the water over? A few families who had circled up their carts on the drier meadows at Ferrytown's eastern edge began to pull their pitches again and move away from the fire. The wind was favorable, but if it came round to the west a little more and they stayed where they were, there was a danger that they might either be driven into the river by smoke or, if the vegetation caught, be burned alive, trapped between the water and the fire. They would have to move out farther with their panicking horses and their vulnerable wooden carts and join their comrades on the fireproof shingle beach.

But despite the disturbing stench, none of them truly feared the fire that Franklin had started. It seemed right, in fact—respectful, even—that the town should become a crematorium. The fever would be wiped out by the fire. The flames would allow the passage of the dead. Why should that bother them? The past was burning at their backs. The fire was in the west and not ahead. Hadn't that always been the prophecy—that mother would abandon daughter to the ashes, that father and son would depart from one another in flames, that before the doors of paradise could open there would have to be a blackened, hot, and utter silence in America, which could be quenched only by the sea and would be survived only by the people of the boats?

When Franklin staggered by with his loaded barrow, coughing on the smoke, his shoulders ashy, his ear still bleeding, nobody offered any help. He was the young man in the unforgettable coat, a companion to the fever victim, and should stay away, no matter if that meant remaining on the edges of the town, where it was becoming difficult just to breathe, let alone lift and push heavy goods. It didn't matter that the shaven-headed woman was no longer in his company. The migrants kept their distance, waved him on, warned him to keep away, showed their staves and bows, and picked up the stones and shingle that they would use again if he came too close. They did their best to avoid even catching his eye, for that also might be enough to catch the flux.

But in a sense they all already had a fever just as murderous and treacherous: emigration fever. It was burning them up and driving them on. This was one of those clarifying points in their migrations (during which the push of here and the pull of there had been equally persuasive) when any remaining instinct to return to their homes went up in smoke. Here was where disease was in command. But there'd be no fever where they were going, would there? They

wanted to believe it. There'd be no ague or calenture, no tick disease
or cholera, no canker or malaria. Why, they had persuaded themselves, illness would be so rare on that side of the ocean that people
would travel for a day just to watch a man sniff.

Margaret was almost insensible when Franklin finally reached her
late in the afternoon. Her fever had returned, taking advantage of
her tiredness. She'd done too much already that day. She had just
about enough energy for growing hair, but little else. Franklin simply lifted her—she had no weight—and put her on the boat barrow
next to the pot of mint, together with the few possessions they had
brought down from the Pesthouse earlier that day.

"We have to get away," he said, although he suspected she might
already be too feverish to hear him. "It isn't safe. It's . . ." He raised
his hand to signify that there were too many unsafe things to list—
the fearful, living emigrants with stones; the fire and smoke that,
once they had the height and confidence, would stop only at water;
the spores and pollens of disease; the ghosts of all their families
which, riding on the stallions of grief, might at any moment come to
lasso any stragglers; the fast-approaching dusk; the haunting possibility that Jackson might discover them.

"There is a way," she managed to murmur. "A secret way."

She had a stunning revelation. High on the bluffs, between the
cascades and the downfall from the lake, where the river was at its
narrowest, hidden by the undergrowth, was a wooden bridge, wide
and strong enough to take the weight of a horseman. It would certainly support their laden barrow. "Just follow this path, up."

"A bridge?" repeated Franklin, unable to believe her. This was
startling, if it was true and not some product of her illness. He'd
never suspected that there was anything other than a ferry crossing.
An expensive ferry crossing! So much per person, so much per animal, so much for each barrow, stage, or cart. A troublesome and un-

safe crossing at which there always was a holdup. A line of people was waiting hopelessly there at this very moment. "How can there be a bridge?" he asked almost angrily, pushing Margaret's arm to make her wake.

"The bridge is for the townsfolk only. Was," she explained, struggling with her tenses. "It's there for us if anybody wants to go across, though no one wants, or wanted to, these days. We keep it, kept it, to ourselves, of course."

"Of course." He laughed, not because of Margaret's struggle with words but because one of their immediate problems had suddenly been solved and also because the people of Ferrytown had effected such an audacious deceit. "I understand! What idiots we are. What clever people you've been. Where is the profit in a bridge? You'd simply pay a modest toll and walk across. But a ferry crossing, now— that's a lot of trouble. A ferry crossing can't be cheap . . . Pay up, pay up, you have no choice. The river must be crossed. Yes, you were better off as Ferrytown. A place called Bridgetown would never have made you rich!"

Margaret was too tired to smile. She wanted sleep more than anything, because she hoped to escape the wretchedness of leaving home, of consciously inhaling the airborne, burned remains of Ferrytown. But when Franklin began to push the barrow up and along the riverside track toward the secret bridge, toward the hidden wooden bridge, she managed to add just one encouragement: "Giddyup." She understood how little time there was, that if the undergrowth caught fire, as well it might, then the bridge would be destroyed by flames as well. She dared not feel hopeful, she could not be well, she would beat back her grief, until the far bank had been reached and they were out of harm's way.

What was it that stopped Franklin from running back to that small group of emigrants who were waiting, helpless, at the ferry point, watching the mud-charged, storm-flushed river, the water almost thick enough to plow, it seemed, but sadly—they'd tested it—

too thin to walk across? What stopped him from telling them that there was a bridge which they could use for free? He wasn't good at keeping secrets, usually. He'd always been quick to pass on anything he'd spotted, even if actually it would have benefited from a blind eye. He was not devious but naively straightforward. That made him enemies, not friends. But on this occasion—revenge, perhaps; the small wound on his ear; the threats they'd made—he instinctively felt that salvation was in short supply, that the world was in such a state of anarchy and spite that it might allow nobody to escape, and that his and Margaret's best option was to slip across the river unnoticed and unannounced. If he ran back down toward Ferrytown calling out, "A bridge, a bridge," who could tell what forces might be listening, what demons might rush ahead with their thin hands to tear away the bridge and throw its timbers into the stream?

No, Franklin's head was full of warring flies. Their clamor was deafening. He forced himself to concentrate on the now unwieldy, human weight of the boat barrow and on the awkward balance it demanded as they progressed upstream, avoiding chokes of rock and finding routes around the thickest undergrowth. Then, once he had reached the wider, beaten path above the cascades, where the ground was flatter and easier, he busied himself with an inventory of everything in their possession that might help them on their way.

What could they sell? The silver cup, certainly. Finding that had been a piece of luck. The silver cup could make them rich. It could secure them places on a boat. And there was his coat—yes, *his* coat now, perhaps, though parting with it would seem like a further act of treachery. He shook the thought away. There were the partly prepared skins. It was likely, too, that the carved dining platters he had rescued from Margaret's family compound would be attractive, if not here in this land, where everybody seemed to be on the move, then possibly across the sea, where there were doubtless many opportunities to feast and many reasons to celebrate.

Then, of course, besides the few clothes he'd brought for Margaret and his own two pairs of everything, there was, or he hoped there was, though he could not remember where he had packed it, the little cedar box containing her three lucky things: the silver necklace that she had shown him as he drew the flux out from her feet; the square of musty, colored cloth, too delicate for him to touch with his big hands, she'd said; and the coins from the old America. The necklace might be valuable, but would she want to part with it? Would he even dare to say she should? What price good luck? Margaret ought to wear the necklace, he decided, and let it hang well out of sight (between her breasts), where it could work its charms without attracting pilferers. In fact, she ought to let him hang it there himself. He could imagine working the chain around her shaven head, lifting it over her exposed ears, and guiding it down to settle at her throat. He would find the cedar box and pull out the necklace for her to wear as soon as they were settled.

They had their riches, then, to trade. And in the meantime they would not starve, not for a while or two. He'd filled their four water bags in the river from the fishing platform where he'd left Margaret earlier that afternoon. It would be enough for several days, if they were moderate. Besides, they had the three flagons of pressed fruit juice that he had rescued from her house. And there was honey to eat—or sell!—and enough dried or salted blocks of meat to see them to the coast, surely, and possibly beyond. He even had a scrap of salted pork left over from the provisions that Jackson had entrusted to him all those days ago, and a handful of dried fruit, the final edible reminder of home and Ma.

Thirst and hunger seemed unlikely, and anyway, in this relatively undamaged land, more forested and fertile than the country he had fled, only the sick and lazy could easily starve. He was well equipped to find their dinner if there was any dinner to be had. He was a farm boy, after all, even though he had mostly been an unenthusiastic one. He knew what was welcome in a pot and what was poisonous; he knew which parts of plants were tasty in the fall and which were fibrous and troubling. He knew his mushrooms pretty well.

Again he made a list. What had they got to help them eat? They had a good-sized weighted net to fish with. (He even had the fisherman's wading boots to make the task a dry one.) He had a bow and good arrows should they chance upon deer, game birds, or rock goats. There was enough rope somewhere on the barrow, under Margaret's body, to make lassos or trip-snares. Anything they caught or trapped could be butchered and prepared with his two knives. And anything they cooked and ate would have the garnish of some fine fresh mint.

He could imagine it, the two of them, their faces warm above a fire, their backs defended from the cold by Margaret's blankets, dining on some venison he'd caught and butchered. And then, when they retired to sleep, they'd have the barrow as their raised cot, too high for dew to bother them as they held hands beneath the tarps, their bodies separated only by the necklace at her throat.

"We have enough," he told himself out loud as he proceeded on an easy but narrowing path into the woodlands on the high bank of the river. Soon they'd be across and they could rest. His dream became more complicated and more comfortable, more settled, oddly. No huddling round a makeshift fire, no venison, no cold night air, no boat barrow. Instead there was a clearing in the trees, a little soddy built of boulders and wood and earth, a narrow bed, and just the two of them, asleep, a curl of smoke from their shared hearth, his fingers wrapped around her toes.

The light was weakening when they reached the bluffs where the falling torrent from the lake had etched a deep, unclimbable gulch into the hillside. They could go no farther on this bank of the river. Franklin, not wanting to wake Margaret before he'd delivered her to a safe place, left her sleeping in the barrow while he went in search of access to the bridge. From lower down the path he'd spotted its slatted wooden sides swaying high above the water. A fall from it would be fatal. But once he'd reached its level, the bridge seemed to have disappeared. He had to clear away some wood and debris from the deep undergrowth and pull aside a screen of branches. It could not have had much use in recent months.

Thankfully, the bridge was wide enough for the two wheels of the barrow, and it seemed firm, too, despite the swaying. A little weight would steady it. The crossing actually was easier than he had feared. The planking of the bridge was smooth, and sagged slightly downward toward a lower mooring on the far bank. Franklin had to concentrate only on keeping a good line with the leading tip of the barrow and trying not to let himself or his load tilt to the side. He was not fond of heights. He'd never been a boy for conquering trees or swinging out on ropes. He counted heartbeats as they went across, taking one step for every other beat, and hadn't reached a hundred before he was able to bump his load over the last impediment, a strut of raised wood, and put his feet and the barrow wheels on solid ground. His first step in the east. He should have felt proud of himself. Triumphant. Mightily relieved. He should have felt brave. But he did not. Rather, now that he no longer needed to be determined, he counted himself weak, dishonest, craven, and troubled by disloyalty.

Something had happened that he did not truly understand. Not the slaughter in the village—he'd never have an explanation for that, except what he had always known, that life hangs on a spongy spider's thread that can stretch only so far but then is bound to snap. Not his own unexpected secrecy about the bridge, his failure to inform the other travelers. Not even the likelihood that, even if Jackson had managed to survive, he would never take another step at his brother's side, or slip his long arms into the sleeves of his own goat coat. No, what troubled Franklin from the moment he reached the east side of the bridge was the fear that he had made a big mistake, that where he truly should be traveling was westward, back to the family hearth, back to Mother waiting at the center of abandoned fields. If instead of taking the path eastward down Butter Hill that morning, he and Margaret had fled westward, heading back to his mother's house, then his brother—and all the people of Ferrytown—could be alive in their imaginations, at least. They could forward him by their best hopes to the coast and then propel him by wishful thinking (quite a gusty friend) toward the new lands over there. If Franklin still hoped to be a true and dutiful son, he should take Margaret back home with him to introduce her to his ma, to have those ancient hands touch his and hers and give their blessing. A mother could expect no less. How had they ever left her there?

Franklin looked back along the woodwork of the bridge. For the moment, it seemed to him that crossing the river had been an act of abandonment. Certainly he was not able to contemplate his own journey eastward anymore with much degree of hope or self-respect. But equally he recognized the nonnegotiable truth. Going home was not an option. It's fearful men who go back home to be with Ma. Only the crazy make it to the coast.

Franklin shook himself. So he'd be crazy then. He'd force himself to be. He'd not allow himself to fail. He had—again—to do the mean and foolish thing. Not out of spite, more spite, toward the other travelers. What did it matter to him whether their journey to the coast was easy or hard? Not simply to protect the safe side of the river from the burning one and keep the flames from skipping across the bridge like imps. He meant to cut himself off from his own timidity.

He took the sharper of his two knives and went back to the bridge. It was slung across the river and tethered only, on the eastern side at least, to several sturdy tree trunks. It would not be a complicated task to cut it loose. The mooring ropes were thick and greasy, toughened by the weather, but they responded to his blade, each strand and ligament springing back as Franklin severed its tension. The whole bridge slumped to one side when he had entirely cut through the first rope. Anyone crossing it would have been tipped into the water far below. The second rope was easier and springier, as the weight on it had doubled. Soon the secret bridge was freed from its eastern shorings. With a little help from Franklin's powerful shoulders, it slithered and bounced down the rocky bluff above the river, breaking up a little as it fell and then finally settling in the water.

There was no longer a secret bridge from Ferrytown. There was instead a steep, timbered slide into the river on the western side of its coulee. A dangling trail of timber. But not even that for long. The racing waters began to tug on the severed end of the bridge, smashing the planks against the rocks. Within a month, much of the debris would be swept away.

"We have enough," Franklin said aloud again. He was thrilled and appalled by what he'd done, in equal measure. But he did not want to examine his feelings too deeply. He'd have to put his doubts behind him and concentrate only on the journey. There was a job to be done: to find a safe place in the forest or beyond where they could pass the night. He had to make the most of what little light remained. Once more he put his weight behind the barrow with its obliging, well-oiled wheels and made good their escape from Ferrytown by climbing up through sunshine along the river bluff until he reached the eastern shoreline of the lake, the silver pendant that he'd only glimpsed before from Butter Hill. He'd never seen a spot more beautiful.

⊰ eiᏩht ⊱

This was no place for a barrow, especially such a heavy one with a fragile human cargo. A sledge would have been better: a sledge loves mud. Or even a rowboat, though preferably one with oars—and an oarsman—tough enough to scull through mud and leaves.

The downpours that only three nights previously had shaken the vapors out of Ferrytown lake might have dried out in the open country around the settlements and on sloping ground. But on the east bank of the river, where the water table was high, the going was wet. The flat forest paths beyond the wooden bridge and the lakeside were still drenched and swollen. Here, away from the thin, rolling soil of the mountain passes and the well-drained scrubland of stocky junipers and tangled laurels that labored for existence on the lower slopes, rain could not drain easily or quickly. Where could it go? It had to settle in and spread itself and deepen.

These wet, silt-rich forests, a mixture of chestnuts, marsh oaks, maples, and hickories, which at this time of the year were exchanging green for oranges and reds, were distended with water and therefore so fertile and tightly undergrowthed in places that not even a mule could pass. What might look from a distance like startled outstretched hands were antlers of pink lichen, a breathtaking and magical sight, especially in this dusk, with the sun finding angles through the hammock to pick out strips of foliage and blaze its reflection in puddles. Even this late in the day and this late in the year, the sun's heat was strong enough to coax a gauzy vapor from the forest floor.

Margaret was still too exhausted and unwell to pay attention to her grief, let alone to notice the beauty all around. And Franklin, after all his efforts, hardly had the strength to lift his head from his hard work and waste himself on leaves. The barrow, with its two thickly rimmed wheels and hefty, shallow-sided deck, had been designed only to transport skiffs the hundred paces between the boathouse and the fishing jetty. And it was meant, too, to be managed by two men, not one. It certainly was not intended to be both an emigrant wagon and a transport for the sick, especially in soil so soft and giving that Franklin feared that if he stopped pushing for only an instant the ground beneath would swallow the barrow whole, and Margaret with it, but if he continued pushing he'd only be plowing furrows, deep enough to plant potatoes. The countryside appeared to him, in fact, not in the least beautiful. He was more used to the wide-lit, open country of the plains. Such a crowded mass of trees did not seem natural. It did seem sinister. Here was just another challenge to be braved.

His knee had noticeably improved. It shifted in its socket once in a while. But it was much less painful. And it was hardly swollen. Nevertheless, every step Franklin took still seemed burdened not only by the weight of his own body and the lesser weight of Margaret and their possessions but also by the load of sorrow that finally began to take its toll on him. He had been too shocked and overcome by disbelief when he'd first observed the many dead. Then he'd been too busy in Ferrytown itself to feel much more than numb docility. But here, now that he was rid of Ferrytown and the sight of any corpses,

the grief was overwhelming. Brother. Ma. He bore the weight and
pushed against the water and the mud. He also wept. Just tears, no
sobbing, no heaving chest. He felt as inundated as the landscape he
was pushing through. The tears leached from his eyes, drawn out by
gravity alone, it seemed.

Franklin could not tell if Margaret was watching him. Her eyes
seemed wet as well, and hardly shut. He knew he ought to care if he
was being observed by a woman, but he did not.

"I'm unhappy for my brother," he explained to the body in the
barrow. He could not use the word *crying*, although he was certain
now that Margaret had been watching him. Such feebleness as his
could never pass unwitnessed.

Jackson would have been appalled, especially as this display of
weakness and emotion was partly in his name. His death or disap-
pearance had occasioned some of the tears. No, Jackson would have
said that weeping was undignified and cowardly. It showed a lack of
self-respect.

When he'd been small and keen to keep up with his brother,
Franklin had submitted himself to all the usual boyish rituals: allowing himself to be cut to bond a friendship with blood, submitting to
being marked on the forearm with a smoldering twig, letting the
dogs take meat scraps from his lips, handling ill tempered snakes.
Risks without purpose, he had thought. But Jackson and his comrades, quick to intimidate the smaller—well, the younger—boy, had
always warned him against refusing or admitting pain, or flinching.
"Be calm and silent. Be undismayed," they'd said, the last word being one they'd heard the adult men use approvingly. Dismay was
something for the girls. If you could cause dismay in girls, then that
was satisfying. But Franklin could not be calm and silent in the face
of dogs and twigs and snakes and knives. He could not bully girls.
And certainly he was never undismayed. He had let Jackson down
too often. He had always been dangerously close to tears. He still had
the all-too-minor burn marks on his arm to remind himself of that.

Margaret, in fact, had hardly paid any attention to Franklin or anything he'd said since the middle of the afternoon. She was recovering in sleep. She would not even remember crossing to the east bank of the river. She had not heard the crashing and the splintering of the bridge. The boat barrow had been too safe, and nearly comfortable. Franklin's hand was steady, his voice was soothing, and consciousness was hardly bearable, so she had clung to sleep. She could not say exactly what her dream had been, but this was certain: when she woke, the bridge and village were far behind and marked only by distant plumes of smoke. Her head was full of animals and frights and characters: three beds confused (the one at home, now ash; the Pesthouse bunk; the barrow, bucking like a ship, her feet caressed, her scalp torn free of hair by devils with wooden hands, the smell of death and vinegar); two bearded men (that Abraham, and that other, younger one but just as tall, her toes pressed into him); two birds (one pigeon burdened by the weight of plague, tumbling with its failing wings to crash among the sleepers at the foot of Butter Hill, and one of her neighbor's doves, its neck broken and black blood crusting on its beak).

But now that she had slept enough, Margaret could hear Franklin's voice, driving her beds and men and birds away. His word *unhappy*— "I'm unhappy for my brother"—had woken her.

Her eyes were open slightly more, he noticed at once. Her chin was pointing at him attentively, and so he raised his voice a little. "If he was here, if he was still alive—he *might* be still alive—he'd tell us what we need to do. He'd know the way." She almost seemed to move and nod. "And you're unhappy for your whole family. More unhappy than I could ever be. For just one brother. I still have a little hope. I understand."

He saw now that he, or at any rate the mention of her family, now not whole at all, had made her cry. Full tears. Her cheeks were red and wet, and he felt better—no, *relieved*—for seeing them. Women are fortunate, he told himself. They are allowed to weep. They are

encouraged to. That was how the duties of the world had been as-
signed. Crying for the women. Spitting for the men. Jackson could
spit a fire out if he wanted to. "My brother wasn't frightened of anything," he added under his breath. A curse almost.

That aunt, the aunt who had strapped the healing pigeon to
Franklin's feet when he was a sick boy, had not been very fond of
Jackson and had judged his fearlessness to be infantile and foolish.
"Your brother's like a child, to be afraid of nothing," she'd said, when
Jackson was already bearded. Franklin had felt both ashamed and
validated to hear her speak so disloyally. "If his bed was on fire, he'd
rather sleep with flames than run for water. Like a fool. If there was
plague in the house, he'd rather die than cover his nose." Franklin almost smiled to think of it. She'd been the perfect aunt for any nervous boy, because she had considered determination and bravery
dishonest. (Although when she herself had died, among the thou-
sands during the Grand Contagion when Franklin was just starting
on a beard of his own, she'd departed without a murmur of complaint, indifferent to death's indifference.)

These moments with his wise, dead aunt brought Franklin's
weeping to an end. Wishing her or Jackson back on earth again,
wanting to return to Ma, fearing the future, would not solve anything. Regret would not reveal a route ahead, and fighting for his
manly dignity would not help. Dignity does not provide a supper.
But he would at least attempt to remain undismayed for once. He
had to find the confidence to deal with their immediate problems. If
he wanted to survive himself and also take good care of Margaret,
like a neighbor, like a suitor, he would have to toughen up and
sharpen up.

First he'd need to understand the territory, to remember how to
find his bearings from the polestar and the sun without his brother's
help. And when the sun or stars were hidden by clouds or mist, he'd
have to read direction from winds and birds and lichen. Only then
could they decide a route that might take them to the drinking places

and the beds and the supplies of food and forage for travelers. What sort of welcome would they get now that they were among not their own people but "the others," who might consider that they had no right to water or to go in peace or even to be alive? That they'd find out as they went along.

Franklin listened to the forest more intently now. He needed its advice. He felt lighter, weaker suddenly, less able to manage the barrow and its cargo. He had to stop and rest. It was almost too dark to go on anyway. He had already given up any hope of reaching a welcoming community with beds for hire for that night. They were still too deep in the woods. Besides, there could be no welcome for a woman as ill as Margaret would still seem to be to any strangers. He had held out a little hope, however, that there could well be a trapper's habitation among the trees where they might bargain the use of a shed or beg hot food. Or an unused night shelter, possibly. Or a woodsman's abandoned soddy, where they could be as snug as they had been inside the Pesthouse what seemed an age ago. He worried that Margaret might not survive a night without some shelter or some heat, even with the barrow as their bed. And he could not imagine lighting a fire for her or constructing a dry, roofed refuge in such deep mud.

In the end—the end of that day's light—they had little choice but to spend the night out in the open. There would be no habitations for a day at least, and Franklin was too tired to take another step. He did as much as he knew how. He let the barrow stand in open ground in water only ankle-deep and as far from falling leaves and timber as was possible in such a busy wood. He gathered up their bulkier possessions—the clothes, the cattle skins, the coil of rope, the weighted fishing net—and made a pillow out of them at the head of the barrow. He stowed the valuables and the food, such as it was, in his own back sack and hung it from a branch that he hoped would prove inaccessible to animals. He suspended the water bags, too, and the flagons of juice.

Now there was room on the barrow for the making of a double bed, with a blanket, the second tarp, and his brother's goatskin coat as the coverings. Finally Franklin placed the pot of kitchen mint at the end of their bedding, just beyond the reach of her feet. He climbed in next to Margaret, his two knives at his side, the hunting bow and arrows within reach. He stretched out, fully clothed, trying not to miss his supper or feel the unexpected cold, as all too quickly the forest yielded to the darkness that it loves.

Margaret was asleep again but breathing evenly. He joined her without difficulty. The day was failing, and there was nothing else to do. Either sleep or lie awake and shiver. He should not complain that Sister Sun had denied him candles and warmth for this night when she had already provided so much daylight for free, and so much fine, unseasonable heat. And there they slept, back to back, the pale-faced shaven woman and the younger man, in their great wooden wheeled bed, between the canopies of trees, like children in a fairy tale, almost floating, almost out to sea. So, finally, some happiness.

A cold night had burdened the trees in frost, the season's first, and stiffened the standing water and the pools of mud with a glazing of ice. The couple had slept well. Margaret was the first to stir. She woke alarmed. All she remembered at first was that everything was either dead or up in flames. She could not remember what had happened the previous afternoon, after Ferrytown, or how they'd ended up enveloped by such unexpected woodland. It took her a moment to focus her eyes, as usual. The distance always looked as if it needed a wipe, and she had trouble telling faces from afar. But she could soon see and appreciate what Franklin had set up for them the night before: the clearing in the wood, the barrow as a bed, the tarps and coat that kept them warm, the familiar pot of herbs, still flourishing in spite of everything, at her feet. She sniffed the frosty air. Her nostrils were clear. Her body seemed to ache a little less. Her hands and throat were reassuringly cold.

There was a moment of unease, or at least apprehension, when she saw Franklin at her side, in bed with her to all intents and purposes. She'd never even been kissed by a man other than a relation. Until a few days previously, when Franklin had massaged her feet, she had hardly been touched by one. She understood that these were pressured times when conventions and proprieties didn't count for much. She felt as well that Franklin was most likely a man to trust. His laugh—how it shook his whole body down to his knees and fingertips, rather than simply creasing his face, how it seemed to loosen him and soften him—was attractive and unexpectedly womanly. She had seen him weeping, too, the day before, and that had been heartening in ways she could not begin to understand. He was a decent boy, she thought. A little nervous, possibly, and kinder and gentler than his size might suggest. She probably owed her life to him. He had become her plague-removing pigeon in her imagination. And she allowed that she might owe her future life to him. But these were only daydreams and too comforting. For the moment, at least, she needed to be tougher, to chasten herself as coldly and as bluntly as she could and to acknowledge how grave her situation was, Franklin or no Franklin. Ferrytown was history. Her family were ancestors. Her home was ash. Any chance she had was in the east, beyond the ocean. Most of her countrymen and countrywomen had already realized that. Her journey there had already begun. That was clear, and non-negotiable. She'd have to make the best of it.

Margaret pulled on her sandals and swung her legs over the side of the barrow. She ought to test her strength, she had decided, before her fellow woke. The trees were noisy with a rising wind and the susurrus of leaf fall. The ground was soft and reluctant to bear her weight, but she succeeded in taking a dozen steps around the barrow, touching anything she recognized. The pot of mint was heartening. She was relieved by how strong she felt: not strong enough to walk a great distance, perhaps, but sufficiently robust to busy herself around the clearing, checking what provisions they had got, what clothes he'd brought for her, what food and drink there was. There was no sign of her cedar box with its three talismans. Franklin had put it somewhere safe, no doubt. She was surprised only to find the platters and the silver wedding cup, touched to see that he had packed a comb and brush for her, and glad to discover the flagons of juice. This was juice that she had squeezed herself from apples and berries.

By the time she'd drunk more than her share from one of the flagons—her thirst was still not satisfied—Franklin was awake and sitting up in their shared bed just watching her.

"I've decided," she said, resolving as she spoke that she would, at the very least, take him as a brother.

"Decided what?"

"Decided that I'll call you Pigeon. That's my name for you. Franklin sounds too dignified."

"You think that I'm not dignified?"

"Not with that limp. How is your knee today?"

"It's better than it was . . ."

"And I'm better than I was as well, so then . . . you see?"

"So then, what should we do?"

"We eat, of course. You have a bow. Shoot something for our breakfast. Suddenly I'm starving."

While Franklin was out of sight in the forest, though hardly silent, Margaret stretched their coil of rope between two trees and hung the net from it. She would fish for birds and with any luck would have food already cooked when he returned. His catch could be their supper. She found the spark stone and the pouch of tinder, but there was nowhere dry enough on the ground for her to start a fire. So she emptied the mint plant from its pot, that doorstep friend from her old home, and replanted it in the heavy silver cup, which had been a showpiece heirloom in her family for a hundred years and more but never used before. Now the plant had to be the best-appointed mint in America. She firmed it in with extra, muddy soil around its tangle of stringy roots, then smelled her hands. That made her even hungrier.

The empty plant pot was big and strong, and glazed enough to withstand heat. Margaret was an old hand at striking fire. Soon—a dozen chit-chits at most—she had a flame and then a smoky oven in which to cook their breakfast. She was an old hand at fishing for birds as well, although the first few captives were too small to pluck and cook. But by the time the sun was high enough to offer some heat to the day in exchange for a little steam, Margaret had netted a fair-sized quail and a bird that she could not remember seeing before, dappled brown and black but fat and edible. She broke their necks and snapped off their wings, trying not to think either of home or of her dream birds. She split the carcasses open with Franklin's knife. It was not easy or pleasant to pull out the bones or tug away the skin and feathers. Rather than spoil the breakfast with down and fluff, she threw away good meat among the inedible waste. The forest is always glad of carrion. The remainder, all clean breast, she wrapped in the greenest leaves she could find. Now she had only to construct a spider trivet out of twigs and hang the bird meat from it over the pot fire, where it could cook in smoke.

Franklin didn't come back empty-handed, but he hadn't found the chance to use an arrow either. Rather than disappoint Margaret, he had spent too much time and effort lifting fallen logs to see if anything tasty was living underneath. The logs were mostly light and flaky, but the overnight frost had iced them in and made them almost unshiftable. He'd had to rock them free. But all his efforts did not produce as much as a snail. He had mushrooms, though. Mushrooms he could trust as safe. And a few nuts. He was disappointed to have failed as a hunter while she, evidently, had managed so easily to trap fresh meat.

They sat together on the barrow, eating breakfast off carved ceremonial plates. They talked about the day ahead. They were almost eager to get on. "I've heard," Franklin said, trying to joke away his failure in the woods that morning, "that on the far side of the ocean, no one uses bows and arrows. Hogs run through their woods ready-roasted, with forks sticking out of them. All you have to do is take a slice whenever you're hungry."

"But first you have to make the pig stand still," Margaret replied. "And that's not easy." She liked it that he treated her as if she were a girl, easy to amuse.

"These pigs are trained. They come to you like a pet dog, if you whistle, if you know the proper whistle. And then you tell them, *Sit*. And then you put a little salt on them and dine like gods. That's what I heard."

"That's what you hope."

"That's what we have to hope."

"You're a booster, then. A good-luck man?"

"Well, yes," he agreed. He liked the thought of that, to be her optimist. "I always hope that the best has yet to come. I think that this"—he spread his hands to take in everything, from the sunlit forest to the mint, newly settled in its silver cup; he flexed his recovering knee—"all this bodes well for us. We'll be lucky." He didn't add that nothing could be worse than yesterday. It wasn't wise to challenge fate.

Franklin's mention of good luck reminded Margaret of her missing cedar box. "You have to wear the necklace," he said, getting up to find it for her but also fearing he might not. "I can help you put it on." An odd offer for a man, she thought. But even though they hunted high and low among their few possessions, checking every bag, shaking out their clothes, examining the ground underneath their barrow, neither the box nor any of the three talismans was found. Margaret could remember touching them when she'd been at the Pesthouse. She could remember pushing the box under her bedclothes there so that Franklin's large hands could do no more damage to her piece of fragile, ancient cloth that he'd been rubbing with his thumb. But since? No, everything had been so hurried and disrupted. There had been no *since*. But she was angry with herself, nevertheless, and her loss was such an ill-timed setback, coming just when their improving fortunes seemed assured.

"It must have dropped out on the other side," he said. "We'd not have noticed it. It's just a little box."

"Where? On Butter Hill. When I was on your back?"

"Perhaps. Or maybe in the orchard where I left you, below the bridge, by that fishing platform," Franklin suggested, his optimism under pressure for a moment. He blushed. He knew in his heart that the loss of the box had been his fault. Perhaps he hadn't even packed it when they left the little hut. "I'm sure we can't have left it in the Pesthouse, Mags," he said.

"Do you remember bringing it?" Margaret looked childlike suddenly. Her eyes were huge. He'd called her Mags and that was melting her.

He nodded, shook his head. He wasn't sure. "I'll go back if you truly want me to. I could do it in a day," he said. He meant it, too. He'd run each step of it. He'd be glad to reunite her with her things and earn her gratitude. Then he remembered what had happened— what he had done—to the wooden bridge. He couldn't do it in a day. Maybe he couldn't do it at all. Maybe the river was uncrossable. But actually it wouldn't matter either way, crossable or not. Much to Franklin's relief, Margaret wasn't looking angry or tearful or child-like anymore. Her eyes were small again and she was smiling at him now, a smile worth any box of treasures. She was not so greatly troubled by her loss but happy that a man would offer such a thing to her, that he'd go back, he'd do it in a day, if only she said yes.

She said, "You can't go back, Pigeon. You'll have to be my good-luck charm from here." I'll run you through my hands, she thought, I'll rub and stroke each piece of you.

NINE

Neither Margaret nor Franklin had seen or imagined such a straight
and broad road before. People here must have land to waste, they
thought, although there wasn't yet much evidence of people. They'd
not encountered any settlements or signs of active farming since
they'd descended from the forests after their three days of rest. The
country was discarded. It had been abandoned long enough ago for
fences to have flattened, for walls to have slipped and lost their shape,
and for tough scrub, already chest high, to have colonized what must
have been good fertile fields.

It had taken them the best part of the morning to leave the taller
trees behind and enter the open lands. But thankfully, after several
days without rain, the going was much firmer and less arduous. The
barrow wheels did not sink into the earth. And it was lighter to push,
as Margaret, now greatly strengthened by her convalescence in the
woods, had volunteered to walk much of the time on her own two
feet, though with the help of one of Franklin's sticks.

Franklin, too, had been greatly restored. His shoulders were no

longer fixed in pain as they had been after his one day of piggyback-
ing and barrowing. His knee was strong again. So—though it was
little cause for satisfaction—he could tell himself that Jackson had
been incorrect to say that his recovery would take a month and therefore spoil their chances of getting to the coast before the final boats.
Franklin had predicted "three days, four days," and he had not been
far off. Getting to the boats in time was still a possibility.

There had been animal trails that they could follow through the
forest, but it had proved more difficult to find a beaten path across
the scrub. They had to weave their way between patches of less stran-
gled ground and along the sides of creekbeds. For every hundred
steps they took they seemed only twenty closer to their destination.
So when, from a raised fold of land, they spotted in the distance what
looked like a long, straight escarpment relatively free of scrub and
evidently heading eastward, they made a beeline for it, hoping to lo-
cate a freer route, less snagged by undergrowth.

The distant escarpment, after their first observation, had not been
clearly visible for much of their journey that morning, so it had come
as a relief and a surprise when they had crested an oddly regular esker of oval hillocks to gain their second view of what seemed now, on
this closer inspection, to be an unnaturally shallow, flat valley, without a river but flanked by parallel mounds as regular as the best
plowed furrow—except that no plow was big enough, not even in the
fairy tales, to throw aside so great a swath of earth. Initially, they
were merely baffled. This was no escarpment provided by nature,
unless nature had on this one occasion broken its own rules and failed
to twist and bend but had instead hurtled forward, all symmetry and
parallels. But soon their bafflement was overcome by astonishment.
What at first they might have mistaken for cattle turned out to be a
horse-drawn carriage traveling at an unusual speed along the center
of the valley surface, as if the route had been designed specifically for
wheels and hoofs. Margaret, who could not see as well as Franklin,
shook her head and looked at him. Something worried her about the

escarpment. But Franklin said, "I've heard of it. This has to be the Dreaming Highway. It takes us to the ships."

They rested on the esker top, lunching on the nuts that they had gathered in the woods and on cold bird meat. They watched a pair of travelers with a string of eight laden mules progress without impediment or any deviation along the same track the carriage had followed.

"This makes me hopeful," Franklin said. The optimist.

Margaret shook her head again: "It worries me, Pigeon." This nickname tease of hers, which thoroughly amused her when she applied it, was so disarming for Franklin that he broke into a smile and reddened whenever she said the word. "That road makes me nervous now we're close to it."

"What is there to be nervous of?" A question, not a challenge.

"It's just too bare. I don't know what it is, but . . . it's open ground. You know, *exposed*. There's not a tree on there to hide behind. I feel we shouldn't even step on it. Not one single toe. We have to find another way. We have to hide ourselves."

Franklin was impatient to move on swiftly, as the mules and the little carriage had done, and thereby reach the ocean soon. "Why hide ourselves? You only have to hide your head. That blue scarf of yours should do it. No one need know that you've been ill. Your color is healthy today. Just cover up."

"My scarf won't make us safe. The roads on this side of the river are dangerous, all of them."

"Who told you that?"

"Everyone in Ferrytown."

What "everyone in Ferrytown" had known, according to Margaret, was that the journey to the coast, rather than becoming more straightforward once the river had been crossed, became more hazardous and deadly. "Why do you think we kept that wooden bridge a secret?" she asked. "Not just for the ferry fees. But to stop anybody from fleeing back to our town on the safe side of the river." She'd heard her father talk about it many times when he was working on the ferry. Once in a while—too often for comfort, actually—bodies would be pushed onto the shingle landing beach or caught in the weed beds, the bloated corpses of people who had tried to swim back across to Ferrytown and drowned. And every few days a little group would be waiting on the eastern side, terror on their tails, begging to be taken back to the settlement by ferry.

She said, "I've heard of people there with gaping wounds, and widows with the pieces of their murdered men and sons in sacks, and tales of little boys and girls, hardly big enough to climb down off their mothers' laps, who've been taken by gangs and sold or put to work. We had to turn them back, of course."

"You turned them back?"

"Well, yes. Don't frown at me. There wasn't any choice. That's what our consuls said."

Ferrytown's failure of charity to these westward refugees, according to Margaret's uncomfortable explanation, was simply a business decision. The town was geared to take in paying emigrants from the west, help them part with some of their wealth, then ferry them out eastward as speedily as possible. Any westward refugees who made it back to Ferrytown would be not paying guests but "beggars and schnorrers." All they'd do, apart from eat and use up moneymaking beds, was spread alarm. With their stories. And the expressions on their faces. And their wounds. The far side of the river would become a place to fear.

"Pigeon, think of it," she instructed him. "What would happen if the migrants learned that Ferrytown might be their last safe place? They'd never leave us, would they? Would you? Imagine, then, how huge our town would be. Big and poor and as crowded as a beehive. And think, if people found the wooden bridge, we'd wake up to an even larger herd of strangers, with not a scrap between them to pay for their beds and suppers. We couldn't let them cross. It's unkind, yes, I know it's unkind, but that's the truth of it."

"Why have the wooden bridge at all?"

"For us. Not them. Who can say when we might need to run away ourselves? Or on what side of the river safety will prefer to live next season? The bridge is our security."

Franklin laughed uneasily and pulled a face. *Is*, not *was*? She hadn't even guessed, then, what he had inflicted on her bridge. He wouldn't tell her, either. What difference could it make, except to have him seem a fool? He wouldn't be her Pigeon anymore. He'd be her turkey, big, stupid, and clumsy. Instead he steered their discussion back to the long straight track where some time ago, he supposed, great vehicles and crowds had hastened between the grand old towns—*cities* was the word he'd heard—and the people of America had been as numerous and healthy as fleas.

He found, in his eagerness to change the subject from the bridge, an uncharacteristic bullying and determined tone to his voice. "This will speed us to the boats," he said. "We have to take a chance. The winter's closing in on us. You've seen the frosts. The snow is never far behind. And anyway, this barrow is exhausting me. You think that because I'm big, I can't ache?" He began to blush, embarrassed to sound so much like his brother—except that Jackson would not have admitted to aches or exhaustion.

Margaret held up her hands in comic submission, but conscious, too, that for the first day, at least, she'd not made the barrow any easier to push. "Let's not make the big man ache," she said.

"We'll either have to throw out half of our possessions, ditch the barrow, and carry what we can, and that is not a good idea. We've not got much, but what we've got we need," he continued. "Or else we'll have to find a path where wheels are helpful rather than a hindrance. In other words"—he pointed toward the disappearing train of mules—"that road. Our wheelbarrow will fly along that road." That dreaming road.

It did not take them long to reach and climb the first of the two parallel mounds that protected the road from the wind and then to descend the sloping, grassy berm, varicosed with gopher trails, to the flat corridor itself. It was almost as wide as the river at the ferry point in Ferrytown, and that made no sense at all. The widest transport that had ever passed through Ferrytown was only three horses wide, while this great swath of track would easily take two teams of horses, each fifty wide or more. It had to be the pathway of a giant or else to have been designed to carry something huge and heavy—those wooden war machines, perhaps, that Margaret had heard talk about, the ones that broke through walls, or shot boulders in the air, or hurled fire.

The road, indeed, seemed built—by how many laborers and over how many years? at what immense cost?—to take great weights. Its now damaged surface, much degraded by the weather and time, comprised mostly chips of stone, loose grit, and sticky black rubble, which only the toughest of plants—knotweed, sagebrush, and thistle—had succeeded in penetrating. Along the verge, behind thick curbs of fashioned rectangular rock and what seemed like rusted metal fences thinned to a finger's breadth by corrosion, were clumps of jimson, not yet cut back by the frost, their summer trumpets rotting at their bases. There was nothing edible for travelers, unless they craved hallucinations and stomach cramp or could, like beetles, dine on rust. The going, though, despite the often uneven rubble, was almost as easy as Franklin had hoped. Margaret could climb on board again, to rest herself. ("Don't let me make you ache," she said.) The barrow, aided by a slight decline in the easterly direction, was quick and easy to maneuver. Franklin only had to lift it a little by its handles and it almost rolled forward on its own, anxious to make progress.

To tell the truth, Franklin's chosen route, though fast, was tedious. Protected by the mounds of earth, it was impossible to tell if any breeze or stormclouds were building up on a far horizon or even if there was any danger in the wider world. Margaret had resigned herself to feeling a bit uneasy on the highway, but she had allowed her Pigeon to win their dispute about her fears and so would have to make the best of it. She had not minded Franklin's unexpected tone of voice. Her brothers, though they were both much smaller men than Franklin, had been greater bullies in their time and much louder in their arguments, so she was used to bombast. She would have been more surprised, and perhaps a little disappointed, to have gotten her own way easily. It was better, all in all, to be in the care of a man who was strong and determined to have his way than to place her trust in what was known by the women in Ferrytown as a lily liver, whatever that might be exactly. Franklin had expressed himself. She had allowed him to. Now the responsibility was his. She could hold him to account if anything went wrong.

Late in the afternoon, with the sun too low to light the road but the sky still brightly blue beyond the escarpments, they caught up with the mule train and its two attendants, a boy not much more than twelve years old and his father. One of their mules carried their personal effects, including a large canvas tent. The other seven were laden with jugs, pots, and crocks.

Margaret had been persuaded that she ought to wear her blue scarf, hiding her shaven head, so that unless a stranger scrutinized her eyebrows too closely, her recent illness could remain a secret. The potman and his son did not seem too alarmed when finally they halted the mules with their sticks and turned to exchange greetings. The size of Franklin could not have been reassuring from a distance, but his manner was mild, and his smile—something Margaret had noticed with increasing satisfaction—was disarming. She might, she thought when they were sleeping side by side in their barrow bed that night, allow his hand to hold hers, or even let her head rest on his shoulder, the bristles of her scalp against his beard. What harm could come of it? A man who would go back for her, to rescue her three talismans, a man who was so sweetly timorous, a man who could remove the flux with his enormous thumbs, must surely deserve something more than words of gratitude.

Franklin and Margaret introduced themselves to the potman as Ferrytowners and, instinctively, as brother and sister. A woman of her age could not admit to traveling with an unrelated man. But claiming to be husband and wife would have been not only embarrassing to themselves but unconvincing to strangers. There was their age difference, for a start. Six or seven years, possibly. And then the careful, respectful formality that still existed between them and would not persist between lovers and certainly not between spouses. The potman raised an eyebrow, though. "You're not exactly twins," he joked, surveying the immensely tall, black-bearded man and the pale, tiny redhead, scarcely reaching his chest.

"Different mothers," Margaret said. "Mine died." That much was true.

They traveled together for a short distance, until the escarpments at the edge of their road flattened out entirely into a broad, barriered semicircle and provided them with daunting views across a debris field of tumbled stone and rock, stained with rust and ancient metal melt. Colossal devastated wheels and iron machines, too large for human hands, stood at the perimeter of the semicircle, as if they had been dumped by long-retreated glaciers and had no purpose now other than to age. Hardly anything grew amid the waste. The earth was poisoned, probably. Twisted rods of steel protruded from the masonry. Discarded shafts and metal planks, too heavy to pull aside even, blocked their path.

Margaret had seen a lesser version of such things before, in the historic north of Ferrytown, where once there'd been—or so tradition claimed—a vast workshop that produced shoes in enormous numbers, though why people could not make shoes for themselves in their own homes was never clear to her. The flaking bodies of machines were still buried there, and as Margaret knew from her own experience, even to that day if anybody turned the soil in that area, she'd be unlucky not to find shiny buckles or little metal eyelets, presumably for bootlaces, among the loam of rotted leather. But she, and certainly Franklin, had never encountered such mighty metal blocks before or such a profligate display of waste by these ancestors. The smell was oily, acidic, and medicinal, the sort of smell even a skunk would avoid. This had to be the junkle that she'd heard reported, third-, fourth-hand, from stories that had managed to cross the river back to Ferrytown, even if the storytellers hadn't.

In Ferrytown, metal things were sometimes prized and always hard to come by. People could manage without. Margaret's family had owned only the silver cup, some bluish pewter cooking pots, some knives, a crude iron grate that Grandpa said was owned by *his* grandpa and half a dozen grandpas beyond him, a hand-beaten kettle, a very useful shovel, and an ax. Margaret herself possessed, or had possessed, her silver necklace and the coins she had found in the river shale when she was a child. But that was all. Carts could not get by entirely without a little metal toughening. On wheel rims, for instance. And boatbuilders and carpenters could manage wood more easily with sharp-edged tools. But generally metal objects were not preferred to those fashioned out of timber or leather or bark or root or withies or cane or wool or gourds or clay or fur. There were so many obliging materials that one could use without going to the time-consuming and dirty trouble of mining and smelting.

It was fascinating, if disturbing, to stand now among the bludgeoned stones and rusting cadavers, trying to imagine what America had been all those grandpas ago, while the potman and his son hunted for any thin metal scraps that they could scavenge and use as staples for fixing broken shards of clay. Margaret and Franklin did not speak. They retreated, shaking their heads, baffled but excited by the presence of so much antiquity, until they noticed signs of life on the outskirts of the junkle. Smoke was rising from the entrance of a sheltered cave of debris beneath an overhang of collapsed stonework. An elderly man in his fifties with a graying beard came out into the daylight, looked across a little nervously at the potman and at Margaret and Franklin, and finally called out a word of greeting.

Franklin, as the younger man, would have to walk across to introduce himself. He left Margaret in charge of the barrow and the lead rein of the mules and made his way across the debris. As he got closer and could see into the deep darkness of the shelter, he recognized the little carriage that they'd spotted earlier that day. A pair of carriage horses were tied against a wall of squared stone, mossy green, at one side of the cave, where pools of greasy water stood. The old man's family—his wife, a son—were sitting around their fire, warming their knuckles. There was a grandchild sleeping in a reed-weave basket with a mattress of fishnet.

They spent the night together in the dry shelter of the stone-and-metal cave, all of them, three "families" sharing their provisions as travelers should, sharing the fire, and glad of the company. When they had eaten and Margaret had handed round her taffies as a treat, especially for the potman's boy, they took it in turns, according to their seniority, to tell the stories of their emigration so far.

The carriage family was from a riverside community much farther south than Ferrytown and on the opposite bank. There was no work or trade for them anymore. The river was narrow there, and so, while it had once been good for fishing, it was not suitable for ferrying and profiting from travelers as Ferrytown had done. The old man, Andrew Bose, and his wife, Melody, had been net and creel makers, employing eight hands and growing rich from their efforts. Their son, Acton, had been a fisherman and fish merchant. "Also doing well for himself," added Melody. "He was much admired." But when the village started to empty as striking out offered better prospects than staying put, the fish and net trade beached itself. Acton became his parents' last remaining customer for nets. They became the only ones to buy his fish. The Boses hoped to sit their problems out. Things would get better. Only a fool would leave the riverbank, because whatever happened there, you would never run short of water or food. But then their daughter-in-law died in childbirth, and Acton determined to leave for somewhere less ill-fated. His parents were too old to stay behind alone, though their son had not insisted that they join him and the baby. On the contrary. But it was time for all of them to "face the facts and leave." So once the child had been weaned by the last of the village pay-moms and cut her first two teeth, they'd shuttered up their house and joined the exodus. Andrew had his tools with him, he said. There was bound to be work for a net maker as soon as they reached water. Net makers were always valued and respected wherever there were boats.

The potman and his son, both named Joey, had traveled from the south from a market town where, once the region's farms had failed and folded and their owners had joined the emigration, there was no work, no market, no demand for pots, and so no supper on the family table. The elder Joey had made the future easy for himself by sending his wife and their three other children ahead in the company of neighbors. Then he'd traded some silver for the mules, loaded up his stock of finished pots, his tools, and some powdered fixing clay, and followed on, taking his time. He and his son had survived during the two months of their journey so far by doing pot repairs in exchange for food and lodging. The Joeys had been in Ferrytown ten days before, and they had sealed the cracks in several of the guesthouse's earthenware water ewers and stapled broken plates and dishes in many of the wealthier homes. "My wife knows it's her job to break as many pots as she can, ahead of me," he said. "She does the damage. I do the repairs." In just a few days' time, he hoped, he'd meet up with his wife again, somewhere on the coast. "I'll find her, you can bet. She's got a laugh can shatter clay. That's why I married her."

Any plans that Margaret had for heads on shoulders and holding hands had been postponed. She and Franklin had made up beds at the back of the shelter a little distance from each other, as brothers and sisters, and certainly *half*-brothers and -sisters, must. But their knees had touched for several heartbeats during their evening at the fireside, and they were content to stay in this good company until their eyes dropped shut. It was such a pleasure just to listen to and talk with friendly strangers. But Franklin, avoiding the true story of what had happened to them and their families in Ferrytown, had hardly started to amuse the net makers with his account of how Margaret had fished for birds in the forest when—silently, appallingly—the band of rustlers arrived.

How had they been so careless? The eight travelers must have been half blinded by staring into their fire and deafened by their conversation and their laughter not to have heard so many heavy feet surrounding them or to have picked up on the sound of horses. They realized that they were snared only when, suddenly, the remaining brightness of the night from the moon and stars and metal luster was blocked. Too ill-prepared for trouble, too shocked to stand and run, they could only sit exactly where they were and look up at the silhouettes of six or seven well-armed men, who, attracted—invited, almost—by the smoke, the flames, the throb of human voices, had crept up as evenly as wolves on a sheepfold.

Everyone could see enough by firelight to know what kind of men these were. Their faces were too weatherbeaten for them to be townspeople. Their clothes were not the clothes of emigrants, designed for warmth and durability, but the highly colored, quarrelsome garments of men keen to be noticed and alarming. Their beards were tied in braids with ribbons. Their legs were bowed from a life on horseback. They were not clean. Their smiles were far too sharp to promise anything but cruelty.

"Stand up," one of them said, a short man in a long yellow canvas coat. He was a little older than the others and evidently the one most feared.

The travelers did as they were told and tried to stay expressionless as another one of the group stepped into the shelter to inspect each of them, turning them round, feeling their arms, even touching the women and the baby. He touched Margaret too much and looked her too directly in the eye. He whistled through his teeth when he felt the strength and size of Franklin's arm. He fingered the piebald coat and laughed. "Give me that," he said. Franklin handed over the coat, hoping against reason that it would prove to be the only loss of the night. The coat was passed to the short man, who put it over his yellow one. It sat so high on his shoulders that the bottom hem reached only the top of his ankles.

Two of the other men went into the darkness of the shelter with brands lit from the fire to see what they could find and take. Another led away the horses and the mules. Another smashed the potman's pots that his son had unloaded, and, not doubting their safety, left in view for anyone to steal or damage.

Franklin and Margaret had no choice but to watch their barrow being unloaded, their mint plant being dashed onto the ground, and the now empty silver cup—their greatest wealth—and the ornamented platters being thrown into sacks along with the Joeys' and the Boses' best possessions (of which there were many).

Now the short man came forward himself to take a look, oddly awkward in his many clothes but doubly threatening. "Not her," he said, referring to Melody Bose. "Not him, too old," he added, meaning Andrew Bose. "Not that"—the granddaughter, hardly nine months old, not walking yet and so no use. "We'll take the rest." His companions came forward with rope and started looping it around their selected captives, beginning with the potman's terrified son. They made nooses for their necks and wrists, so that the Joeys, young Acton Bose, Margaret, and Franklin could be joined and led away like the mules had been, in one long train.

Franklin's last action before he too was bound and haltered by the rope was not exactly a heroic one, but it was thoughtful and intelligent. He saw a chance for Margaret. He reached across, not so quickly as to cause alarm among the men, and pulled the blue scarf off her head. They backed away at once. Few men are so tough or so intent on rape that fear of illness doesn't caution them.

"Not her," the short man said. "We don't want her."

They gathered up their plunder as quickly as they could. Then, almost as suddenly and silently as they'd arrived, the silhouettes disappeared. The Boses' grandchild hadn't even woken to see her father taken as a slave.

❧ ten ❧

The child, named Bella after her dead mother, was the only dreamer on the Dreaming Highway that night. The three adults judged valueless by the rustlers did not have any rest. For the first time since leaving the Pesthouse, Margaret spent the night alone, too shocked and frightened to sleep but not allowed to offer any comfort to the net makers or to seek from them any comfort for herself. The Boses had found a narrow, ferrous crevice, damp and unwelcoming but dark enough to hide them from any further passersby. Margaret had tried to squeeze in with them, but they had pushed her back with their feet and elbows, not wanting even to touch her with their hands. Their only conversation after that had been shouted, and brief, just long enough for Melody to warn Margaret to keep her distance "or else." She'd armed herself with a heavy piece of metal. If Margaret came too close, Melody was ready and prepared, she said, to do some lasting damage to Margaret's shaven head.

The night was not silent. Andrew Bose, chirring like a katydid, kept up a muttered chorus of curses against humankind for its cruelty and its treachery and against his own mother for ever having given birth to him. Melody soothed the baby and herself with rocking and repetition, "Son. Son. Son . . . ," not daring to invite more misfortune by naming him out loud. And all around, the relics made noises of their own. Trash disturbed by all the recent hoofs and feet settled back in place. Degraded concrete slabs shifted and wheezed as the night grew cold. Insignificant animals with outsized, moonlit eyes that were only scavenging for scraps sounded to Margaret and the Boses as large and dangerous as horsemen. The taller metal shapes picked up any wind in their hollows and their tubes and played their fluty monotones with it, competing to produce the saddest and most spectral sound.

Margaret was trembling for a long part of the night, too shaken by her loss—her losses—to settle on a single emotion. In just a few days everyone she loved had been carried off. Bitterness piled up on bitterness. She had not expected to get any sleep, but nevertheless, once the Boses had rejected her and she had exhausted herself with weeping and vomiting, she had moved her bedclothes onto the barrow and stretched out on her side, resting an arm across the empty space where Franklin had slept. Another good man gone, she thought, as if somehow it was her fault, that it was as inevitable that misfortune would attend Franklin once he was in her company as it was certain that the men in her family would beat with sticks that older, fine-mannered stranger who had proposed a midnight meeting with her all those years ago. Maybe it was correct what everybody said: "Red hair, bad luck." But then, she had been lucky in other ways, hadn't she? Like no one else from Ferrytown, she was alive. Yes, thanks to Pigeon, thanks to him. His touch had rescued her twice, first when his strong slow fingers had massaged her feet and then again when his sudden, quicker fingers had pulled off her scarf.

She should not be angry with the Boses. Margaret knew that, despite her spinning emotions. They had a right to suspect and fear her shaven head, even though her hair was now a few days old and visible, an orange fuzz that felt like the nap of some fine cloth when she ran her palm across her skull. She almost had eyebrows, spiky and stiff. But still she could not expect them to risk exposing a child of Bella's age to a disease, even if that disease was clearly in retreat. Nor could she expect them to show much sympathy to her for the loss of her "half-brother." How could that compare to their loss of a full son and their granddaughter's loss of a full father? Nor could she expect them to stay quiet during the night, when their grief, their shock, and their terror were so burdensome. Yet she was angry with the Boses. She was angry at the way they had turned hostile and despairing so quickly, creating more conflict instead of staying calm. She was angry that only a short time after sharing a fire and their life stories with her, and at a time when the four of them should be unified and thinking of ways to help or rescue their men, they were threatening her with a strip of metal. Not that such a threat was frightening. The Boses didn't have the pluck or strength to do her any harm. They didn't have the character.

Margaret's anger made the time pass more quickly. It kept her warm and busy. *Keep your distance or else?* The threat was so infuriating and unkind that Margaret succeeded in persuading herself that it would be easy, a pleasure even, to take the metal out of Melody's hands and give her graying braids some sharp, painful tugs. Or else she would happily find a strip of metal of her own and put an end to all that "Son. Son. Son . . ." Melody, the crowd of emigrants who had stoned them on the shingle beach at Ferrytown, the short horseman who had stolen Franklin's coat, anyone ahead of her who'd dare to block her path, they all became one body, dropping to its knees under the thrashing weight of Margaret's metal strip.

As soon as there was some light, Margaret wrapped her blanket around her shoulders and clambered up a high rampart of rubble to make sure that the junkle was deserted. She could not trust her eyes entirely, but she listened carefully, turning into and against the wind. No whinnying. No brays. No dogs. No men. Not even birds. For the time being they were safe. Safe enough to run away.

The Boses watched her from their hiding place. They seemed so weary and so old suddenly, so frail and defeated, that Margaret, against her instincts to tell them nothing, called out to inform them that she was moving on, and that if they wanted to—and if they had any sense at all in their old heads—they could join her. "At a distance, if you prefer," she said. "Otherwise you'll have to manage on your own. Make up your minds." She sounded like her mother for a moment, impatient and practical, when what she truly felt was desolate and hollow.

"Where will we go? How will we get there?" Andrew Bose asked eventually, after a whispered conversation with the ill-named Melody.

"We walk. How else?" They might be in possession of a carriage and a boat barrow, she reminded them, but without any horses to pull the former or anyone strong enough to push the latter, they had no choice but to leave behind anything they could not carry easily and go ahead by foot.

"But where?"

"I don't know where. Don't ask me where. We go. We carry on. That's what we have to do." Again she recognized this tone of voice, not her natural, more respectful way of speaking, and not her mother's. It was the voice her brothers had often used to bully her. It was the voice she'd heard from Franklin just the day before, when he had made her take the highway despite her worries. It "will speed us to the coast," he'd said. Well, he'd been wrong. Horribly so. And she'd been right. I'll never take the advice of a pigeon again, she told herself—and it almost made her smile, just to imagine for a moment that she was truly saying it to him, that he was still there with her to be teased.

Well, now she had the chance to take her own advice, to leave the old wide track and all the hard lands thereabouts and follow country routes, ones too narrow, preferably, for horses or groups of men. But Franklin needed her. She was not free to take her own advice. There was no one who'd look for him if she didn't. So what she'd have to do was try to find where he'd been taken, no matter where it was, even if it meant continuing along the highway.

"Okay, it's true, I don't know what we ought to do," she called out to the Boses. "And nor do you. All I know is that I want my Franklin back." She fought her sobs. "And you must want your Acton back, too. Her pa. So what's the choice? There isn't any choice. We find the horse scuffs and we follow them. What happens then will happen then. We can't stay here. So let's pack up our bags and go. Before those men come back for us. Or something worse."

The Boses were persuaded by those last two words.

They dragged their remaining possessions and the few things left by the Joeys out into full view from the darkness of the rubble cave and made their choices. Any food they had to keep. And water bags. But otherwise the hard decisions were their own. Margaret kept her fishing net, one of Franklin's knives, his spark stone, a thin blanket, one tarp, the comb, the hairbrush, the green-and-orange woven top that had been rescued from her room in Ferrytown, a spare undershirt, and her blue scarf. She forced them into Franklin's back sack, leaving enough space on top for what was left of their salted meat, the honey, and her remaining taffies, as well as some damp tack from the potman's stores. The cattle skins would have to be abandoned. They were too bulky, as were her father's wading boots, which Franklin had for some reason rescued from the house, and—she hesitated—the coil of thick rope, which might prove useful but was heavy. She hesitated, too, about the bow and arrows. Franklin would want to keep them, she knew. But she could not use them herself. Women were never trained to hunt, so taking them would be an empty gesture—as, possibly, would be the inclusion of Franklin's change of clothes. She did not want to challenge fate by adding them to her load. If she and Franklin ever met again—which, candidly and with bitter resignation, she doubted that they would—then a change of clothes would not matter one way or the other. But if she took his clothes with her, it was guaranteed—they were so capacious—that they would weigh her down and use up space and energy. Throwing them out was shamefully distressing. A murder of a sort. Again she had to swallow tears.

The fruit-juice flagons were also too heavy to carry, even the empty one, but she filled a water bag with juice and hung it on its lanyard around her waist, together with the larger bag still nearly full of now stale water from the river at Ferrytown. Then she filled her stomach with the remaining juice. She offered it across the clearing to the Boses, but they shook their heads and wiped their lips defensively, as if the mere mention of sharing a spout with her were enough to smear them with contagion.

The little clay pot over which she'd cooked their breakfast birds while she and Franklin had been resting in the forest was not worth keeping, she thought, and then she thought again and remembered a chilling moment from the night before. Those metal scavengers, those people rustlers, whatever they were, had thrown out her mint plant, the one intimate thing that she had shared with her family remaining in her possession. Margaret stepped into the cave with the clay pot and felt around with her foot until she located the earth and the plant. The mint was damaged, both by the assault of the previous evening and by the season. Few leaves were left. Soon there would be none. The mint would draw back to its roots until the spring. But still she scooped the earth and the plant into the pot and nestled it among her clothes at the top of her bag. This was not sensible, she knew. Why bother with a plant that grew wild anyway? But Margaret was determined to defy the scavengers, in some small way at least. The mint would live.

It did not take her long to find the traces of the horsemen and the mule train. Pack animals are not discreet. Their bowels leave steaming messages. Their hoofs leave runes. And mules can never pass a scrap of bush without tearing at it with their gravestone teeth. The men—this much was clear—had gone back to the highway with their pillage and their hostages and, lit by the moon and the night vision of criminals, had headed east like everybody else.

Margaret led the way and the Boses, grumpily—and with good cause, Margaret had to allow—followed twenty paces behind, stopping whenever she paused to examine the track, looking away when she glanced back to see if they were managing. They did not wish to catch her eye. She had become a dangerous mystery to them. Why was she so angry and unreasonable? Why was she impolite? Why didn't she pull that scarf back on to hide herself? They did not understand her lack of respect, and she could not be bothered to shout out her explanations: that she was angry because anger was purposeful, that she was impolite because courtesy was an impediment, that her scarfless head—and this surely must be welcome—would keep strangers at a distance.

The Boses followed on, taking it in turns to carry their granddaughter in a sling across their chests and taking it in turns to complain about the burden. They were glad at least that they didn't have to gaze at Margaret's unnerving bald scalp. Their view of it was obscured by the few mint leaves that protruded from the top of Margaret's back sack and tickled the nape of her neck when she walked, a touch of green against the red of her new hair, a combination that anybody not as beset by troubles as the Boses were might recognize as beautiful.

So they followed the highway from sunup until sundown, hardly exchanging a word all day, not sharing food and not daring to rest in case they fell too far behind their abducted men. There were no other travelers ahead of them for Margaret to frighten off with her bare head, although in the afternoon, behind them to the west, they could see and hear from a rise in the road that a convoy of farm carts, a large number of travelers on foot, and some cattle were moving slowly in their wake. Apart from hoofprints and dung, the only, chilling evidence they found that other emigrants had passed recently ahead of them was an abandoned cart with the bodies of a half-dressed woman and a dog draped across its deck and its load of household furniture and effects scattered around. The boxes had been kicked open, the bags turned inside out. And possibly any man fit enough to work or sell had been added to the line of captives that already included Franklin, Acton Bose, and the Joeys.

The woman's body was warm. She'd died that morning. The blood on the crown of her head was sticky, and her limbs were not yet stiff. Margaret covered her face and legs. The dog was alive but injured badly, though still vigilant enough to growl and show its teeth when Margaret went to it with a piece of tarry stone to finish what the rustlers must have started. She knew that what she'd have to do was ugly, and probably unwomanly in the Boses' eyes. But she would not regret it. She thought of her own dogs, Becky and Jefferson. Better to be ugly and unwomanly than to leave a loyal dog to suffer. She guessed it had done its best to protect its human family. This was its recompense. It took three blows.

They spent the night away from the road, crouching in the undergrowth under a makeshift tent of tarps and branches and taking it in turns to stand guard. They knew from the pillaged cart and the dead woman that the rustlers were still in the neighborhood. That was both reassuring and alarming. But they dared not light a fire, although the temperature was wintry and there was a wind. Margaret was allowed to occupy the shelter with the Boses, though not to sit too close or to share their food. She chewed on dried meat with a slab of the potman's tack and drank a little juice, which had already grown bitter from the journey.

Andrew and Melody whispered to each other as they did their best to make their granddaughter accept her meal of cold water porridge with mashed fish. Margaret presumed from what little she could hear that the Boses were discussing her, what their attitude should be. They must have recognized how well and fit she'd been that day. Hardly a flux-ridden invalid. And what a leader she had proved to be, taking the decisions, selecting the route, quietly valiant. Even her unbecoming killing of the dog was oddly reassuring to the Boses, she gathered. It showed she was a woman who would not turn away from problems or challenges, and that if pressed, she might defend herself and anybody in her company. What was clear to Margaret was that the Boses had come to fear her slightly less. On the whole, they could now allow that they were better off in her company than out of it.

The Boses would have preferred it if Margaret had walked a little slower that day and for less time and with more rest breaks, however. Bella had turned out to be a heavy, struggling bundle who would rather be on the ground, learning how to bend her knees and crawl, than strapped to an irritated grandparent and not allowed to move. The effort of taking care of her and of themselves, after the undemanding luxury of riding in a carriage, had come as a shock. Perhaps, if they could persuade themselves to overcome their anxiety just a little more and convince Margaret to cover her mouth, then she could take her turn with the baby. Yes, it would be in their interests to talk to her, to broker a period of peace. They'd not find Acton on their own. Even if they did, they'd not know what to do. Whereas Margaret . . . well, Margaret was "knotted from strong twine," the highest praise from net makers.

So it happened that when they set off the next morning, after a night in which the baby would not hush or sleep and the adults could not stop shivering, the gap between Margaret and the Boses was reduced to a few steps. A workable peace had been made at sunup, with apologies spoken if not entirely felt, explanations offered, comfort and sympathy finally exchanged. Margaret was being sensible. The Boses had dried peas and a good supply of oats, as well as several bags of salt fish. They might not be the finest company, but they were preferable to traveling alone. Six eyes would make better lookouts than two poor ones. Three adults, even if two of them were frail, could defend themselves better than one. Besides, it was Margaret's duty to support her elders. She might not like the Boses much. Certainly she could not admire them, ever. But the little girl was lovable.

Margaret had compromised for prudent and selfish reasons. She wore the blue scarf around her face and head, as she was asked, with just her eyes on show; she made an effort to defer to her elders and to be more outwardly patient; and she was content that in return, they let her carry Bella on her chest. The child was unexpectedly warm and consoling. Her head had hardly any more hair than Margaret's. Her body smelled of stewed apples—sweet piss and bloom. The child was also less difficult in the younger woman's care because she was less bored. They played tug with an edge of cloth. Margaret sang to her, everything from nursery rhymes to laments. She invented new noises by trumpeting farts on the girl's neck or blowing in her ear, a sensation that Bella evidently loved. She gurgled her appreciation, but when she grew tired of that and even of sucking her own thumb, she accepted Margaret's little finger as a pacifier, determined to find nourishment for her small, empty stomach. The baby had not eaten properly since leaving home, and she had not fed truly properly since her mother died and her umbilical was cut. Bella Bose needed milky food. Margaret whispered promises that somehow, and within a day or two, she'd get hold of some for her.

By afternoon the Boses had decided that they could walk with Margaret, shoulder to shoulder, and tell her what a fine life they had had back home before the migrations began, how respected Andrew had been, and wealthy. His creels would last for years—and they were beaver-proof. His nets were the best. You could snag them on rocks and it would be the rock that lifted and not the net that tore. Fishermen from the far bank of the river would risk the rapids just to get across and purchase a Bose net. He owned a good part of the riverbank. He owned a carriage and had a dozen boats for rent as well as the canoe that Acton used for fishing. He had more land than any farmer in the neighborhood, which he rented out for one fifth of the crop. "Now look at me," he said, handing over Bella for the umpteenth time that day. "A bag of oats, that's all we've got worth anything."

The road degraded. With every step of their journey the highway became more damaged and disordered, its top shell cracked and coming apart. The route was losing its clarity. A watercourse that had once flowed along a man-made culvert had broken through its false banks years before and flooded, every time it rained, onto the road, tearing out the surfacing and, with the undramatic patience of water, shifting blocks of curbstone and rubble scree. It became easier to walk along the berms and margins than to scramble through the detritus. This was no longer a route for vehicles or even for horses. If there'd been no rustlers and the Boses had made it to this place intact, they would have had to find another route or abandon their carriage and their animals.

Margaret was glad to leave the highway at last when what was left of it turned to the right in a great arc, heading for the south. She had found no traces of the band of rustlers since midday. No fresh horse dung, no scuffs consistent with a line of men or a string of mules, no more bodies sticky with blood. So she did not feel that she had abandoned her duties toward Franklin when she finally led the Boses away from the old straight road and through the debris fields surrounding it, with rainclouds at their backs, and onto a narrower, less exposed pathway that was more truly pointing to the east but that was also virtually unused and therefore likely to be safe.

Before long they found the ideal place to spend the night, replenish their drinking bags, and revive their spirits: a disused cow barn backing onto a creek in which minnows and darters evidenced how sweet and safe the water was. Even better, the cow barn still had half a roof, so not only could they be certain of a rain-protected stay and a warmer one than on the previous night, sheltered from both the wind and the sky, but also they were blessed with kindling wood, the splintered, hollowed-out remains of roof beams that were feather-light and dry and would produce hardly any telltale smoke.

Soon they had a decent fire as their companion and were making the best of their pooled food. Bella refused most of her meal again. The salt fish was too strong and the oatmeal was too weighty for her stomach. She was distressed, as well, and colorless. Her olive skin seemed metallic.

Margaret was happy to share her blanket and the tarp with the child, though surprised that the Boses seemed to have abandoned their health precautions so thoroughly in the space of just a day. They had, indeed, said, "Let little Bella spend the night with you. She's better off with you. You're young." But their thorough change of heart was soon explained. They were whispering again at their end of the cow barn, and Melody was sounding oddly sweet and childish for a change. They did not seem able to settle and were constantly arranging and rearranging their bedding. Margaret might have called out to them to keep quiet, that there was a testing day of walking ahead of them, and that she for one would welcome a good night's sleep. But when she heard the rasping notes in Andrew's throat, she knew that the Boses were making love. She'd heard the sound of it before, from her father, and from her younger sister's husband, Glendon Fields. She'd heard it from her neighbors' windows at all times of the day, the selfsame loss of breath and pigsty squeals, high-pitched and not quite male, the shushing sounds, attempts at secrecy, the creaking timbers of the bed, and sometimes panting from the woman, too. But she'd never seen anybody making love, and so her sense of it was constructed only out of sounds, which seemed both distressed and joyful at one time. It was a mystery that, because Franklin had been taken, she felt would never be solved for her. She'd live a maid, not touched by anyone, a listener to lovers.

Margaret hadn't thought the Boses could be lovers. Lovers as well as partners. Lovers as well as grandparents. It wasn't just their age and frailty or (when it suited them) their stiff good manners that made their passion so unlikely, it was also the current shape of their life. Their son was missing, all their wealth had been taken from them, their lives were draped with fear, anxiety, and grief, their bodies were exhausted by the walk, they had not truly eaten well for a month—yet still they had the will to kiss.

Margaret lay as still as she could. Soon the breathing at the far end of the barn was back to normal. Then the snoring started, and the rain, beating on the roof slates noisily. Little Bella began to stretch her legs and cry, invasively. She wanted to crawl and try to seize anything that caught her eye in that dim light. The supper was making her restless, so Margaret put her little finger in the girl's mouth and let her suck on it, and then she let her snuggle to her breast. The cow barn settled to the night. Soon everyone was sleeping. Another day, then, passing without incident.

First they noticed that pockets of land around the pathway were cultivated and that within easy reach were clusters of unabandoned wooden huts, some with plumes of smoke and hostile dogs, others with washing lines, others with a tethered cow or two and goats. The farms around the homes were dying back for winter, but still the practiced eye could recognize where rows of beans and corn had been, and see that apples had been in such abundance that year that the ground was squelchy with windfalls. This was almost the America that they had all been born in. It was reassuring finally to discover such normality, but it was unnerving also, especially for the Boses. If everything was normal here, then who was to say that their flight from their fine shuttered house and those lucrative riverside employments that had provided wealth and respect had not been precipitate? Had Acton been the price they'd paid for haste?

Margaret tied her scarf tightly around her head and under her chin, left the adult Boses in charge of their bags and possessions, and went, with Bella sitting on her hip, to find out what she could about the way ahead and beg some baby food. She avoided the first two huts. Their guard dogs, both on long leashes, were a warning to stay away. But at the third building, a single-story cabin with a slate roof similar to the one that had kept them dry the previous evening, no dog was in evidence. There was, though, a washing line with children's clothes on it and the bulky figure of a woman sitting on the stoop and work-ing on a reed basket. Most important, they had a yard of nanny goats with young. There would be milk to spare.

Margaret was not noticed until she lifted the rope tie on the gar-den gate and began to walk slowly down the ash-and-clinker path toward the house. Then she coughed and waited. When the woman looked up, startled, it was clear that she was younger than she ap-peared, a girl, probably less than twenty years old. That made Mar-garet the elder, so instead of going forward to introduce herself, she stayed where she was, as was the custom. To do otherwise would be to insult each other's dignity. If you are alone and they are in com-pany, then you salute them; if you are sitting and they are standing, they greet you; if you are walking and they are riding, you acknowl-edge them, and certainly it always was the case that the young should defer to anybody older. So Margaret waited while the heavy girl put down her work, struggled to her feet, and came forward toward her visitor. She called out "Pa!" before addressing Margaret.

A man, her father, fat and tall and with a curly, close-fitting beard, came to the door, holding a stick. "What does she want?" he said.

"Well, I don't know."

"Just ask her, then."

"What do you want, he says."

So this was hardly normality. For all their goats and windfalls, their garden gates and washing lines, these people were living with fear, a fear that extended even to a single woman with a child. If this had been a village in the America that Margaret and the Boses had been born into, she could have expected a smile, a little curtsy from the girl. Her father would have reached his door not with a stick but with the immediate offer of a bench to sit on and a cup to drink from. In small communities like this, if not in places such as Ferrytown, where there were too many people for these observances to survive, passing guests could expect a dozen offers of a bed for the night.

Neighbors would have competed "for the honor" of having her dent
in their mattress. Who could be more generous? Who could promise
most?

Margaret could remember being told by Grandpa that when he'd
been young—and that was going back a bit! What, fifty years?—
he'd gotten lost high in the hills during a blinding storm. But he'd
been taken in by a family of fur trappers and allocated their only bed.
They had no meat to give him for his supper, and so the father of the
family had walked across the valley in the rain to his nearest neighbor's quarters and, finding him asleep, had stolen a hen and brought
it back to pluck and roast for Grandpa. When the neighbor showed
up early next morning to protest about the theft, the trapper simply
said, "We had a guest. He had to eat. We thank you for your hen. I've
got a herd of sheep, still out in the pasture half a day from here. You'll
know which ones. My sign is three green bars. Next time you pass
them, take two, take three, whatever you like. It makes no difference.
We had to feed our guest." That used to be America.

But all Margaret was getting from this small, fat family was hos-
tility. Showing them the baby made no difference. Her offers to undertake any work that needed doing were ignored. Her smiles and
her determined cheerfulness were wasted. And every time she made
to take a step closer to the girl, her father lifted his stick and growled.

It was a struggle, but in the end she got her way, though only after pulling off her scarf and threatening to sit in the middle of their
path "until the both of us, my kid and me, are full of worms." She
liked the sound of that, "my kid and me."

"I feel sorry for that child, and that's the only reason," Pa said
eventually, justifying his surrender to the bullying and evidently dangerous young woman. Now that he had seen her scalp, the man was
desperate to find some way to compromise and give his visitors a
good excuse to leave. So finally he let her sit on the garden wall,
among the woody stalks of dead vegetables, and feed Bella a little
goat's milk sweetened with honey and simmered. "We'll not want

that pot when you've done with it," he said. "Just throw it down. I want to hear it break."

The girl stood and watched, breathing heavily, too uneasy to ask any questions of her own.

"How far is it before we reach the ocean?" Margaret asked her.

"I've never even been."

"Ask your father. Has he been?"

The answer was a shock if it was true. Perhaps he was lying, giving Margaret false hope, just to see the back of her. He'd never "witnessed" the ocean himself, he said, calling from the safety of his front door, and he hoped his fortunes would never make him want to or need to. He touched the end of his surprisingly elegant nose for good luck. But he had been to the nearby town many times—a one-day walk—to trade the produce of their farm, and he had heard that less than three days forward on foot from there, in the direction of sunrise, was a river that was widening and salty and that breathed in and out twice a day, spreading to its banks and then receding, as if its lungs were being pumped by some outrageous giant "a thousand times my size—and that's not small."

"Is that the ocean there? Is that where we can take the ships?"

"It's near. It must be near. When there's salt in the water, there'll be ships in water, too. Sea ships. That's what I've heard," he added, repeating what everybody who'd never witnessed the ocean said about it, that you know it "like an old friend" when you come to it, that it roars at you like a cougar, that it smells like blood, that the ocean's got only one bank, that if you drink a cup of it your piss turns blue.

Only four more days to reach the salt? The Boses did not seem to know whether this was good news or bad, nor did Margaret. At this rate it was possible that they might make it onto one of the last boats before the sea packed in for the winter. Exactly what they'd wished for. But four days was too soon to abandon any hope of finding Acton and Franklin, of just discarding them like cornhusks and getting on with life as if they'd never been born. How could they go aboard a ship and say their farewells to America without first knowing what had happened to their men? asked Margaret as they progressed among the little fearful farms toward a skyline that seemed to promise larger habitations.

"What other choice is there for us?" asked Andrew Bose. "We can hardly ask the sailors to wait around to watch the sea block up with ice while we stay on shore hoping for a miracle. There never is a miracle, in my experience."

In Andrew's view, the country was too wide and long for them to be able to pick out a single group of horsemen. And even then, even if they ran the rustlers to ground, they'd need another miracle to free their men, if they were still alive. "No, Melody and I have already thought it through. If Acton were still a child, then maybe things would be different. You have a responsibility to a child. But he's a man. A married man, or was. He's taller than me. He's got more years ahead of him . . ."

"Let's hope that's true," said Margaret.

"Let's hope it's true, sure. But also let's be sensible. Acton could be anywhere. Your Franklin could be anywhere. They could be two days to the south by now. They could be on a ship already, as far as we know. You think they'd be squandering their chances for us? You think they'd hang around for us?"

"Your son could be fifty paces down the road and looking for his daughter."

"Don't argue, Andrew, not with her," said Melody, and then went on to justify herself. Whatever choice they made would be a cause of misery, so maybe it was wiser that they made the choice that took them to a better place. "That's what Acton would want us to do, if he was here. We've got the girl to think of, haven't we? It's not a selfish thing. It's you that's selfish in my eyes, just thinking of yourself and disregarding us."

Margaret would not express an opinion yet. She listened to the

Boses but would neither nod nor shake her head. They were not at the coast. They couldn't see the ocean. They couldn't guarantee passage on a ship. They couldn't even guarantee a ship. So it was premature to punish themselves with cruel and difficult decisions. Anything might happen between here and there. She adopted her bullying voice again. "Come on," she said. "There's walking to be done. Let's get on with it."

So the subject of Acton and Franklin was dropped from their conversation (not to mention the subject of the unfortunate Joeys: the potman's wife was probably at that very moment cracking jugs and water ewers on their behalf with no suspicion that her husband and her son had been picked out of their lives as easily as berries from a bush). Margaret and the Boses simply pushed ahead, keen to discover if there was any truth in the big man's promises that the salt water was only four days distant.

That afternoon they almost reached the market town that he had mentioned. They could see its pall of smoke and what appeared to be a log tower, with a banner flying from it. But the days were rapidly shortening, and so, too early in the afternoon, they had to hunt for shelter. Their quarters for the night—a sheep pen—were cramped, no room for lying down, no room for lovemaking. They had to eat and then sleep with their chins on their knees. Margaret did her best to hold a cheerful conversation. She retold the story that she had been reminded of that day, with her grandpa and the stolen chicken and the sheep with three green bars. But the Boses—how could this be the same couple who had made love so noisily just one night previously?—seemed preoccupied and unamused. They thought the trapper's hospitality had been foolish and unbusinesslike. "I'd take three sheep for a single hen anytime," said Andrew. "Any fool would." He did not understand why Margaret laughed and why his wife, after a moment's reflection, joined her.

Margaret had recovered from her illness now, but she was exhausted and roughened by the journey and by the trauma of losing both Franklin and her family. Was she thinking only of herself and disregarding others, as Melody had claimed? What the Boses had said about taking passage on the first available boat might seem callous, she thought, but they were probably right. Franklin might have been taken in any of a thousand directions. He might already have met any of a thousand fates. If she had a duty now, it was only to herself and possibly, in the short term, to little Bella. Obtaining goat's milk for the child that day had been immensely pleasing, especially when the girl had settled afterward and slept so contentedly. Carrying her had been easy.

Tomorrow Margaret would do the same—identify the safest house that had a cow or goat and use her wiles to procure more milk for her charge. She could not imagine parting from the child. She had nothing else, and there was no one to value. Bella was her only friendly flesh. So maybe she was now obliged to bite her tongue and stay on with the Boses, whatever they might decide to do, just to make sure that their granddaughter was given the attention—and the future—she deserved. It was strange, was it not, that a man whom she had scarcely known for seven days and a child whom she had known for only three should hold her thoughts, and perhaps her prospects, in their grip?

The rain outside the sheepfold was thickening and sleety. Margaret set her back against the corner of two walls and twisted her body so that Bella could lie across her lap and they could share the scarf, the blanket, and the tarp. It would be the coldest night so far. She offered her little finger to the girl's hard gums. But Bella pushed the hand away. Her lips were chapped and sore from the salty food she'd had and from the cold, so Margaret dug for wax in her own ears and applied the honey-colored secretion as a lubricant. The child licked her lips, stopped crying for some moments when she tasted sweetness, and then cried out for more wax, tugging at Margaret's fingers with her tough and tiny hands.

❧ eLeveN ❧

Margaret needed to bully for milk three more times before her fortunes changed. For the better and for the worse. She valued these trips away from Andrew and Melody, and she knew they were glad to be free of her for a while. It was their chance to rest and recover their strength, as well as an opportunity to talk and complain freely behind her back. Having Bella entirely to herself, helping the baby to stand for a moment, rolling stones for her to crawl after, allowing her to explore her mouth, ears, and nose, tickling her—all that mothering was a joy.

Margaret had promised to reward the girl with milk, so over those few days, by trial and error, her begging and beseeching skills improved. She'd tie her scarf, put Bella on her hip, and head for anyone with goats or cows. She was ready to exploit the twin forces of a hungry and appealing child and what could be taken by the fainthearted as a diseased skull to get her way and get her milk and any other food that might be going spare.

The least neglected habitations were the best for begging. Untidy homes, she found, and homes with little to boast of were unlikely to part with anything as prized as milk unless someone was holding a blade at the owners' throats. But tidiness suggested composure and respectability. Tidy people were more easily coerced. They had more to lose. They evidently had more to prove. Why else the public display of houseplants or painted fences or trimmed hedges on their land?

Men were easier to browbeat than women, Margaret soon discovered. For men, a child was a mystery. She had only to tell a man, "Look at my poor girl's dry lips—that's thirst. And look at her skin. Those blotches on her nose, you see? That's hunger rash. My darling's only got a day or two to live, just feel her bones," and he would rather part with his big toe than stand accused of heartlessness. How Margaret loved her newly invented, inventive self, and how powerful she could be with certain, tidy men. But a woman, and especially one who'd been a mother, would know that just a little redness around the nose was common to all children of that age. Some kids are red around the nose for fifteen years and never hungry once.

So Margaret chose her victims carefully. Once she'd seen a man on the land, preferably near a well-kept house with livestock, she would approach, first greeting him in the old American way, then showing him the child (her beauty first, her hunger next, and then the red nose and the dry, chapped lips), and finally, if all of that had failed, dragging off her blue scarf to show the evidence of flux. This last act always had the greatest effect. Men everywhere fear illness more than women do, she supposed. But it was more complicated than that. She could not know—especially now that Franklin was not around to tell her—that as the days passed and her hair grew a little longer, she became more strikingly unusual. In the first days after the shaving, she would have seemed ugly to most men. Her color was not good. The illness bleached her. Her lids and brows, though, were red from where each pinch of hair had been plucked out by the women in her family—her mother, her two sisters. But except for the

scabs where her grandpa's shell razor had nicked her skin, her scalp
had been oddly white and ailing from never having been exposed to
light before.

But now her color was a healthy one. Since Ferrytown she'd had
good exercise in open air, if not good food, and she had what country
people call "ripe cheeks, sweet enough to pick." Even if she did not
remove her scarf, anyone could see she was a handsome woman. Her
eyebrows were light and thin as yet, but that need not declare her as a
recovering invalid and possibly contagious. The black-haired people
of America did not expect those rare, unlucky redheads among them
to have the forceful facial hair of normal folk. But with her scarf off
and her history of contagion clearly on display, her attractiveness was
enhanced instead of betrayed. By the fourth day of her begging her re-
grown head hair had become tufty enough to hide her scalp entirely
under a soft, springy carpeting, but not long enough to hide the good
shape of her face, the candor of her forehead, the set of her mouth.
Her great green eyes, which might not see too well over long distances, looked to any observers—and there would be many—as if
they were the largest eyes they'd ever seen. They'd wonder whether
they would dare to sleep with her. Was such rare beauty worth the
risk? It was.

So on her last trip into the final farmlands of America in search of
milk, on the morning before she and the Boses expected to reach the
salty, giant-pumped river, the man she found mending his harnesses
outside his neat wood cottage, with its pen of three fatly uddered
cows, was easily—excessively—seduced. When Margaret arrived
with Bella and called out her greetings from the boundary fence, the
man, like all the others before him, took hold of something with
which to defend himself (in this instance, a weighted leather strap)
and ordered her to stay exactly where she was and state her business
unless she wanted to be driven out of the county with blood on her
back.

Margaret was used to these immoderations. The man—as old as

Margaret's father by the look of him, and not as tidy as his house—
did not seem alarmed. Just aggressively cautious. She gave her name.
She smiled. She was polite. She introduced "her" child. She said how
hungry they both were. She asked if there were any chores, anything
at all, that she could do in return for a little milk and some food, and
then, before he could actually suggest any suitable work, she pulled
down her scarf and let the blue material puddle on her shoulders.

She saw the startled look on his face and expected him, like all the
others (at least once their wives had shown their faces), to order her
to keep away from the house while he brought milk and then to feed
the child and leave his land immediately, or else. But this man
stepped toward her, calling out to someone in the house as he did so.
And then she realized, not from experience but from base instinct,
that pulling down her blue scarf, together with her smiling offer to
do "anything at all" in return for milk and food, had been taken by
this man to be an invitation to advance and put his hands on her. Her
hair was not short enough to scare him off. "You'll have the milk," he
said. "You'll have it twice." Another man appeared behind him at the
door.

When Margaret and Bella had not returned to their rendezvous tree
by late afternoon, Andrew Bose acted out of character. Anxious, fretful, and exasperated by Melody's demands that he "do something on
his own account for a change" rather than just cussing their misfortune and feeling sorry for himself, he volunteered to do exactly what
she suggested and risk "a little scout" into the nearest fields.

He left his wife in charge of all their possessions. She would, she
said, make as much smoke as she could if the missing couple were to
return in his absence and as much noise as she could if a stranger approached and offered her "any inconvenience." She was pleased with
herself for sounding so spirited in such worrying circumstances. In
fact, she had discovered, and liked herself for it, that she could be

tougher—*steelier*, to use the older word—than she had expected. Acton first. Now Bella. She still felt strong and calm and ready to be tested further, although she acknowledged in her heart that the prospect of Andrew's being the third loss to the family was one that was mildly amusing to her imagination only so long as it didn't actually happen. He was thin water, though. No denying it.

Her husband set off across the strips of field toward the wood cottage that Margaret had identified, just before noon, as promising. Andrew, whose distance eyesight was still sharp despite his age, had clambered onto the same tree trunk as Margaret and agreed that, yes, her eyes were not deceiving her, that was a man outside the house and those were cattle, though he could not specify whether they were shes or hes.

"Take your knife," Melody instructed him, but he thought it better to arrive at the dwelling empty-handed. He doubted that the inhabitants would want any nets mended—they hadn't passed a decent river for days—and knew for certain that he would not be able to use a knife effectively for any other purpose. He had no plan in mind, other than to take no great risks. He'd satisfy his wife's challenge and no more. He would walk as quietly as he could, keeping to the shade and to the low ground as much as possible, and see what he could see from a safe distance.

He did not approach the house directly by its path but followed a line of trees and then a highish loose stone wall that provided good cover. The only sound he could hear, apart from the entirely natural disharmony of birds and wind and branches, was the half gate of an abandoned hut that was swinging noisily on the last of its leather hinges and repeatedly banging its jamb. But by the time Andrew Bose had reached the end of the wall a dog had begun barking. You can't creep up on a dog. Andrew waited. There was no point in running away from a dog. He expected it to arrive with its inquiring nose at any moment. He would do his best to charm it. Perhaps he should have brought that knife. Stabbing a dog would be no more difficult, surely, than gutting a good-sized fish. But not only did the dog fail to arrive, it also stopped barking after a while.

Andrew counted to a hundred before he dared to stand a little and look over the wall toward the house. There was a dog, its head between its paws, safely leashed at the side wall, but no one was looking out across the land to discover why his guard had been making such a din. The only movement Andrew could spot was from the back of the house, where there were at least three cows in a deeply slurried pasture. For a moment he was tempted just to stand up and call out Margaret's name. If he shouted loud enough and then ducked behind his wall, he would be able to hear any reply but no one would be able to see who'd done the shouting or where from. But they might untie the dog. And, as he had seen, the dog was a large one. Even if they did not release the dog (and a clear sense of *they* had already formed in his imagination: *they* were the same group who had already taken Acton), if they decided to chase after him, what chance would an old, tired man like him stand? No, he would stick to his current policy and stay both quiet and hidden. He skirted the front of the house, still pressing close to fences, walls, and hedges, until he reached the boundary of the cow paddock, on the opposite side of the house from the dog. There he could hope that his odor might be masked by stronger ones.

He waited for another count of a hundred, watching for any movement. There was nothing. He felt reasonably satisfied that unless the rooms were occupied by drunks or men without legs or hostages tied up, the only living creatures within the grounds of this house were the cattle and the dog. So, thinking not only of the heroic tale he would be able to tell Melody later that day but also of how he would never forgive himself if this first chance of finding his granddaughter was refused, he walked across the pasture, using the cows as shields as much as possible, and pressed himself up against the rear of the cottage. Again he waited and listened. Nothing, other than the sounds that empty houses make. So, with his heart racing and his mouth dry, he peered between the shutter boards in the larger of the two windows into the long, single room, half expecting to find Franklin, Acton, and Margaret trussed in ropes, with little Bella crawling in the dust. But all he could see was a table with a pair of leather boots on it and two bed boards covered in a tangle of blankets. Otherwise the house was unfurnished and certainly not permanently inhabited.

Now he was confident, though disappointed. He walked around to the front of the house by way of a side gate, and—this surely was courageous for an aging net maker—went inside. Other than a damaged harness and a leather strap that somebody had dropped on the doorstep, there was nothing more to see than he had noticed from the rear window. Just leather boots and bedding. But fresh hoofmarks in the earth outside suggested that horsemen—only two or three, so far as he could tell—had recently departed, probably only that afternoon. There was nothing to suggest that Bella and Margaret had even reached the house or that there was anything there to be feared, other than a tethered dog that now, for reasons of its own, began to bark again. Andrew thought he heard shuffling and a voice, a baby's cry, perhaps. A bird? It was time for him to flee.

It was dark by the time Andrew found his wife again. She was shaking and hardly able to breathe. Her period of mild amusement on her husband's departure had been short-lived. As soon as he was out of sight, she could no longer admire herself as tough and steely or ready for greater tests. Without her husband's timidity to measure herself against, she soon felt unprotected and exposed. Even though there had been no strangers to offer any "inconvenience," every bird and every cracking branch terrified her. Every shifting shadow made her jump. She'd never known such fear and anxiety before. What if neither her husband nor her granddaughter came back to her? That would be worse than losing Bella's mother. That would be worse than losing Acton. It was not that she loved Andrew better than her son (indeed, she did not) or was so deeply attached to her granddaughter that the thought of life without her was impossible. It was rather that she was alone.

Melody was relieved to see her husband fit and well, despite the dreadful fates that she had imagined for him, and to know that she herself would not be left entirely on her own in the middle of a hostile land, a widow and a destitute, with not a hope in the world. But she was still distraught when he returned and she saw that he was unaccompanied. She listened to his account of finding only an empty house and no sign of their granddaughter or Margaret. She kissed him and embraced him, glad of his warmth, but she was annoyed with him again. "Did you call for her? Did you shout her name?"

"I did everything. There's not a sound. There's no one there."

"A woman and a baby just don't disappear without a trace. Something bad's happened, I'm sure of it now . . ."

"There were horsemen there."

"There were horsemen? Andrew, you never mentioned horsemen. Did you speak to them?"

"I didn't see them. Just fresh marks."

"They're lost. I know it in my heart. They're lost." We all of us are lost, she thought, unless we make it to the boats.

Margaret hadn't had to run like this for years, not since she'd been a girl and dodging boys in games of free 'n' freeze or taking part in races to and from the lake. She'd never had to run with a baby in her arms, taking care not to let the child's head bang against branches or walls but still not slowing down to pay attention to her distress. But she was younger than the two giving chase and marginally more desperate.

Before the first man at the front of the building had managed to grab hold of her arm, she had instinctively run forward and to the side of him. If she had turned and run away, he would have caught her at the gate and hauled her back onto his land. Then what? But he was not expecting her to rush toward him and then take off just out of reach. Now he had to waste a few moments of advantage to turn himself around and take stock.

Margaret headed for the cottage door. The second man, a little younger than the first and simpleminded to all appearances, or maybe half asleep, just stood and watched. He hadn't any idea who she was or why his elder was now calling out, "Bring her down!"

Margaret veered again and took the path that led around the east side of the house and into a horse paddock. A dog, which had been sleeping, shot out at her on its leash and missed her calf with its teeth by the thickness of a reed. She felt its breath. A moment later the first man cleared the corner, too, but snagged his ankles in the leash and hit the earth. The simpleton followed after, just sauntering, in time to see his buddy rolling on the ground, the dog beside itself with fury, and the fur-haired woman climbing the back fence, already too far gone to hear him say, "Blue devils, Charlie, what's goin' on?"

Charlie soon explained. "You'd better wake up, boy. We missed our chances there. We'll get her, though. She owes us now."

"She's got a kid."

"So it won't be nothing new for her." Any woman was a rare commodity for squatters like them. A beauty was too good to lose. They wanted her.

It did not take them long to saddle up their horses, equip themselves with cattle prods and rope, and ride around behind the house in search of Margaret. The men spread out, riding fifty paces or so apart, close enough to shout out to each other and to control a wide stretch of the land. Margaret, with Bella wailing, more frightened by the dog than by anything else, had scrambled through a choke of rocks and ended up above the house, looking down on the roof timbers. She was breathless, and angry, mostly with the men but partly with herself for having been so dangerously and laughably ambiguous. "Anything at all." Not the wisest of remarks. She'd cracked her knee during the climb and caught the back of her hand on a thorn.

She sucked the blood away, quieted Bella with a little finger in her mouth, and tried to think what she should do.

It was tempting, actually, to pick up several rocks and see if she could put some holes in their thin roof, or even damage their milk cows. She thought that probably her danger would prove to be brief and somewhat comical. Perhaps her only problem now would be getting back to the Boses by a circuitous route, though the thought of trying to amuse them with an account of her adventures was not promising.

It was only then that Margaret saw that the two men had mounted up and armed themselves. They had not spotted her yet, but a golden rule of hunting said that nothing from a bee to a buffalo could evade two mounted men for long, except three mounted men. Her first thought was to try to reach one of the other habitations in the neighborhood and beg for help. A young woman with a child, escaping from two likely rapists, could surely expect the offer of help and safety from any normal home, if there were other women, anyway. She could see the roofs of two small steads within easy reach, though no sign of people. If she could see another woman or a child, then she would head that way. But there was no one. There wasn't even any smoke. For all she knew, these places might be abandoned. Most places were abandoned nowadays. Perhaps these two men were simply passing through. Their high-tacked horses seemed to suggest so. Maybe they had rustled their three cows and moved into the empty cottage for a day or so of butchery. Salt beef would see them and their dog safely and fatly through the winter. Perhaps the other buildings were harboring similar men, from the same band of riders possibly. Margaret did not need reminding how cruel and murderous such groups could be. She'd seen them take her Pigeon away. She'd seen the woman on the highway, raped and stoned to death. No, Margaret dared not take her chances at another house. The best thing she could do was get away from humankind and horses altogether. She had her breath back now. She made a sling out of her blue scarf, wrapped it around Bella, and tied the child to her back. She'd carry the baby the way Franklin had carried her down Butter Hill.

This would be a game of hide and seek. Margaret's best plan was to avoid open ground entirely. A stand of trees reached into the flat land around the farmsteads and spread along the low escarpment in patchy clumps, not thick enough to frustrate horses but offering shade and camouflage. But then again, she thought, that is exactly what the men would expect her to do—run for cover. She'd do the opposite.

The countryside was undulating rather than hilly, and the under-growth was thick though low, so it was good for riding and not so good for walking. There was an open meadow just before the trees, cleared by farmers years before but long disused. Margaret looked behind her to see if she was in sight of the horsemen, but they had not cleared the escarpment yet. She ran into the middle of the meadow and, after some long moments of panic, found a hollow big enough to lie down in. She pulled as much dry vegetation and dry foliage as she could find within reach over the two of them and lay on her side, cradling Bella. With one eye, she watched the sky for shadows. She was good at lying still and breathing silently. All she could hope for now was that Bella wouldn't cry and wouldn't want to play.

As she had hoped, Charlie and the simpleton kept to the edge of the trees, peering in among the trunks and pursing their lips to make those "Come to me, cat" noises that men seem to think are flirty and seductive but that are menacing for women. The nearest they came to Margaret and Bella was forty or so horse lengths away, but the baby, placated first by a finger and then by a little sweet ear wax, kept quiet, happy, it seemed, to stay in the undergrowth and watch the clouds with Margaret.

Margaret had no comfort for herself, nothing sweet to take her mind off the fear that raced her heart and cramped her stomach and seemed to want her both to weep and to belch. She could not say ex-actly what she feared. *Rape* and *death* were only words to her. *Pain*

she understood a little more. But there was something in the faces of
those men that she'd been born frightened of. She was shaking but
could not steady herself. She held the baby far too firmly, until Bella
opened her mouth to cry in protest. But by that time Margaret could
hear the horses heading away, growing fainter. Their hoof treads on
the snapping twigs and dry fall leaves would mask Bella's noise, so
Margaret let the baby cry a little and allowed herself to shake and
weep and belch.

It was tempting to take this opportunity to break cover and run
back toward the Boses. Her hide was damp, cold, and uncomfortable. But Margaret's legs were jelly. And she could hardly breathe.
Besides, she knew enough about horses to realize that a woman with
a child to carry would be seen and caught up with before she had a
chance to reach the hem of the meadow. Even if she did reach the
Boses, that would be no guarantee of safety. Those men could knock
them all aside like cornstalks if they wanted to. Andrew and Melody
had only sharp tongues with which to defend themselves.

Margaret had no choice but to wait until sundown, when the light
would be more on her side, and then, skirting the cottage and the
cows, stumble back down to the track and the company, if not the
safekeeping, of Bella's grandparents. They'd have to move on
straightaway. In these circumstances, none of them would want to
spend the night in such a risky spot. They'd be dreaming horses. She
could almost hear Franklin's voice, saying to her, *You'd have been better off sticking to the open highway*.

Late in the afternoon, just about the time that Andrew was checking on the farm cottage, when the shadows of the trees lengthened to
reach the place where Margaret had gone to ground, she decided it
was time to move. She listened carefully, distinguishing the natural
creaking of the trees from any human voices or horse sounds before
judging it safe to make a dash with Bella for the forest edge. She
peered through the gloaming down the slight incline and beyond the
roof of the cottage, hoping to recognize the route she had followed

earlier that day when she had left the Boses under a rendezvous tree on her usual quest for milk. The quickest way to safety, she saw, was to drop into the small pasture where the three cows were kept, pass close to the house, and then follow the shared path between the group of mostly uninhabited buildings. She held her breath and tried to steady her eyes. She was hoping to see no horses. No horses probably meant that the men had not returned, that they'd probably lost interest in their hunt for her and gone after fur of some other kind. They'd certainly be back by nightfall, so now was definitely the time for Margaret to run for it.

She and Bella had reached the choke of rocks above the house before Margaret heard a sound below and immediately took cover again. A small man, not young, was peering through the shutter boards of one of the rear windows. The light would have been too poor in the shadow of the house to see him clearly even if her eyesight had been good, but he was not large enough to be one of the horsemen, she thought. That did not mean that he wasn't just as dangerous, however. Margaret would have to retreat. She waited until the man walked around the house and through the side gate to the front. When he went inside, she came out of her hiding place among the rocks, noisily dislodging a scree of small stones. The dog, still tied at the side of the house, began to bark. She had not been careful enough. The dog could have seen her, smelled her, heard her.

Now Bella started to protest, a cry of complaint. She had had nothing to eat or drink since the morning, her eyes and mouth were full of leaves, she hadn't played all day, she hadn't been allowed to crawl. There was milk to be had just a short distance away, but this was no time to be a milkmaid. Margaret hurried back the way she'd come. This time, protected by the deepening twilight, she kept to the edge of the trees, her finger in Bella's mouth. If she was spotted by the horsemen now, she could at least disappear into the trees and hope to find a narrow trail that horses could not follow.

This was the worst night of her life, hollower even than her first

night in the Pesthouse, more despairing even than the night of the
Ferrytown dead, when at least she had had the company of Franklin.
She had not brought her bedclothes with her, or the tarp or anything
to eat. She wrapped Bella in her blue scarf and cradled her, tucking
her tiny feet inside her tunic top, and waited for the time to pass.

After she saw the two horsemen returning in the last light of the day
to their house, Margaret pushed as deeply as she dared into the trees, far
enough for Bella's now constant crying to be deadened by the trunks.
The darkness was blinding. She could not see a star. Even the moon
had been blocked out by the thick hammock and canopy. The trees
were less than silhouettes. But Margaret would not allow herself to disappear. The child would not allow it, either. Margaret knew—had not
the nursery rhymes told her so when she was just a few years on from
Bella's age?—that if there was no light, still she could create a candle in
her heart and with that candle she could "beam her meanings/On eter-
nity/And shine a purpose/On the Night."

She whispered all the rhymes she knew to Bella, and when the
girl finally fell asleep, exhausted by her own hunger, Margaret, too
gripped by darkness, cold, and fear to sleep, forced herself to light
that candle in her heart and make its meanings and its purposes en-
velop her in light. Now for a few moments, despite the awful im-
mensity of her troubles, she could still pretend to be an optimist. In
that imagined brightness, she could picture, beyond the nighttime
and the trees, beyond the horses and the men, a place of greater
safety, but not outside America. There were no saltwater boats or
gulls. There was no Promised Land. Her place of greater safety was
a soddy on a hill. She could envisage dying there, an ancient girl, her
hair as long as the bed beneath her, with hands—more hands than
she could count—in touch with her, and faces she could recognize
and name, all saying *Margaret, sweet Margaret, you loved us, and we
loved you in return.*

Her eyes were now accustomed to the night, and she could see.
She could see the child's face. She could see her own tough hands.

She could see the fretwork of the trees, and finally a moon and owls for company. She could not stop the tears from flowing then, nor could she keep her hands and shoulders from shaking. She made owl sounds herself, sniffing and gasping for air. She felt expended and ashamed.

But weeping was a speedy sedative. Soon Margaret was calm enough to take stock of her situation. It had been a frightening day, certainly. But nothing irreparable had happened. As the night deepened, she ran each detail through her head. Apart from that scratch on the back of her hand, she'd hardly hurt herself. That idiot of a man, who'd presumed to frighten her and who would have forced himself on her given half a chance, had actually not even succeeded in touching her. The only body he had damaged had been his own, when he tumbled over, snared by his own dog leash. Now all she had to do was take good care of Bella, remain patient until the very first light, and then get back to the Boses and away to safety before anyone else was out of bed.

The rest of the night passed more quickly than Margaret had feared it would. She even dozed, although by the time dawn came she was so cold and stiff from standing with a tree trunk as her backboard that moving at all was difficult. Finding a sure route was impossible. It was easy to tell east from west, even before the first sun rays had penetrated the woods, but anything more precise than that eluded her. Besides, knowing east from west was not a lot of use for someone who could not precisely remember the position of the sun the previous afternoon when she had gone into the woods. She should have paid more attention and marked her route in some way.

Margaret studied the ground at her feet, expecting to find evidence of her walking, footprints and snapped twigs, but if they were there she couldn't see them, not in that half-light, anyway. She was a town girl, not a countryman's daughter. She'd not had to track any animal before. But still she could not stay where she was. She would, she decided, head east. That at least would take her in the direction of the ocean and ships. She would still be sharing a destination with Bella's grandparents, even if their paths did not cross at once. As soon as she reached open ground, she could take stock of the landscape and any buildings that she found and get back to the Boses before they were sent crazy with anxiety. She could imagine their anger. But what else could she have done but make sure that their granddaughter was safe?

Margaret was oddly calm. She felt for the first time in her life as if she were impregnable and strong. There was so much evidence. Only she from Ferrytown had survived the flux. Only she of all the younger and fitter travelers of their campfire group on the highway had not been taken by the rustlers. And yesterday, unlike the woman displayed on the deck of the cart, she had not been raped. She was still alive, and only lost. What was more, she had an independent purpose in her arms, a girl too small and young to walk or talk or even feed herself. She didn't need a cedar box of lucky things. Bella was her priceless talisman.

Margaret was so composed and certain of herself that she did not mind that she wasted the greater part of the morning reaching the edge of the woods, for they were beautiful, and that once she broke through to a clearing, nothing familiar was in sight, not a single building, not a reminiscent shape, not even any cultivated land, and only the footings of ancient walls and lines of metal spikes, rusted thin, as evidence that this had once been farmed many years before but now was wilderness. People had been there in better times, had lived there possibly, had died, but there was little chance that anyone would come again. People were becoming scarce. America was emptying. The land was living only for itself.

The clearing sloped a little to her right. She would not climb. That made no sense. The ocean was at sea level, as low as anyone could go. Even the place where the Boses had spent the night was on a track lower than these forests and lower than the group of treacherous farm buildings where Margaret had almost been attacked. She

turned downhill, and even though she hadn't eaten or slept, she had
the energy and spirit to walk pretty fast, bouncing Bella as she went
and crooning to her all the songs she'd ever learned and some she
hadn't. To be alone would have been frightening and miserable, but
having Bella made her strong.

Margaret suspected the extent of her mistake only when she
reached a low ridge with good views across the territory. Now she
could see what seemed to be the rooftop outline of the cottage she had
visited, but it was far away. She must have walked at right angles to
where she'd wanted to go. Now she'd have to make up the distance.
It could take another half day if the going was complicated. But she
set her sights on the rooftop and struck out for it, determined to get
back to the Boses by sundown. She had not counted on the snow. It
offered only flakes at first, too wet to settle. But soon the flakes light-
ened and fattened and fell so thickly that it was hard to see ahead.
Clear landmarks disappeared. That distant roof was whited out. The
track was filled with snow, and when the wind came up in the afternoon, the open ground ahead of her changed shape. It would be
crazy to labor on against the weather. And end up where? Again
Margaret and Bella would have to spend the night away from the
Boses. At least they had meltwater and some mashed berries for their
supper, and an overhang of wind-bent conifers to give them shelter
and a roof. Margaret lit the candle in her heart again, and slept.

Next day, Margaret was up and walking by dawn, feeling slightly
drunk on tiredness and hunger but also exhilarated by the beauty of
the snow-neatened land and the sharp cold light that gave clear views
of where she had to head. It was mostly easy going, but wading
through the deeper drifts was fun.

Once she reached the familiar open ground a little farther out
from where she and the baby had earthed themselves the day before
last, she did not even bother to keep to the shadows. She could not see
any men, and she would hear if there were mounted horses. The little
cottage looked asleep as she walked past. Two horses were tethered at

the front, breathing steam and already sweating under their cover of blankets. The shutters were closed, and so the three men—she included the small man she had spotted from the choke of rocks—must be sleeping, she thought. The dog was sleeping, too, out of sight on the far side of the house—or, if it was not asleep, it was ignoring her. Her scent was now familiar.

If she wanted, she could probably stop to milk a cow. If she wanted, come to think of it, she could find a good-sized stick and give those men a beating in their beds and be gone before any one of them could lift a finger to defend himself. If she wanted, she could help herself to the two horses, to punish the men for their repulsiveness, and make her journey to the coast a little speedier. But Franklin had explained to her an age ago how horses were an expensive complication for a traveler.

"What, worse than a barrow?" she had asked.

And he'd replied, "When did you last see a barrow stabled? When did you last see a barrow eating hay? When did you last see a barrow rear up, or run off, or nip its owner?"

So Margaret just walked by, within sight of the cottage, leaving her deep footprints in the snow for anyone to follow, being reckless in the interests of speed, but keeping quiet. She was still afraid. It was wise to be afraid. But as she passed she saw an opportunity too good to miss. Only men could be so careless with their food. There was a cold larder on the veranda at the front of the house, with snow swept up by the wind against it. In a moment she was opening it. In the next moment she had helped herself to milk in a jug, a damp wrap of sour cheese, and, joy beyond joy, three hen's eggs, already boiled hard and just a crack away from eating.

No one caught her stealing food, and no one heard her stealing away. Soon she had left the little fields behind and was back on home territory. There was the tree that marked the place where she had left the Boses. They would have spent the last two nights somewhere close, just waiting. Quite soon they would be reunited with their granddaughter. They would be angry. They would be shaking with anxiety. They had a right to be. But Margaret had a tale to tell. And there were eggs and cheese to feast upon.

Andrew and Melody Bose had left the meeting point only at first light that morning. They had spent two almost sleepless nights in a makeshift tent that they had rigged up, using Franklin's tarp and Margaret's thin blanket as weather shields and their own finer blankets as bedding. There had been nothing they could do except eat and wait and argue, once Andrew had returned from his expedition with no news of their granddaughter or "that diseased woman" to whom they had recklessly entrusted her. They'd finished Margaret's taffies and the last gobbets of Ferrytown honey. They'd used up too much of their own salt fish, hoping to placate their nervous stomachs by constant feeding.

Once in a while Andrew had ventured out, armed with Franklin's knife, which was larger than his own net maker's knife, to see if anyone or anything was moving. All he had seen the previous day had been the three cows, pressing up close to the cottage walls for warmth. Then, once the snow had begun to fall, the only sign of any living things other than themselves had been a distant curl of smoke from a chimney that was out of sight.

They made up their minds, talking in whispers through the night. If the child was not returned by first light, they would be coldly sensible. They could presume the worst had happened. Waiting any longer would be pointless. It made no sense to sacrifice themselves to whatever horrors had befallen Margaret and Bella during the past two days and that had previously befallen Acton and the other men. Wise people do not stay, as the valley floods, to witness for themselves how high the waters will reach. They get away. The Boses, then, would do the same.

Margaret found her sodden blanket and the tarp immediately.

She didn't have to look around or call out any names to guess what had happened or what their reasoning had been. She could tell that the Boses had left only that morning. There were footprints in the snow, recent enough not yet to have lost their unambiguous shape. Later—indeed, for the rest of her life—she would wonder how easy it would have been to have caught up with them if she'd set her mind to it. If she had left immediately, then probably within just a few moments she would have been able to see them from the slight brow of the path. They would not have moved very quickly, especially without the fitter, younger Margaret to urge them on.

Margaret, though—could she ever admit it to herself?—was not inclined to hurry after Bella's grandparents. To catch up with them was to relinquish the child, and that was something she was not impatient to do. It might have crossed her mind during the previous few days how joyful it would be to have a child of her own—this child. The thought of stealing Bella away might have stained her daydreams briefly. But Margaret would never actually have done it. It would have been wicked. She would have felt guilty to her grave. No matter that the immediate parents were dead or missing, or that the grandparents were selfish and uncaring, or that Margaret would provide the girl with a kinder future. The theft of a child was unforgivable, even though the ties of every family in the land were already hanging loose.

But for the moment, now that Bella seemed to have been delivered freely to her by the adversities of travel, Margaret did not feel wicked in the least. Or even compromised. She was not stealing a child. She was merely being slow. Anyway, she told herself, the grandparents had made their own decisions—good ones, possibly— and they had willingly abandoned Bella, or at the very least relinquished her. Margaret had kept to the rendezvous. Margaret had returned the child to the promised place. It was the Boses who had walked away, heartbroken, no doubt, but of their own free will. They probably had not believed that their son's daughter would show up again after such a prolonged and baffling absence. They would have shed tears. They would have argued about what was best to do. But in the end they must have felt that they had little choice but to protect themselves and press on with their journey. Already they would be getting used to the loss of their granddaughter. They were not to blame. Hard times make stones of us all.

So Margaret did not hurry on to catch up with the grandparents. She dawdled. She persuaded herself that her first duty was to feed Bella with some stolen milk and mashed white of egg. Then she had to feed herself with cheese and Bella's yolk. Then there was her blanket to be wrung out and her possessions to pack.

She realized at once, when she lifted up her back sack, that it was emptier than it ought to be. There was a water bag inside. There was the died-back mint, still in its pot. Her comb and hairbrush had not been touched. There was the spark stone and the fishing net, which Andrew Bose had dismissed as "the work of ten thumbs." But her taffies and her scraps of food were missing. So was Franklin's knife. Margaret dug into her clothes and checked each item, getting increasingly annoyed and upset when she could not find what she was looking for. The green-and-orange woven top that her sister had made for her and that she loved and wore only for best was not inside. Margaret hissed to herself. She could imagine Melody Bose wearing it as if it were her own. She muttered out loud a thought she knew was hollow, but because the theft of her clothes had come before the keeping of the child, it allowed her to feel that what she was about to do was justified, if only thinly—that her top was payment for the girl, a fair exchange. So now, in Margaret's readjusted view, the Boses were not innocent. They were to blame, after all. They had brought this loss, this separation, on themselves. They'd crept away like thieves, abandoning their blood.

"I'll love you, though," she said to Bella, and pressed her own wet face against the child's.

❧ tweLve ❧

The narrow country path preferred by Margaret soon joined a wider and more regular track, with way markers and mounting blocks for riders. Her route became a little busier and then much busier, and not only with emigrants heading eastward and impatient for the first hint of a salty wind. There were farmworkers with baskets of produce and barrowmen with sacks of late-season silage for sale and trappers going into town to trade in hides and tallow, hogs and fur. There were unhurried horsemen with panniers of goods and children riding backsaddle, and hurried horsemen riding in and out with documents and messages, taking little care to avoid pedestrians and the droves of sheep and goats destined for the slitter's knife. There were journeymen—weavers, skinners, coopers, carpenters, wagon makers, shoemakers, hatters—with tools, and bands of hired hands, all competing for a day's labor, as well as beggars, hucksters, and salesmen waylaying anyone who was unlucky enough to catch their eye. Please help. Please buy. Please give.

The only travelers who were not pursued by the pesterers were a pair of what appeared to be, according to the loop of white tape tied across their shoulders, Baptist pilgrims, looking as beyond reproach as they could. Baptists never helped or bought or gave, so they were rarely bothered. They'd freely pray for anyone and express their pity. But prayer makes the weakest soup. And pity doesn't settle any bills.

Everyone on that wide road was going to or coming from Tidewater, a town that had to be passed by anyone hoping to escape America from those flat quarters of the coast. It was the sort of busy and attentive place where you would find it hard to travel faster than the news of your coming. Beyond Tidewater's buildings and beyond its double set of defensive walls, the ground sloped gently to the scrub-covered shores of the estuary, so much slower and broader than the river at Ferrytown, browner too, and turbid with silt. For once the groups of emigrants were outnumbered by people who had not yet decided to depart from their birth country but who, like the residents of Margaret's town had been, were more attracted by the prospects of local wealth and consequence than by the distant promises of life across the ocean.

The first stranger to hold Margaret's eye, despite her best efforts to hide her face, was a nut-brown man carrying two geese in a basket. He put on a show of admiring Bella, though he didn't try to hold her fingers or touch her cheek as true admirers would. Margaret had to lean close to hear what he was saying. He had what was known as a Carolina twang, that is, a way of speaking that suggested words were rubbery and could be bent and stretched, though only once he'd softened them with chewing.

"Your boy's very sweet," he said, cooing theatrically but mistaking both the child's gender and her parentage. "What's the little fella's name?"

"His name is Jackson," Margaret said. Why not, indeed? Better not to give the child's actual name in case the Boses were inquiring thereabouts.

"Now that's a good old Yankee name."

"His father was a good old Yankee man."

"You don't want to buy a good old Yankee goose, by any chance? A fine and meaty bird." He pointed at the smaller of the two.

She laughed. "Is it fine and meaty enough to take us on its back and fly us east, across the sea, and put us down in some safe place?"

"She would have been, if I hadn't clipped her wings. She lays five eggs a day."

"And if I buy your obliging goose, where should I go with her? Where can we spend the night, within a day's walking from here? Can you suggest a winter lodging place if we don't make it for a sailing?"

She was not sure, but Margaret understood the goose man to say, "The Ark's ahead, on the far side of the town. You could be there by this afternoon. There's always work to be had in there and food for free, if you can settle for the rules and do your bit. Though there're no eggs or geese in there, as far as I've been told. Best get one now."

"Did you say *ark*?" she asked. She didn't recognize the word.

"The Blessed Ark. It's where the Finger Baptists live. It's safe, at least. You'll not be touched." The man laughed, as if he'd made an unusually clever joke. "No, that's for sure. You'll not be touched in there."

"Do you advise me, then."

"I'd say you're best off going to the Ark and seeing winter out on this side of the water rather than risking a passage now, especially with the kid. The weather's up and running, and it can only get worse. They say a ship departed yesterday at sunup but came back in again at sundown, full of green faces. Couldn't keep their stomachs down in waves like that. The ship had just been tossed about. Too overloaded, see? Couldn't even ride the tide. And far too small. They'd send a sieve to sea if they thought there was a profit in it. The bigger ships start to come again at first blossom. That's four months yet. A goose—two geese!—is what you need to see you through."

Margaret took the man's advice but not his goose. She would make her way to the Ark. He'd said that it was safe, and after the horrors and abductions of the past few days, that was what she wanted most. She was relieved, in fact, to be advised that her departure from America would have to wait at least until the spring. She did not follow the obvious and quickest route through the middle of the town, though. She was certain that the Boses would be there, and they might have parked themselves at the town gate to see if their granddaughter showed up. Surely they would do that, at least. Margaret tried not to give them too much thought. She'd not abandoned them, after all. They were the deserters. The honor debt was theirs, not hers. She'd follow her instincts, even if they were selfish and undutiful, and try not to burden herself with doubt or guilt. She'd just spend a little extra time walking around the outer walls rather than passing through them, into the clutter of people and buildings.

At least the longer route was free of beggars and salesmen, and it took her past Tidewater's wells and middens, where she found rotting scraps to wash and eat. A woman who leaves her home and family must end up as either a prostitute or a destitute. That's what the Ferrytown widow who narrated doom-laden stories each evening had told the diners in the guesthouse on several occasions. Well, what was eating rotting scraps of food if not the habit of a destitute?

It took Margaret until the middle of the afternoon to reach Tidewater's eastern gate and the road that led along the riverbank toward the sea. The birds were mostly dressed in white and either screamed like ghouls or scampered in the mud in synchronized groups, as if they had only one brain to share between them. The smell of water was overpowering, both energizing and nauseating. The wind was sharper than any wind she'd known before. It cut into her face and made her eyes water. It chapped her skin. It tugged at her scarf. It deafened her.

Margaret could sense the sea beyond the distant dunes, although now that it was close she could not imagine it. The largest stretch of water she had encountered so far had been the lake above Ferrytown. She could stand on its shore and easily see banks in all directions. But an undulating, salty lake without banks? That was not within her dreams. She could press ahead, of course, a half day's walk, and see the ocean for herself. But her legs would not oblige. She knew that she had reached the point of ultimate tiredness. All she wanted now was rest. The ocean could wait. Every step she took was painful. Bella had not gotten any fatter—how could she?—but it felt as if she had. The baby, well breakfasted, for once, on eggs and milk and sleeping happily, felt as heavy as a stone. Margaret's walk had become semiconscious and mechanical. It was as if just the smell of the ocean, or perhaps the crust of salt on her lips, were a sleep-inducing drug.

Margaret saw the Ark way before she and Bella reached it. At first it seemed to be little more than a massive palisade made out of cut but unworked tree trunks and arranged in a perfect rectangle, too high and smooth for anyone to climb. But as they drew closer, the roof planks and roof weights of several long buildings could be seen, and a half-constructed stone tower at their center, with scaffolding and men at work. It did not look entirely welcoming. The palisade was defensive and discouraging.

And this was odd: in the approaches to the Ark, great trenches had been dug and mostly filled in again, as if there had been an epidemic and a thousand bodies were being buried, had been buried, there. The trenches were not graves but dumping grounds, as far as Margaret could tell, for objects that these Finger Baptists evidently did not want. In the one open trench within sight, she could see some harnesses, a beaten copper tray, and some cans, as well as something small and silvery. Such waste was unnerving. Had she been less tired and dispirited, she might have turned away and gone elsewhere. But she walked on. "It's not long now," she said to Bella. "Then we'll be safe." What could they hope to find inside, she wondered, apart from not being touched? Free food, at least. The goose man had said there'd be free food. A bed? A winter roof? A place out of the wind, that was for sure. And time, finally, to teach the girl to walk.

. . .

There was a single entry to the Ark, a great timber gate, closed but with a smaller door set into it. All who sported the loop of white tape came and went as they pleased, but Margaret and Bella had to get in line. They joined about thirty other travelers who were seeking shelter until the spring and, not daring to sit and sleep, waited their turn. Two keepers moved among the hopefuls, turning away anybody wearing jewelry who would not agree to throw it out or any man wearing a sword or knife or hoping to enter the Ark with any kind of vehicle. A family with a short barrow hung with tools and implements salvaged from their abandoned cart chose to press on and find other winter quarters rather than sacrifice their forage tines, a drag chain, an ax, a kettle, a shovel, clouts, and linchpins, as well as sufficient nails and hames to equip another cart if only they had horses. Another who had hoped to take his horse into the Ark for stabling was told he either had to stay outside or lose his metaled saddle, the horse's shoes, and his bit and bridle, which had been handed on to him through generations of riders. He chose to stay outside.

The determined survivors, fewer than twenty in number, were allowed through the smaller door into a courtyard between the inner and outer palisades. There they had to form another line, which passed between two long timber tables minded by devotees with the now familiar white tape around their shoulders and carefully expressionless faces. Were these the Finger Baptists? Margaret wondered.

"Nothing metal, nothing metal," one of them was commanding, walking up and down the line, repeating his instructions and devotions to every group. "Remove all metal from your hair—no antique combs—no knives at all, no silverware, no ear or finger rings, no pans. Metal is the Devil's work. Metal is the cause of greed and war. In here we are, like air and water, without which none of us can live, the enemies of metal. Check your pockets. Shake out all your rust. Remove your shoes. Unlace your bags."

Margaret watched as the members of one of the two families ahead of her in line were frisked by devotees in gloves and then required to empty out their bags, every single item, and put their shoes and belts onto the tables. A spoon and a bracelet, wrapped in felt, clearly valuable and probably loved, were thrown into woven baskets under the tables. The father of the family shook his head, hardly able to control his mounting anger when the buckle was snapped off his belt. A coat whose buckle would not tear free from its cloth was thrown out entirely. Their shoes were inspected, and either any brass eyelets or clips were pulled free and jettisoned or, if they would not loosen readily, the whole shoe was thrown out and replaced by a pair of stitched moccasins. Metal buttons were snapped off their coats and pants by expert gloved hands. Seams and hems were checked for hidden metal valuables. The children had to part with toys that they had made from found scrap, and the family dog—a cousin, in looks at least, to Becky, Margaret's missing terrier—was stripped of its studded collar.

The father, though, was keen to preserve at least a little of his dignity. He was not prepared, he said, to lose the short sword that he had hidden among his blankets, which was discovered by the sorters with a look of disapproval and triumph. Losing it and any ability to defend his family in the future was too great a price to pay, he argued. It was wrong of them to insist, even though the family would have winter food and accommodation as recompense. "We've already given up our few valuables. Enough's enough."

"It's your decision," he was told. "If you don't like us, you can go."

"I like you well enough. But you're robbing us. What you're doing isn't much different from stopping us on the road and holding knives to our throats."

"We never have knives."

"I know that, yes." The father was getting exasperated. "A wooden stick, then, if you held that to our throats," he added hastily, trying to be sarcastic, and then realized how foolish he must sound.

"Well, something sharp at least, for heck's sake!" He glanced at his short sword, still lying on the table and within easy reach. His wife put her hand on his arm, a gesture of both solidarity and restraint. She could see how tempted he was—and not for the first time—to support his indignation with a blade. She could also see that these Baptists were fit young men who seemed ready to defend their high principles with their fists and feet.

The white-taped man who had been walking up the line listing forbidden objects and giving instructions to the applicants and who had seemed to be the most senior of the devotees now approached the family at the table, clapping his hands for silence. "Enough's enough, indeed," he said, spreading his arms to show that the way ahead was now barred to them. "Please gather your possessions and leave. We have no place for you."

"Who'll sew the buckles back? You've damaged everything. Who'll mend the shoes?" the father asked.

The man shook his head, entirely calm. "No one," he said, making his meaning very clear. Their metal already in the baskets would not be returned.

"Hand me back my mother's bracelet, then." The emigrant's wife hoped to salvage what she could. "And let us have the silver spoon. That's all the currency we have."

"And give me back my sword."

The calm man shook his head again. "Metals equal weapons equal death," he said.

Now the wife was heated, too. "Then you're thieves, for all your piety."

"We don't steal from anyone. We put the metal back into the soil. We bury it. That's not theft. That's restitution. We require our winter residents to observe our practices. Neither your broad sword nor your arguments are welcome in the Ark." He took the father's sword from the table and dropped it into a basket with as much ceremony and measured finality as he could. "You should leave now. The inner door is closed to all of you."

The next family was careful to cooperate and not argue. A much-loved, battered cooking pot and their leather-working needles plus their wrap of bone-handled tools—scissors, cutters, blades—which might have provided them with a livelihood on the far side of the ocean, all ended up among "the stones of hell" in the wastebaskets, with every other scrap of pewter, copper, battered steel or rusty iron, gold or silver, lead or tin. They had made up their minds swiftly. On the whole their sacrifice was worth it. They'd not survive the winter on the cold side of the palisades. They could survive without their tools.

Margaret offered Franklin's bag. She could not think that there was any metal inside. Her comb and hairbrush passed inspection. They were wood and bone. They checked the pot of died-back mint for staples, too, but found none, though for a moment Margaret feared that they intended to tip out the earth and check for hidden scraps, but clearly soil was something that these devotees approved of. Nothing grew in metal, but any soil was natural and sanctified.

Perhaps it was just as well that the Boses had stolen Franklin's knife and that she had lost or left her cedar box in Ferrytown. It would have been heartbreaking for her to see two of her lucky things, the coins and the necklace, flicked away as if they were as worthless and unpleasant as ticks. Now the devotees checked her body and the clothes she was wearing, her hems, her seams, her tucks, her folds. It was a humiliation that was only partly eased by the fact that the checker closed his eyes while doing so and repeated his apologies. He felt her head through her blue scarf but did not require her to remove it, nor did he seem to detect the shortness of her hair. He then examined Bella, though he smiled and stood back as soon as she grasped his little finger in her wet fist.

"These two are untarnished," he said finally.

Margaret, then, had nothing to declare, not even a brass button. She was, they let her understand, the perfect applicant for entry to the Ark. She and "her son, Jackson," registered their names and birthplace (Ferrytown) and were allocated lodgings in the Kindred Barn for Women and given a wooden token to exchange for food.

Now they were free to go ahead as residents through a second wooden gate into the inner courtyard. Inside on a roofed terrace was another long timber table loaded with bedding, towels, bone spoons, and water jugs, and black headscarves for any woman whose hair was still on immodest display. An older devotee gave one of each item to Margaret, his hands arthritic and trembling, his voice constricted. Bella was too small and young to warrant a set of her own, he explained, and then he examined the signage on their token before directing Margaret across the open ground toward the sleeping sheds. "The farthest to the right is yours. Take any bed and crib that's not in use," he said. "These are the rules: Exchange the token for your meal. Reclaim the token when you have completed your tasks tomorrow evening. You will not be able to eat again without handing over a token. You will not be able to depart from the Ark without presenting a token. You will not receive a token unless we are satisfied. We will not be satisfied unless you work well. You will not work well unless you eat." He waited while the logic and neatness of her new regime sank in, and then he added, "Yes, we have devised a circle of effort and reward. And if you provide good service within the circle, you may be asked to help the Helpless Gentlemen themselves."

Margaret was too exhausted to inquire further. Her daily tasks? The Helpless Gentlemen? The Finger Baptists? She would find out in due course. At least, for the first time since the onset of her flux, she was not even vaguely fearful. *You will be safe*, the man had said. And she believed that to be true. Here was an odd but organized community. She could smell roasting meat. She could not see anybody running. There were no raised voices. The wind, and therefore much of the winter cold, was blocked out by the palisades. The loss of metal was no great sacrifice to those who did not mind cooking without pans or sleeping without a knife at their side.

Margaret walked across the great paved courtyard, soothing the now fretful and always hungry Bella, toward the place where they would spend the winter. Now that she could see the Ark's inner courtyard in detail, she could only stare openmouthed at the half-completed low stone building at its center. Never in her dreams had she seen a place more decorated or more beautiful. The finished stone itself was grained and worked as intricately as a wood carving, with images of animals and plants and the round faces of people who looked as wide-eyed, calm, and expressionless as the devotees. The wooden window frames were glazed with pieces of colored glass, stained with the reds, greens, and blues of blood, moss, and sky. The entry was an archway with a capstone that seemed too heavy to be so far from the ground. At least ten masons and carpenters, all with the white tapes of devotees, were working on the buttresses and doors, and a dozen or so other men and boys, evidently winter guests like Margaret, were earning their keep, helping with the unskilled labor or holding the timbers steady while artisans fixed them into place with trunnels instead of metal nails. She raised a hand in greeting, and though no one called out in reply, she was responded to with several honest smiles. Now she relaxed. The Ark, whatever its purpose might be, would rescue her and Bella. It would be their first home together.

The women's sleeping shed was cobble-floored and timber-sided, with loose roof planks protected from the mischief of the wind by stone weights. It creaked as she entered, a sort of greeting to the newcomers but a nailless greeting, as once again the building was pegged and framed with wooden joints and hinges. There were no windows. The only light came from the open door and through gaps in the timber. There was no fire or grate, but it was warmer inside than outside, and certainly drier. She recognized the homely smells of women, washing, tobacco, and hog-fat candles.

Margaret chose a bed that was not already made up with a blanket and covered with possessions. She found a crib for Bella. The hut was empty of other residents. All were working, she presumed, maintaining their circles of effort and reward. The mattress was a luxury that she had almost forgotten, cotton ticking stuffed with chaff and moss. She fell asleep at once, with Bella on her chest, and neither woke until the daylight had gone entirely, robbing the shed of any definition. They slept until someone passed by with a mallet, beating on beams and doors, and calling out between the drumming of wood on wood, "Let's eat. Let's eat."

It was not hard to find the dining hall, even though it looked exactly the same as the sleeping huts. Everyone was going there, holding his or her bone spoon. She followed, keeping her distance, not yet wanting to talk to anyone or introduce herself, but once she had handed over her token, climbed the three steps, and was inside the hall, she found a decent smile to wear and tried to look as if she belonged and was not at all embarrassed by the company of so many strangers, divided as usual into tables for men and tables for women and a circle of low planks for the children. The two tables nearest the door were reserved for pilgrims, devotees, and anyone else entitled to a loop of white tape.

Margaret should have known that her discomfort could not last. A woman with a baby, especially one as beautiful as Bella, is always welcome at a table of other women. Within a moment she had been summoned by another mother, whose child was old enough to handle his own spoon, and she was sitting among friends, with Bella on her lap. There was more good food in front of her than she had seen since Ferrytown. But no one was eating yet. One higher table at the side of the building was still unoccupied. They would have to wait, it seemed, for the latecomers.

When she saw them, it was not immediately clear how the Finger Baptists had earned their name. They wore long sleeves, long hair, long beards, and seemed to have trouble walking with any strength or commitment. There were exactly twenty of them. One had to die before another devotee could be elected to their group. Twenty was the holy maximum. They took their seats at the higher table, paying no attention to the crowded hut, and one of the attendants struck his mallet on their table to beat out the blessing, wood on wood, and to indicate that dining could begin. Margaret mashed some of the softer food for Bella first, and added a little milk to make it into a digestible paste. She broke up a piece of chicken into safe shreds and let the girl suck it while the paste was cooling, and then she took her too-large spoon and began to feed the stolen child, her boy Jackson, her girl Bella.

It was only when Bella was eating that Margaret looked across the room and saw that what she was doing was mirrored at the higher table. The twenty Finger Baptists were the Helpless Gentlemen. They did not want to feed themselves, it seemed. They sat before their food, their arms hanging loosely at their sides, their beards and hair pushed back, while devotees—one each—spooned food into their mouths and wiped their lips with cloths. The devotees lifted cups of water and juice and waited for their masters to sip. One was holding up a chicken leg for his Gentleman to gnaw. Another offered dry beans, one at a time, as if he were hand-feeding a turkey.

"What are they doing?" Margaret asked the mother who had befriended her.

"The very same as you."

"So I see. But why?"

"Has no one told you yet? They're not allowed to use their hands. The hands do Devil's work."

The Devil's work, Margaret soon found out, included not only fighting and stealing, both of which indisputably required dishonest hands, but also art, craft, cooking, working, and the age-old and best-forgotten practices of technology for which all metal was the chilling evidence. The Helpless Gentlemen had set their minds and bodies against the country's ferrous history. Wingless and with withered arms, they'd earn their places at the side of God.

So the winter passed. It was an oddly comfortable existence for Margaret and Bella. Much of the doubt, regret, and danger had been

removed from her life, though what replaced them was mostly dull.
In this respect, the Finger Baptists were proved correct—no blades,
no blood. The emigrants were honest, because there was nothing to
steal; sharing, because there was plenty to eat; sober, because there
was no liquor. There were no misers, because there was no wealth to
hoard; they were industrious, because it was work or starve.

As the mother of an infant, Margaret's duties were long but light.
It was her job to sit from sunup to sundown at the Ark's water supply, a shallow well, protected from the cold by a three-sided shelter.
For most of the time there was nothing for her to do except be patient
and keep Bella amused and out of mischief. The girl was an adven-
turous crawler and then a reckless walker, who, like the worst puppy,
would take any opportunity to slip away behind Margaret's back to
investigate and taste anything that caught her eye, whether it be a
dangerous splinter of wood or a shard of ice or a scrap of crust or
mud. Then Margaret had to clean out Bella's mouth with her finger
and force open her fists to remove any trophy. The child was growing, becoming more interesting and more difficult, first learning to
recognize the word *no* and then learning to resist it. Once she had
discovered how to pick things up and use them without help—her
cup, for example, her spoon—it was not long before she devised the
game of throwing things down for Margaret to fetch or simply to enjoy the sound of tumbling, rolling, and breaking.

There were busy times when Margaret had no choice but to strap
Bella to her back and deal with the peak demands for water. The first
to arrive were those emigrants whose duty it was that day to fill the
family water jugs. There were eighty-two overwintering families in
all, including Margaret and Bella, and so the line for water was often
long and unruly, with impatient boys trying to jump the line and
older men demanding precedence, especially as the first waters of the
morning were the least cloudy and the sweetest. Margaret had insti-
tuted the Ferrytown method to prevent arguments. As people arrived at the well, they threaded a loose rope through the handles of

their jugs. That fixed the line beyond question. Then they had no choice but to be patient and talk to each other rather than argue, or to play with the child.

Margaret's still-short hair was long enough by now to be revealed to the women in her sleeping shed. She could safely recount to them the story of her illness and some details of her journey to the Ark. She could relive out loud and weep again at the horrors of Ferrytown, that rock-hard memory: every member of her family dead in sleep. Now she appeared to the women as a survivor, as someone who had once been alarmingly dangerous but was no longer. They were the only ones who saw her bareheaded, though, and they were the only ones, too, who inevitably saw Bella naked. So Margaret's pretense that Bella was a boy called Jackson was short-lived. No, Jackson was a girl's name in her family, she'd explained, despite the sound of it, its final unfeminine consonant. So she had begun calling Bella Bose "little Jackie." It was more convincingly girlish. Bella did not seem to notice the change. Indeed, it wasn't very long before she did not even respond to the word *Bella*. She became Jackie to herself. And Margaret was known to her as Ma, a not entirely dishonest pretense, given her first name. Ma for *Margaret*. Ma for *make-believe*.

Jackie was not a predictable baby. She was ready to grant broad smiles to any woman or child who paid attention to her but was more reticent with men, especially the workmen and the craftsmen from the half-completed tower, who came throughout the day, smelling of sweat, stone dust, and timber, to fill their buckets. And when any of the twenty Finger Baptists came and required Margaret to draw water for them, Jackie was prone to burst into tears and hold on to her ma as if these Helpless Gentlemen meant to do her harm.

Margaret thought the girl was disturbed by the Baptists' long gray robes, but actually she was smelling Margaret's own uneasiness. Their greatest marks of holiness—their flaccid arms and lifeless hands, which had weakened over the years for want of use—were usually hidden in their sleeves. But when they came from their ablutions (where, according to the gossip, though no one had witnessed it, they cleaned their intimate parts by squatting in a shallow bowl), they liked to have their hands washed as well—force of habit from their less devout childhoods, she supposed—and Margaret had to hold back their sleeves while they dipped and trailed their emaciated fingers limply in the water. Then she had to take the washing block and soap them, sometimes as far up as their armpits. Their arms, especially those of the residents who had been there longest, who had not so much as picked their own noses for twenty years or more, were wasted from the shoulders down and weighed less than a strip of feather wood. Once the Baptists had washed, she had to dry them, too. She found the whole procedure unpleasant and disturbing. Their hands were weak and useless but not shrunken. In fact, with so little flesh and so much prominent bone, they seemed huge and corpselike.

Margaret tried to keep her eyes lowered and maintain silence when the Finger Baptists were at the well. She did not want to be selected as one of the emigrants who had the honor of serving these men in their private quarters. She'd heard—more rumors, possibly, but disquieting nevertheless—that duties might include massaging and masturbating them, washing them down all over, washing their hair, providing pellets of food, pulling their clothes on and off, cleaning their teeth, and helping the fatter and the older ones to sit and rise. But only once in those winter months had Margaret been asked to do anything more intimate than draw the water and wash and dry the arms. On that occasion, one of the younger Helpless Gentlemen, who, although his arms and hands were useless, was very mobile elsewhere, a speedy walker and a man with fat, expressive lips, had lifted his face toward Margaret and, with a series of commands— "Higher," "Lower," "Aah, just there!"—required her to attend to an intolerable itch on the side of his face.

"Count yourself lucky," one of the women had commented that evening. "A man can itch in many places."

There was no escaping the evening sermons, mostly delivered by a Baptist aspirant while all the families were eating. Metals were the cause of weaponry and avarice: "Think on iron, think on gold." Metals were invaders in a world otherwise designed from fire, air, water, earth, and stone, all of which were more or less compressed versions of each other and indestructible; "Metal has brought death into the world. Rust and fire are God's reply." Sometimes the emigrants, their mouths oily with food and scarcely able to restrain their laughter, were required to repeat some favorite Baptist lines out loud. The diners were always happy to join in, though hardly any of them truly felt that tins and sins were quite the twins that the Baptist songs made them out to be.

Otherwise, Margaret's life in the Ark was without problems and without external incident. The trickle of new arrivals—which, luckily, did not include any Boses—stopped as the snow thickened and the cold intensified. The world beyond the palisades became a memory of hardship and sore feet. She did her best not to dwell on Franklin or her family in Ferrytown. The devotees, pilgrims, and disciples who had arrived during the fall kept to themselves in the evenings, preferring to concentrate on their rites and religious ambitions rather than consort with people who were less hostile to the old ways of America than piety and reason demanded. Once in a while a group of devotees, expressionless as usual and wearing their sorters' gloves, disturbed the domestic calm of the sleeping huts by enforcing an unexpected search for hidden jewelry or any other trace of metal. A nonobservant mason brought in from Tidewater during the summer because his carving skills were unrivaled was rumored to have hidden shards of metal between the tower walls to undermine its sanctity. The devotees had not found any evidence of that, but their confidence had been undermined. So they took no chances with the integrity of their new building. If anyone was caught with as much as a half nail or a splinter of tin, his or her whole family was expelled at once, no matter whether it was the day or night or in the middle of a storm. The Ark would not abide so much as a fleck of metal.

Margaret had nothing to fear from these occasional disruptions. She had no possessions that might harbor contraband. She did not care about the tower. She was without blemish and, in their eyes at least, lived a blameless life, hoping only to pass unnoticed or, at most, to be regarded as an attentive mother. She exchanged her token for food each day and earned it back by her attendance at the well. She slept and ate and grew more confident.

At mealtimes, when they could be stared at, the Finger Baptists were a source of great amusement among the younger emigrants, including Margaret. Afterward, gathered around the candles in the privacy of the sleeping shed, their faces animated by the warmth and light, the women of Margaret's hut could laugh and joke at will and then exchange their hopes and ambitions for the coming spring.

In some respects, Margaret had never been happier. Of course, her happiness was always haunted by the all-too-recent and all-too-memorable loss of her family, her hometown, and her only man. The very thought of them was crippling. Nevertheless, Franklin had become the perfect husband and father in her imagination and in the stories that she told to her companions. He was her lover and her friend. He was the father of Jackie. She would never look at another man until she was certain he was dead. She could not shake off entirely the receding but nagging shame and guilt she felt for her abduction of the child. But for once she was part of a community that had not known her as a girl, that did not count her coloring as unfortunate, and that could not control the way she lived her life or how she raised her daughter. She was a woman with status, a mother, a wife with a lost husband, a good friend whose wit was appreciated in the hut. Here was a warmth and neighborliness that she had never encountered in Ferrytown, where the only common interests at times seemed to be avarice, jealousy, and competition. In the Ark, among her shed companions, there was the common interest of strangers sharing their directions and their hopes.

Over the months both Jackie and the half-completed tower grew higher and more ornate. The Finger Baptists hoped to move into the lower levels when the spring and a fresh intake of both pilgrims and travelers arrived. Everybody among the emigrants dreamed of walking out through the double gates to see a sail ship in the estuary. Another month would see them free again. A month was nothing to endure. Then America could be a nightmare left behind. Even Margaret began to believe that her best future—their best future—would be beyond the ocean, that taking to the ships would not be cowardly. That dream she'd had, up in the forest on the night when she had lost her way, that dream of being once again a safe and ancient girl in her soddy at the top of Butter Hill, had been a delusion. Yes, happiness was in the east. Wasn't that what everyone believed?

As the final days of winter passed and the moon, losing its hold, retreated back toward midnight, Margaret settled to the thought of finding passage in a ship along with her new friends. It was a comfort, in a way, to have a shared plan. She was distressed less and less by thoughts of Andrew and Melody and Acton, their son, or by recollections of her life and family in Ferrytown. Even Franklin, her Pigeon, became more remote to her, despite the many occasions when her version of him as a father and a husband was offered to the women in the Ark or the many times she dreamed of their reunion. In fact, one morning when she was still exhausted from a restless night of Jackie's teething, she realized she could not remember many details of his face, and she could scarcely recall his family name. It wasn't Lombard, and it wasn't Lopate. She was relieved when, finally, the name was retrieved. Lopez, that was it! Franklin Lopez from the plains. How could she be so ready to forget that part of him, to let him slip away? That was troubling. It was as if the winter in the Ark had enriched her and robbed her at the same time.

The first truly warm day came when snow was still on the ground and the earth was hard. Spring's breath was in the air, crying green. Margaret had checked her pot of mint for signs of life, but there were none as yet. She was enjoying the sunshine at her duty spot beside the

well and dozing, despite the usual hammering of carpenters and masons at the tower and the not-so-usual cries and hammering at the
outer gates of the Ark.

Jackie, now into her second year, was playing push-and-pull with
another toddler. It was she who first spotted the man dismounting
from a horse and running across the courtyard from the entry gate
toward the tower works, followed twenty paces behind by a gang of
thirty or so, all armed with swords and pikes. *Metal* swords and
pikes, some already wet with Baptist blood. But it was not their shin-
ing blades or brass-encrusted shields or the clanking of their buckles
and their armor that most alerted Jackie. It was the first man's
clothes. A pinto coat like his, in such a striking pattern, was bound to
catch a child's eye. She called out, not a word exactly, and pointed at
the man, clearly amused by something. For an instant Margaret, with
her poor eyesight, mistook him for Franklin. She half got up. She
half cried out. But then she saw how short he was, his bandy legs, his
many layers, the colored ribbons tying back his beard. She recognized his face.

❧ thirteen ❧

Franklin Lopez and his forty or so fellows in the labor gang had arrived outside the Ark soon after dawn and set to work at once. They were almost eager for the exertion. Work was their one protection against the cold, the hunger, and the boredom of captivity. The masters had kept their vassals lightly clothed and underfed, but the laborers had been told that this day's work, if it was as richly productive as was hoped, might be rewarded with an evening meal and—possibly—brief access to a fire.

"Make it quick and keep it quiet" was the only instruction for the gang, though that was easier said than done. The winter months had shut the landscape down, hardened it and left it brittle. Even walking through the dead, frost-stiffened vegetation that morning had been far from silent. The ground had snapped and clacked loudly underfoot, protesting at the weight of so much flesh, though so far only telling anyone awake inside the Ark that men and horses were passing by. That was not unusual for these spring mornings, when everyone was impatient to catch first sight of sails. The ships were coming. Any dreaming citizen with any hope was packed and ready for the sea.

Franklin, clumsy and stumbling at the best of times, had made more noise than most as they approached the palisades. He'd been strapped across the neck as punishment and then strapped again when he'd cried out in pain. His masters, he'd discovered, were quick to pick on him and were less eager to punish shorter men. Sometimes, when his anger and his despair became intolerable, he stood and stretched himself and laughed out loud, shaking all his limbs as if his humor knew no bounds. It was a way to shrive himself of all the furies. It was a laugh that did not seem (well, not at first) too impudent. Sometimes his masters laughed along with him, counted him an idiot, called him Donkey. At other times they beat him for his laugh. But usually the beating was good-humored and less painful than not laughing.

Franklin had been relatively fortunate during his captivity. The morning following his separation from Margaret, after a cold, hard night sleeping with the horses and the stolen animals at the fringes of the Dreaming Highway, Franklin, Acton Bose, and the two Joeys had been tugged awake on their leashes at first light and hurried along at the speed of the slowest horse toward Tidewater.

The horsemen did not stop to feed their charges, whose only opportunity to rest and urinate had not been pleasant. The seven rustlers had caught up with a cartload of furniture and farming tools being pulled along the highway by four heavy horses. The three emigrants who owned it, two men—brothers, with identical beards—and one wife, hoped to make themselves invisible by staying absolutely silent and making no eye contact with the newcomers, who had first ridden around them in a circle, whooping like children, and then dismounted to inspect their prey more closely.

The travelers studied their own feet without comment or expression as Franklin and his fellows were forced to sit in a line with their backs toward the cart. The family's horses were unharnessed and their boxes kicked open and their sacks emptied onto the highway.

Only their dog did not understand that nothing could be done to save them or their property. Its barking protests were short-lived. Finally, once all the valuables had been discovered and stolen and anything fragile had been broken, just for the sake of it, the heavy horses were added to the string of mules and the two men were attached to the train of captives with loops of rope around their necks and wrists. But the woman, despite the protests of her husband, who called out her name—"Marie, Marie, Marie"—well beyond hearing distance, was left behind in the attentive care of two of the rustlers. They caught up with their comrades later in the afternoon in high spirits but unaccompanied. When the husband once again called out her name, they shook their fists to silence him and made vulgar gestures. "Make another noise and you'll be beaten," they said, and added, "Like the dog. Like sweet Marie. That goes for all of you. We're in the mood."

On their fourth day of captivity, exhausted by their pace of travel, by their anger and anxiety, and by the meanness of their rations, the six hostages arrived at an encampment in ancient wasteland to the north of Tidewater. The land was far too widely strewn with rubble and debris for many trees to have survived. Only weeds and a few low scrub bushes made their living among the remains of great stone buildings and the tumbled masonry of a grand, dead city. So deep were the fallen remnants of the now shapeless structures that pools of water, little lakes, were nestling in the marble and concrete piles. The horsemen stopped in a steep-sided canyon of rubble and wreckage where the sunlight hardly penetrated. There the captives were tightly bound and shackled to an antique, purposeless engine of some kind, smelling of decay and rust, and—or so they feared—left for dead, without a jug of water or a scrap of food, any protection against the cold or any word of what their fates might be. Their only freedom, now that their captors were out of earshot, was that they could speak among themselves, exchanging names with the husband and brother-in-law of sweet Marie, who made their oddly formal introductions, observing rules of precedence that could no longer have any value.

"I have to get back to my wife," Nike, the husband, kept repeating, as if offering an excuse not to join the others in their enforced adventure.

"We all have someone to get back to," the older Joey said. "I have a wife and other children, too. I don't know where they are." He indicated Franklin. "He has a sister, and Acton has his parents and his daughter. That's how it is for all of us. They're lost to us, we're lost to them."

"You're older than the rest of us," replied Nike, as if age devalued Joey's pessimism.

The younger Joey spent his time either crying or sighing deeply. He was in shock: the beating of the dog had been the cruelest act he'd ever witnessed, and inexplicable to a boy of his age. He'd no idea that anyone could be so heartless as to treat a dog as if it were . . . well, just an animal. But the men, once they had heard the horsemen depart and tested the silence for a while, saw this unexpected abandonment as their only chance to get away with their lives. If there was anyone to get back to, if the wife, the child, the sister, and the parents had survived, then this was the opportunity to seek them out.

The men were too tightly bound to attempt to untie any knots, but with a little wiggling each could sink his chin onto his chest and get his teeth around one of the thinner ropes. It tasted of sweat and smelled of horses and wood. But it was feasible, though not easy, to snap or chew the thin strands. Given time, it now seemed possible that they could bite through this rope, though whether that would set them free or merely damage their mouths and lips remained to be seen. They worked away, no longer wasting any energy on talk. They sounded like six feeding rats.

The best of them had broken through only a fraction of the rope when three of the rustlers, including their short and overdressed leader, still wearing Jackson's coat, returned. They were accompanied by an elderly man who rode his horse sidesaddle and his two armed retainers. They helped him to dismount. He walked along the line of captives, nodding, shaking his head, behaving like a trader in-specting barrels of apples or bolts of cloth.

"Very well," he said. "My offer stands. I'll take those three." He pointed at the brothers and at Acton Bose, but shook his head at the middle-aged potman. "And I'll take the boy. We'll make good use of him until he grows. What name?"

"I'm Junior Joey, mister."

"And this one, too." He placed his finger on the end of Franklin's chin, buried in the hair and the threads of chewed rope. "We'll have them digging coal."

"No, the mountain's not for sale," the small man said. "We're keeping him."

"Well, keep him, then. The more fool you. I would have paid ex-tra for him." He shook hands with the rustlers, handed over the price they'd negotiated, remounted his horse, with help, and led his retain-ers and his four newly roped purchases out of the encampment.

"There's much to do," the little rustler said, inspecting the remain-ing Joey, now trembling with shock and fear. "I own you now, you two. I have you for eternity. Free servitude. Work hard, and then we'll see what rations I might offer you. If you continue to devour your ropes, you'll not be fed, except with rope." He laughed, quite normally and merrily, his beard and ribbons shaking—the very thought of feeding them on rope! Surely they could see the funny side of that. "You call me Master or you call me Captain or you call me Chief. Those are the names I answer to. Let's hear the sound of that. You first."

"Master," Joey said.

"And you, the giant."

"Yes, Captain Chief." The three rustlers found Franklin's answer hilarious. They laughed like teenagers, too easily amused. That name would stick.

"I could have made a shiny profit out of you," said Captain Chief, indicating with a flapping hand that Franklin should squat. Franklin was used to being flapped down to the ground by senior but shorter

men. "I could have sold you with your four friends. Strong men like
you are precious to the quarry barons and the gang masters, who pull
the reins around here at Tidewater. But I've held on to you. Now
why is that, do you suppose?" He took a step forward to whisper in
his captive's ear, so close that Franklin could smell the familiar skin
of Jackson's coat as well as the chewed tobacco on the man's breath.
"We're holding on to you because if you're wise as well as strong, if
you're sensible, we might decide to let you be a brother in our band.
Does that appeal to you, to ride with us when we go out on business?
You look as if you could be educated how to snap a man in half if you
saw any profit in it." He raised his voice, so everyone could hear. "But
if you're *other*wise as well as strong, then . . . Well, then, you'll be the
one who's snapped in half. You won't be mounted on a horse. We'll
have you mounted on a sharpened pole. We'll skin a shield with you.
You have the word of Captain Chief on that."

Franklin felt oddly hopeful after this whispered conversation. He
would cooperate, be wise, be sensible. And then, as soon as he was
trusted, he would try to creep away. He could imagine it, a nighttime
opportunity. He would retrieve his brother's coat. Its theft was a constant insult and a provocation and one that, in his head at least, he
could revenge. Wearing it again might make him as valiant and purposeful as Jackson had always been. He'd be as light and silent as a
moth when he cut loose the rustlers' biggest horse and stole away
with Joey at his back. Then he'd be on board a ship with great white
flapping sails and with Margaret at his side (for he could not bear to
think that she had already gone ahead of him). And all the Boses
would be there, on deck, with wind-pinked cheeks, both Joeys too,
the brothers and Marie, the slaughtered dog, the coastline sinking as
the waters passed around the hull.

Franklin considered, too, that he might slit some throats before he
fled the encampment, or take a chunk of metal to stave in their sleeping
heads. Seeing that cruel and pompous Captain Chief dead in his blankets would be a satisfaction. But Franklin could not concentrate on that

heavy revenge, because the more he tried to imagine it, the less likely it became. He could never make a convincing murderer. His hand was far too hesitant. He'd never be the sort to "snap a man in half," or slit a throat, or bludgeon a head, sleeping or not. He could not make that leap. There was too great a gap between his near bank and his far.

It was not long before the rustlers also realized that despite their expectations, Franklin would not proceed to be a member of their band, a menacing comrade. He was large and powerful, for sure. And he proved to be a useful beast of burden, willing and easily tamed. But making him menacing and dangerous would be beyond the ingenuity of the Devil himself. The man might be big, but he was hardly daunting. He laughed inexplicably and too loudly every once in a while. He blushed like a girl. He did what he was told too readily. Even on that first day of captivity, after he'd been separated from the plague girl, he'd flinched at the slightest prospect of being touched, even though none of the horsemen had yet done more than lightly kick or slap him. Their horses were treated worse than that and accepted it with a flick of the ear. It wasn't long before they gave up any hope that a crueler, tougher side to Franklin would be beaten to the surface. So they beat him idly, expecting nothing in return.

Now, on the morning of their visit to the metal soil heaps outside the Ark, it was hard for the labor gang to stay as silent as the horsemen had demanded. Breaking through the frozen topsoil with metal-headed tools was bound to be noisy, whatever efforts the men might make to dull the sound. But once the surface had been breached, the earth there was less solid than most other open ground in the sea-chilled neighborhoods of Tidewater. It was protected from the worst of the ice and the winds by the Ark's trunk palisade and kept soft by the washing and cooking slops that were drained through sluices from the Ark every evening and were too oily to freeze. There were the first spring sun and a little melting snow to soften the ground further and to provide these raiders and their slaves with their first opportunity to do what they had planned to do for months: harvest the crop of confiscated metal. Even the captives had been looking forward to this. They might not prosper personally from what they unearthed for their masters, but the work would be less dull than the usual tearing down or grubbing out of timber, stone, and metal salvage in the debris fields beyond the town. They were almost boys again as they embarked upon their work. Every rightly constructed boy has a desire to go somewhere and dig for buried treasure. They set about the task almost cheerfully.

Much of the earth had been turned and loosened during the previous fall's excavations and burials. The disturbed ground had not yet settled, and so it was easy to spot the trenches where so many tools, valuables, and weapons had been "restituted" by the Baptists. Breaking into these long mounds was not hard work, especially with a strong man such as Franklin wielding the heaviest mattock. Almost at once his efforts were rewarded with the tuneless clang of his blade on earth-deadened metal. One of the masters shouted out that Franklin should be more careful and use his mattock less forcibly. There should be no carelessness, no damage to their booty.

Once the topsoil had been thoroughly raked away, the labor gang gathered around to clear and search the middens with their bare hands, taking care to check for metals in every palm of soil. The slave masters had laid out three waxed blankets behind their workers: one for swords and knives and any arrow- and spearheads that had been snapped off their shafts and could be mounted and used again; a second for useful objects that might be sold, such as buckets, silverware, and platters, and reclaimable parts of saddles and wagons; and a third for trinkets, silver plate, and jewelry, the abundant riches that were understood to be buried there and that, together with the weapons, would make the masters even more powerful.

Much of the confiscated metal that they extracted had already been damaged in its burial by the Baptists and then crushed further by the months of frost and the weight of earth. Buckets that had gone in round and unpunctured came out flattened and split. Clasps and buckles were degraded. Sets of cheap knives and forks had halved their weight but doubled their bulk to rust. Sets of nails and tacks had been welded to each other by the damp. Once polished surfaces had roughened and corroded. Everything had lost its sheen and color. Everything was acned. The soil itself was dark with rust and stains.

Many of the pieces pulled clear by Franklin and his fellows were inspected, found wanting, and just thrown back into the cleared trenches, but nevertheless there was plenty worth keeping, enough to arm the horsemen from toe to teeth and make them rich. Within a short time the three blankets were heavy with pickings. They were dragged away, tied corner to corner, and lifted onto carts. New blankets were provided. Nothing of any worth could be left behind. By now the men were tired and cold and no longer excited. The treasure hunt was proving as tedious as any other work. They filled their blankets three more times before the sun gained much altitude.

It was, then, almost a relief when the work was finally interrupted by the arrival of the Baptists, a group of fifteen or so, mostly the younger devotees and gatekeepers, distinguished as ever by the devotional white tapes tied at their shoulders. But there were four of the older disciples, too, wearing their calmest faces and carrying the very weakest of the Helpless Gentlemen in an invalid chair with long lifting poles. The younger Baptists did their best to seem imposing and imperious without inviting an assault. They were armed only with their pilgrim sticks, good implements for prodding families, perhaps, but no use against metal swords and pikes. They were outnumbered, anyway. Besides the labor gang and the horses, the masters had mustered more than thirty men, all used to conflict, every one of them inclined to be a murderer.

The Baptists would not offer any short-term violence. Instead they threatened hellfire and damnation for all who soiled their hands and souls with metal. For a while, now that excavations had ceased, the only sounds were the high-pitched, fearful voices of believers and the clacking of the few winter birds that had come to see what they could find in the freshly turned soil. The Most Helpless Gentleman himself called out: "This is the Devil's work. Enough." A very reedy voice. Then there was the laughter of the mounted men, the sound of horses being spurred and turned, the shithering of blades from sheaths. "The Devil's got some better work for us, I think," the short-est of the riders, Captain Chief, said. "Now come on, boys, make meat of them. Prime cuts of Baptist for the crows." Again his men were laughing, too readily amused.

The Helpless Gentleman would have shaken his fists in anger had he had the strength to raise his arms from his lap. He would have used his hands to save himself, despite his vows. He would at least have pressed his palms together and said his prayers. But horsemen were already at his back, determined to see him tumble from his chair. The devotee who dared to try to push away a horse was struck three times across his face and head with a heavy steel blade. The first blow cut into his cheek and across his mouth. The second, aimed at his white devotional tape, severed his windpipe and finished him. The final blow, delivered as the body fell, was just for show. It took the Baptist's head clean off. It would have rolled a step or two had not his long nose wedged against a frozen clod of soil.

Franklin and his fellows—men who'd been added to his group in the last days of fall—were not shocked. This had been a winter of punishments and executions. They'd seen more deaths than they could even remember, including other decapitations. Two overspir-ited young men had tried to escape at their first opportunity, been dragged back to the encampment behind horses, feet first, and then brutally dispatched with an ax. It was a lesson to the others, accord-ing to the one comedian among the horsemen: "If you let your legs run, then we'll make sure your blood runs, too," and "Use your head or lose your head," and "The man who quits is cut in bits. His toes are separated from his nose." He never tired of rhyming threats.

The elder of the two Joeys, the potman, had succumbed during the winter to the cold, the hunger, and the string of beatings he'd re-ceived for being too small and weak for heavy work. He was worthless, anyway. The labor gang was not a charity. All its members had to earn their keep tenfold or they would perish.

Only the most obedient, the strongest, and the fittest could survive such a demanding and relentless regime. Franklin and his forty or so companions who had lasted long enough to serve in that day's metal raiding party were hardened men, mistreated, underfed, but mostly young and muscular. How was it, then, that not one of them so much as raised a hand to save a life that morning? They had only to stretch and help themselves to freshly unearthed weapons from the spoils pile on the waxed blanket. They outnumbered their armed masters and could simply take the horsemen, who were now paying attention only to the group of Baptists, by surprise. Franklin thought of it. He clenched the muscles in his back and neck and thought of it. He thought of pulling free from the pile the heavy ax that he had just taken from the soil. A man could kill with it easily. He would take Captain Chief first, the little fellow who'd stolen and was still wearing his brother Jackson's piebald coat. He'd add another, brighter color to the black and white and brown. And then he'd settle all the scores of winter, cracking the skulls and bloodying the faces of those hard men who'd made his life so bitter. He imagined rolling all the bodies into the trenches among the useless metal and kicking soil to cover them. He imagined kicking them until every bone in their bodies was splintered. But that was just a story that he told himself. He did not free himself. He did not fight. He did not save a life. He did nothing except stay quiet and calm, biting his tongue, watching the carnage as one by one the remaining Baptists were rounded up. How he wished that his brother might appear with his substantial temper to bring this nightmare to an end.

Franklin and his enslaved comrades had learned enough in the previous few months not to risk for even the highest of rewards the anger of these idle, mounted men, their captors. They'd seen too many beatings over the winter, too many throats cut, too many punishments for crimes no greater than muttering under their breaths and being weary before their work was done, to chance any kind of rebellion. They were not fed well enough to have reserved any courage. They were dispirited and fragile. Who'd be the first to call out for mercy for the Baptists? That one might lose his supper for the night, and be denied the promised fire. Which one would call out to the disciples to run? That man might have his tongue cut out or nailed to a tree. Who'd be the first to dare to reach out for a sword? That one might be the first to die. So all the labor gang did was stand and watch as the devotees who'd come to stop the disinterment of the Devil's metal were encircled by the horses. Franklin and his comrades heard the final prayers and the cries. Curses, even. But they rubbed their hands against the cold. They stamped their feet and watched the horses' breath sculpt clouds. A hundred heartbeats and the horsemen pulled away again, to leave the Baptists dead or dying in the snow.

Margaret hesitated. Two opposing instincts fixed her to the spot. The first instinct was to gather up Jackie in her arms and scuttle from the Ark as quickly as she could. She already knew what kind of men these were, even if the only one she recognized was the bandy leader in the stolen and recurring goatskin coat. Their bloody swords and pikes stood for what they had already done that morning and what they would continue doing until the raping and the looting began. After so many quiet and uneventful months, even the sight of these men's perspiring horses, left to graze the paving in the Ark's inner courtyard while their masters went about their trade, was alarming in itself. A horse had never come this far before. But that was nothing compared to the menace of the raiders' cries and the hard set of their faces as they ran across the open space toward the building work and the accommodation sheds, looking first of all for men. These were the Anti-Baptists that she'd heard about all winter, strong-armed and cruel-handed outlaws beyond redemption, intent on forging the blood and metal of the Devil's work, the subject of so many dinner sermons. She and Jackie should run for the gate as quickly as they could, before their moment passed and they were spotted by any of these sinners.

The second impulse held her by the ankles for the moment. That coat was Franklin in a way, or at least it might be a route to him. Just that glimpse of goatskin brought Margaret's decent, blushing friend alive for her after the months of forgetting. She had lightning images of him, his shoulders working between the shafts of the barrow, his big frame at the Pesthouse door, drenching her in shadow, his fingers between her toes. Franklin Lopez, tall and tender, taking care of her. Franklin Lopez reaching over with his outsized hand to tear the blue scarf from her head. She ought to follow the coat. Her heart demanded it. She was in debt to him. She ought at least to beg the small man for word of Franklin's whereabouts, if he was still alive enough for whereabouts. She ought to drag the coat off that impostor's back and press the goatskin to her nose for any trace of her lost and never lover. The word was *lover*, yes, the lover she had never even kissed, and never would unless she called out to the coat. This might be her only opportunity for getting close to him again.

But this was just a passing impulse. Margaret was wise enough to shake it off. Her first duty was to Jackie. She did what any mother would. She put the child before the man and ran, with Jackie struggling under her arm, toward the raiders' loose horses and the exit from the Ark.

As soon as they were among the animals, they were hidden from sight and safe for a moment. Margaret was a town girl, and although her family had always owned a burden mare, she was still a little nervous of horses in a group, their nipping teeth, their kicks. The last time she had ridden had been that day when she'd been taken up to the Pesthouse, almost unconscious with fever, by her grandfather. But now she recognized her opportunity. As anybody knows, making an escape by horse is nearly always preferable to making an escape on foot. The horse provides the speed and the distance and is also saddled with the tiredness. Only a sailboat is faster than a horse and then only when the wind is in a helpful mood.

Margaret shielded Jackie from the horses' teeth and hoofs and pushed her way through the animals to one of the smaller mounts at the back of the group. It was equipped for travel, with a heavy striped blanket for a saddle and leather panniers. She tugged it by its reins. It came readily. She wouldn't mount it yet. She wanted first to get outside, beyond the Ark's outer gate. Then she would shelter under the high palisade and consider her options.

The next few moments would be difficult. If anyone was in the small outer courtyard between the two gates, she could not escape unnoticed. Perhaps she could use the horse as a shield, or as an excuse. "I was told to take this horse outside," she could say. "The small man with the patterned coat said I should." But no one was there to challenge her. She reached the Ark's great timber gate. And it was unattended, with just a heavy block of sunshine wedging it open.

They went outside, the three of them, the horse, the woman, and the girl, into the thin warmth of the morning. There was a breeze, a shell-blue sky, the earthy smell of winter melting, and a sound that she hadn't heard for months, the clatter of metal tools. Had she closed her eyes, she could have imagined she was back in Ferrytown, with everything and everyone well. But still she did not dare to mount the horse. To sit on it was to declare that she had stolen it, and stealing a horse was an act that would earn no mercy. While she was leading it, she could at least maintain the lie that she was being helpful, doing what she was told, making a mistake, that she was muddled, that she had found the horse roaming free—yes, that was best—and was only looking for its master in the hope of getting a reward. She even smiled to herself, relieved to have found a story that might save her, or at least win her time.

There was still no one around to challenge her. She walked between the horse and the timbers of the palisade, with Jackie now growing heavy and starting to snivel in the crook of her arm. The girl reached out and touched the horse's flank, more baffled by its size than scared. "Horse, horse, horse," her ma said, a new word for the child, but it was too strange a word and too unmuscular for Jackie to attempt the sound.

The wind intensified as they came out into the open ground beyond the western corner of the Ark, with its high views along the estuary toward the roofs and curling smoke of Tidewater. Now Margaret could hear the metal tools distinctly, but at first her eyesight was too poor and her face was too beset by the wind to comprehend the scene before her in any detail. She could see three mounted horsemen, turned away from her and looking out across the flat approaches to the Ark. Beyond the horsemen, if she screwed up her eyes, she could make out the trenches that she had noticed on her way in the previous fall. The invalid chair that was used to transport the Helpless Gentlemen was lying on its side. She could make out the flash of white tape and what had to be the bodies of disciples. Just as she'd expected when, earlier, she'd seen the bloody swords and pikes.

She moved to the far side of the horse, out of sight and out of the wind, and hurried on, counting away the moments beneath her breath. Fifty to be past the rustlers. One hundred to be relatively safe. Two hundred to be out of sight and out of harm's way. But something, some half-digested shape, had lodged itself inside her head. She ducked beneath her horse's reins, still keeping her body and Jackie out of sight, and peered again at what was going on among the trenches. Again she saw the horsemen, still with their backs turned to her. Again she saw the upturned chair and the dark outline of fallen bodies. But now, for the first time, she spotted the gang of men on their hands and knees in the earth, some almost buried, or so it seemed, in the diggings. There was nothing there to give her pause, at least not until one of the horsemen blew for attention on an elk horn and half a dozen of the men stood up and looked in his direction. A tall man was among them, thinner than the one Margaret remembered but otherwise just his shape. She could not see his face in any detail, but the beard was right, a little longer possibly, but its jut was reminiscent of Franklin's beard. "No, surely not," she said out loud. Surely it couldn't be him. She understood her hopes were playing tricks on her. They would make her recognize her Franklin in any man of any height above the average. She should not fool herself. That one sight of the piebald coat had robbed her of her reason, and would rob her of her life and liberty if she stayed too long. She had to get away before one of the horsemen turned around on his mount, saw her there, and recognized his comrade's horse from its color and its tack.

She pulled the distinctive blanket from underneath the horse's saddle strap and bunched it up to hide it from the riders, some of whom had matching cloths. She started trotting the animal like a trainer in a corral, with her head close to its and their legs moving in unison. Eighty-five, eighty-six, eighty-seven . . . In moments they would be relatively safe. Then she heard a sound she half recognized and could not ignore. A laugh. A sudden donkey laugh, but from a man. She looked toward it. No tricks of hope. This time she truly found the laughter's shape familiar. It seemed to buckle his whole body. His hands were shaking and his head was down. Franklin's signature.

Margaret knew at once that she'd been blessed. It was a wonder that their paths had crossed again in such a vast and wayward land. It was as well a miracle that Franklin should have laughed at all, for what was there for anyone to laugh at on such a day of slaughter? Without his laugh she would have hurried on with Jackie to Tidewater and been none the wiser. She stepped out of the shadow of her horse and raised her hand to show herself to Franklin.

What next? Margaret hadn't time to think. She'd not remember what happened after that, not exactly, not in all its detail or its order. But there were images that stuck, amid the commotion: one of the horsemen had dug his heels into his mount and was moving toward Franklin with his stick raised, meaning to put an end to any laughter; Margaret was calling out with a reckless abandon, too desperate and elated to be limited by any fear or caution, "Fran Klin! Fran

Klin!"; Franklin was raising his arms, either to wave at her or to shield himself against a beating; a second horseman had already turned and started riding up the slight incline toward her, calling out for her to show herself and put her hands on her shoulders; she was stepping clear of the horse and holding up Jackie, just to show that she was nobody more dangerous than a young mother with a child.

By the time Margaret had looked again across the corpses and the open trenches, Franklin had already taken three blows to his shoulder and a fourth to his head. The next never made contact. Franklin, too stunned to be cowardly, caught hold of the horseman's leg and flipped him from his saddle. Such an easy thing to do. The rider fell heavily on his shoulder and was slow to rise, too slow at least to defend himself against the flat back of a spade, wielded by one of Franklin's comrades in the gang. Now Franklin somehow had a heavy mallet in his hand and was swinging it wildly. The third rider, already off his horse—because he had been dragged out of his saddle or had dismounted—was running for his life toward the Ark.

The second rider, now halfway between Margaret and his dismounted colleagues, was quick to realize that he could not manage on his own with such a large gang armed with heavy tools and waste metal and so clearly ready to be mutinous. He turned his horse and started to ride for assistance. In moments he'd come back with his fiercest friends, and there'd be punishments.

Margaret, too, was moving quickly. This much was clear to her. She had to be valiant. She had to be a horsewoman. Thank goodness that she'd taken such a modest, willing animal. She pulled herself onto its back, tucked Jackie between her thighs, and held her tight with her left arm. She surprised herself by riding efficiently with just one hand on the reins, though more rapidly than she'd intended. The group of men from the labor gang were beginning to look more frightened and confused than exhilarated. These unpracticed heroes were alarmed. What might be the consequences of their hotheadedness? Some, seeing Margaret bearing down on them, were already running toward the cover of the trees. Others headed toward Tide-water, putting their hopes in the distant streets where they might disappear among the crowds. A few had stopped to help themselves to jewelry and valuables. Others seemed too scared to run. They stood and watched the woman on the horse, not knowing what to expect from her.

Franklin had not moved off either, but not because he was rooted to the spot by fear. He was standing with his hands above his head, clapping and still laughing, despite the pain in his shoulder and the bruising across his forehead. Again Margaret called his name. But he'd already seen her. He'd recognized her voice and the redness of her now almost thumb-length curly hair as soon as she had shouted his name the first time. He might have taken that second blow to his head if he had not known that Margaret was watching and would be ashamed if she observed what sort of slave he had become.

The slave master whom Franklin had thrown so easily from his mount was sitting up among the bodies of the slaughtered devotees and was holding his head between blood-red hands. But his horse was loose and for the taking. Franklin had it now. He'd been used to horses on his farm. They trusted him. Before Margaret had reached the trenches on her horse, he was mounted, too. He turned its head and dug his heels into its sides. He was its master now.

Margaret found her way between the open trenches and the spoils heaps, winded and elated. "Let's go," she said, and loved herself a little for her poise. He shook his head with disbelief. There were so many questions to be asked. Where had she come from? Whose little child was this? He rode with Margaret at his shoulder—at his aching shoulder—toward the north side of the Ark, scarlet with pleasure, too breathless even to say a word to her. He had overexerted himself that day, but joy was fizzing in his lungs. His mouth, and hers, were stretched too wide with smiles for them to form a single sound.

⁘ fourteen ⁘

Time now for Margaret and Franklin to take stock of themselves and each other. They'd spent the afternoon riding eastward into the salty scrubland beyond the Ark. Franklin led on the larger horse, with Jackie (as yet unexplained) tied round his bruised shoulders in the loops of the saddle blanket. Margaret, less used to riding, allowed her mount to chase its companion's tail, half expecting at any moment to hear the beats of a pursuit. The slave masters would try to hunt them down, that was certain. It would be a matter of pride, for a day or two at least, Franklin said. So, hardly minding where it led so long as it was away from any building and therefore any immediate danger, they chose to follow a wet and shingled creekbed, where their horses would not leave any trackable hoofprints. When Margaret's horse, a mare, lifted its tail to drop its dung, Franklin dismounted and kicked the still steaming muck away into the undergrowth, out of sight. And when any branch or twig was snapped, he took the time to disguise its clean, pale end with mud.

The couple kept to low ground when they could, but as the afternoon dimmed and quieted, so did their anxiety. Conversation was not easy. Now that they were back together, they were awkward and tongue-tied. This was an encounter rescued far too suddenly from their dreams. So many times that winter they had imagined this meeting, what they might say, how they would hug and weep, but they had never truly believed in it. The world was not as generous as that. This dream-free moment was too great a gift. They felt too ill at ease to embrace each other and exchange kisses of relief. They were not kin, after all. They had not been lovers. It did not seem possible that last fall (though only for a few days) she had been his Mags and he had been her Pigeon. Whatever feelings there had been between them then (and it was difficult to know which memories were genuine and which were fantasies) could not be acknowledged openly yet. It was too soon to express out loud any joy at being free, united, heading east. Instead they concentrated on the practicalities—moving onward as quickly and as quietly as they could, hoping to find shelter and a meal, keeping Jackie amused with softly sung rhymes until, exhausted by the motion of riding and the warmth of Franklin's back, she slept.

Margaret found comfort in the hope that the rustlers would have more immediate priorities than chasing after their absconded labor gang—if any others, apart from Franklin, had had the sense and the guts to run away, that is. Surely new slaves could be seized easily from among the next influx of springtime emigrants, she told herself. So why waste fresh horses and good muscle tracking down those few who had broken loose when there were more pressing matters to attend to? First the loot from the metal burial ground would have to be secured and taken, probably—oh, sacrilege—into the Ark for division or safekeeping. Then the Ark itself would have to be secured or burned to the ground. No doubt all the Baptists were now united with their God and lining up to have their bloodstained devotional tapes replaced by halos. The Helpless Gentlemen would be standing limply at their Maker's side at last. But what of Margaret's fellow emigrants? She could only hope her winter friends were being treated well, though in her heart she feared otherwise. Could she hear human voices calling in the distance? Could she hear other horses sneezing? She turned her head like an owl to listen on all sides. No, nothing. Just the usual sounds of a cooling countryside. Finally, when twisting in her saddle she could see no sign of any roofs or any smoke or any hoof-raised dust apart from their own, she said, "We're free of them, I think. There's no one at our backs."

Franklin knew these men more intimately than she did. The loss of slaves might not matter to them, but the loss of face and the loss of horses would be intolerable. At the very least, the two rustlers on guard duty who had been dragged off their mounts and dishonored in the labor gang's sudden rebellion and the third guard who had ridden for help would want, and would be expected, to put right their blunder. He could almost hear Captain Chief mocking and haranguing them in that deranged voice of his. How could three strong men, mounted on good horses, armed, fail to keep control over that rabble of low-life refugees and farmers? he would want to know. Perhaps these flimsies would prefer it if he found them some less complicated duties in the future. Could he trust them to guard a herd of goats, perhaps, without a couple of the goats pulling them from their saddles? No? Too hard for them to manage on their own? Well, then, did they have the brains between them to take charge of a trussed duck without the duck chewing through its ties and disappearing into thin air with a horse tucked under each wing? He doubted it. He doubted that these three men deserved to have anything for supper except a beating, unless they succeeded in getting back each lost man and both lost horses. At once. Today. "Go bring them in!"

"They're coming for us, never doubt it," Franklin said. His only hope was that the three blameworthy guards would check out the obvious hiding places first: the forest just beyond the Ark, and then the shacks and beds for hire of Tidewater. A second, less likely hope was that if Franklin's labor-gang comrades were recaptured in any numbers, all of them perhaps, then the rustlers and Captain Chief might decide to settle for the loss of one tall man. But two good mounts? Franklin could not convince himself of that.

"They'll come to get their horses back, I promise you," he said after a while, wanting to break their silence. "Good mounts are valuable. A man like that without a horse is not much use to anyone."

"Let go the horses, then," Margaret suggested.

"And walk?"

"We've walked before." The word *before* seemed sensuous.

Franklin thought about her suggestion for a moment before rejecting it. "Can't do that," he said. "A horse will find its masters if you let it go and then lead them back to us. They'll have our scent."

"They're horses, not dogs!"

Franklin laughed. "Only a woman from the town could think that," he said, and blushed.

Nevertheless, Franklin and Margaret dismounted from their horses as soon as they dared. It would be best to keep their mounts fresh and rested, just in case they were discovered by the rustlers and needed to take flight again. They led them by the reins and took it in turns to carry Jackie on their backs in the blanket sling. Franklin liked her fingers tugging at his neck, the smell of her, the weight of her. He'd worn jackets that were heavier. At least the girl, whoever she might be, was warm in her blanket, but it wasn't long into the afternoon before the sun was too low and too obscured by cloud and treetops to offer much comfort. Franklin was in his shirtsleeves and his work pants. He had nothing else. The morning of laboring had kept away the cold, but now he was shivering. He did, though, have a pair of stout work boots that made the walking easy. All Margaret had were some yard sandals, a pair of knee-length socks that she had knitted herself over the winter, a long patch skirt, and a smock tied at her waist. No hat. And nothing personal. Everything had been left behind at the side of her bed in the Ark, including her comb and hairbrush, her spark stone, the fishing net with which she had trapped a bird for breakfast months before, and her beloved blue scarf, that remnant of her youth in Ferrytown.

She had lost her pot of homegrown mint as well, just when it could be expected to show signs of springing into life again. She had a haunting image of it bleached into her memory: their barrow being raided on that dreadful night on the Dreaming Highway when the rustlers had kidnapped Franklin, the mint being dashed onto the ground as if the plant were worthless, and then the sudden spinning of her head as her blue scarf was dragged away. "Not her," the short man had said. "We don't want her." And she was saved.

Franklin seemed to hear her thoughts. He smiled at her and raised an eyebrow. "Go ahead, ask."

"What happened to you afterward?" she asked. *Before* and *afterward*. "What happened to you when I wasn't there?"

"You mean the horsemen? All of that?"

"Everything." Had he missed her? Had he thought of her? Was she in his dreams?

He understood what she hoped to hear—he hoped to hear the same from her—but no, he could not find the words just yet. He spread his hands and blew out air. Overwhelmed and at a loss. Such sudden freedom winded him. There was a lot to tell. There'd been so many hazards to survive over the winter and there was so much distress to put to rest, now that it all—touch wood—was history. "Bad months," he said. "And you?"

"Bad months as well," she said.

Neither wanted to be the first to give an account. So they came to an agreement: the one carrying Jackie would do the listening and the other would talk. But they would take it in turns with the girl and the storytelling, exchanging both of the burdens whenever they grew weary of either.

Margaret was first. It was important to explain the child to him. She told Franklin about her travels with the Boses and the two murderous men in the woods, how she'd come to be Bella's adopted ma,

the Helpless Gentlemen, the hilarious and temporary safety of the
Ark, why Bella had been renamed Jackie, how that morning she'd
recognized the short man in Jackson's long coat, and, last, Franklin
laughing with his great loose arms.

Franklin explained the boredom of slavery. "My story can't compare with yours," he said. "We worked, we slept, we nursed our
bruises. And I was starving all the time. I could have eaten rope. I did
eat rope. And cockroaches." It felt too personal to mention the punishments he'd witnessed, the deaths or the provocations of the man
he'd nicknamed Captain Chief.

Margaret listened with her stomach tightening at the prospect of
any news of Acton Bose, Jackie's—Bella's—father. She was afraid
that she would hear that he had been one of the labor gang in the
trenches outside the Ark and that somehow she would be required,
for duty's sake, to seek him out and reunite the father and the daughter. She was relieved and ashamed of herself to hear that Acton had
been sold to work in mines and could be anywhere. "I haven't seen
him since that day. Not heard a word of him," said Franklin. "Poor
man," she said, but could not truly mean it. She wished Acton well,
but also she wished him far. "Poor man," she said again, and felt that
the second time she had sounded more convincing.

Franklin checked the mare's panniers, hoping to find some better
protection against the cold for himself and Margaret, but there was
nothing suitable, just an empty water bag, some damp nuts, and a
few twists of meat that were almost too stiff and rancid to be edible.
They had to find some shelter very soon, shelter for themselves and
shelter for the horses. At that time of year, the land could not store
the day to warm the night. The early spring heat was too thin a sheet.
It melted almost as quickly as the last light of the afternoon. They
also had to find some food. The adults might be resigned to sleeping
with nothing in their stomachs except a knot, but Jackie would not
understand. The child, already unnerved and overexcited by that
day's events, was bored and fretful, and tired of being sung to. She

wanted her friends, she wanted to play, and she wanted something sweet to suck.

"What happened to those taffies, Mags?" asked Franklin, and Margaret rewarded his familiarity with her broadest smile.

"Those Boses stole them from me," she said, and, once she'd swallowed hard, added, "Pigeon," not quite loud enough for him to hear.

It was almost dark when they discovered the outline of a long, uneven roof with a tall chimney on slightly higher ground above the track that they were following. They could smell smoke and supper, but no lights were coming from the building. Franklin found a stick and went alone to see if there was any danger. After a few moments he called out that it was safe to bring the horses up "if they'll bear the smell."

The building was a row of connected wood cabins with a square stone smokeshop at one end. And it was mostly empty. No fires were burning, and the only signs that it was still a working place were the sheets of scraped leather that were curing and the hands of stiff smoked fish hanging from the rafters of the house, discarded and forgotten remnants of last season's netting. There was no other food there or in the cabins, so far as they could tell in the fading light. A side of bacon would have been welcome, or a butt of apples. But there was water in a deep trough at the far end of the buildings, and some forage drying for tinder that would make do for the horses' evening meal. They were out of the wind, if not the drafts. At least they could stay relatively warm, although they could find nothing with which to strike a fire. Tomorrow when the sun was up they might discover greater comforts.

But for the time being, once they had picked at the smoke-toughened skin and flesh of a fish that they had never tasted before and would pray never to taste again, Margaret and Franklin—Mags and Pigeon—stretched out together as a family on a wooden pallet as far from the stench of the smokeshop as they could, separated only by the girl and sharing the saddle blanket for their bedding. It had been a busy day. They were exhausted, and they slept "midsentence," as the saying goes, with things that mattered left unsaid and drying on their lips.

Margaret woke in the middle of the night and took a moment to remember where she was and who was at her side. She panicked for a bit, but the sounds that she could hear were only breathing and the wind, and the restlessness of horses, and something deeper, far and near, a sort of restful quake. That was a sound she'd never heard before, but still she recognized it from the stories she'd heard. The snoring sea. The grieving sea. The Waters of the Whispering. The river with one bank. The Deep. She checked that Jackie was well covered and kissed her on her forehead. Then she leaned toward Franklin, a large dark shape. She put her hands into his hair and kissed him on each cheek, beneath his eyes. A tiny sin. Then nothing else. He was asleep and could not know how motherly, how sisterly, how *loverly* she'd been, or how her fingers and her mouth still smelled of last night's fish. He could not know how full of sudden hope she was, and warm. They'd reached the ocean, then. She was embraced and heartened by the thick of love.

By the time she fell asleep again, Margaret had decided that she would wake at first light, at the very moment that the owl became the cock, and lead her family outside to stare into the ocean's salty promises. She had little doubt now that her problems—their problems— were largely behind her. Why else would fortune have delivered such a rendezvous? They'd reached the coast. And they had reached it together. And it was almost spring. All they had to do was find an early boat and set sail for that better place, a place she could not even name but where there would be . . . No, she could not say what there would be. But she was clear, in her imagination, about what they *wouldn't* find across the sea. They wouldn't live in fear of Captain Chief. They wouldn't have to battle for their meals. They wouldn't have to travel every day. They wouldn't have to sleep with fish and smoke. They wouldn't have to hide their height or hair. They wouldn't be afraid to kiss. Tomorrow she would break down all the barriers.

There was a heavy mist when Margaret woke and tiptoed to the cabin door. All she could see through the cracks was a steeply falling slope covered in reed grass and a heavy gray haze backlit by a dawn still too distant to provide any shadows. She could not hear the ocean at first. All she could hear was the sound of Jackie and Franklin sleeping, their breathing synchronized, and the horses fretting on the wooden floor. But when she slipped outside, into the cold, in her socked feet, the sea returned. It sounded more placid and less promising than it had done in the night. The mist was out of reach but at the same time touchable. She walked toward it, her hands held out in front. It backed away, without moving. It parted for her hands.

Margaret would not call out for Franklin yet. This was a moment to enjoy, a moment on her own. She could not remember the last time that she hadn't had Jackie at her side, wanting something, needing to be cared for. Margaret would not trade a moment of that care, but still she was relieved to have some steps of freedom. The reed grass was damp and uneven. Her socks and the hem of her skirt were soaked. But none of that counted for anything. She felt only the joy. The joy of those two sleeping.

She might have ventured no more than twenty steps, but already the cabins and the smokeshop, including the smell, had been removed from her back by the mist. The light ahead of her seemed brighter and so she persevered, comforted by the certainty that no one would catch sight of her in such secretive weather. Another twenty steps and she could make out tones among the grays, where true light and reflected light met to make a flat and almost black horizon. More steps and she was clear of the grass and walking on more solid ground, flat rocks and puddles of star-gathered dew. The new smell was slight but overpowering. No longer fish and smoke and timber but something brackish and inedible, something faintly menstrual. She heard a cry that seized her heart and squeezed it. She turned around toward the cabins, fearful for her Jackie. But it was something other than a child. There was another cry, then the curtain of the mist seemed to draw apart, and there they were: the gulls, stocky, busy, laboring, their bony wings weighted at the tips with black.

The ocean itself was a surprise. Margaret could not have guessed how leaden it would be, and lacking in expression. It seemed too hard-surfaced to take a boat or for fish to pass through it, more metallic than watery. It was not until she reached the edge of a crumbling overhang and could look down through the thinning mist onto the tugging of the water on the shore, that she had any sense of the ocean's unremitting, unproductive strength and its patience. Now the leaden surface was alive. What had been flat a little way offshore seemed to resent the unresponding land. It had raised itself up in folds and furrows of water that broke against the beach, flashing their white underskirts, unloading and delivering themselves, time after time, never seeming to progress. The sea was like a great lung, but exhaling and inhaling water rather than air. The gulls breakfasted and squabbled among the underskirts, crying at the waves.

The ocean had changed entirely by the time Margaret returned to the overhang with Jackie and Franklin. The rising light had carted off the lead and left its sheeny residues of blues and greens. The water seemed to have withdrawn, leaving a deeper beach with fringes of green-black weed, and there were yellow banks of sand offshore that she had not noticed previously.

"What do you make of it?" she asked. "It's frightening, it's beautiful . . ."

Franklin shook his head and laughed, that laugh again, those hands, those dipping knees. "It isn't frightening from here," he said. "But heaven's glory, see the size of it. Who's to say how long you'd need on board a ship before you reached the other bank? All day, I'd say."

"All month, and then another month. That's what I heard in Ferrytown."

"Two months?"

"Can you see anything? I've not the eyesight to be sure. Can you see any specks of land?"

They put their hands up to their brows and peered into the sunrise. No, nothing. There was nothing there.

These off-track cabins were the perfect place to camp for a few days and hide from any search parties, though only the smokeshop, too cluttered and smelly for sleeping, was built to withstand the cold or snub the worst of the wind. The wooden buildings were not intended to be lived in. They were just storage sheds, made from a framework of heavy poles with their stumps embedded in the earth and banked on the windward side with sand. The roof was rushes secured by bags of hardened sand hauled up from the beach.

Franklin guessed correctly from the long-dead embers in the grates, the poor condition of the water in the trough, and the bone-dry state of the nets and fishing gear stored there that visitors were rare and seasonal. The smokeshop was probably worked only once a year, in the fall, when what could not be eaten or sold in the summer was invested in the smoke for the leaner months.

A daylight search of the buildings resulted in a disappointing haul of casks and creels, boxes and baskets, fish traps and crab pots, all smelling of the sea. There was a chest of salt, rock hard and encrusted with an orange fungus, and some good lengths of rope with which they could loosely tether the horses in the lee of the buildings and let them graze unhindered, though out of sight of any passersby.

The only food that they could find, to their alarm, was a flagon of sugar liquor that smelled too dangerous to drink and some pressed fish oil that might be good for cooking or for burning in a lamp if only they could conjure up some fire. Outside the smokeshop, at its back, was a stand of logs, used for smoking and curing, and a reeking pile of glossy boulders, evidently employed as weights to press oil, brine, and blood from casks of salted fish.

It was Margaret who spotted the chest resting on the roof beams of the smokeshop. It was heavy to lift down, but it was only a fisherman's toolbox. Inside were a gutting knife, a fillet blade, fire rakes, a mallet, and a skillet that must have been ten ages old, as well as implements they could not recognize. Few of these things could be of any use to them. There was no firestone or anything that would provide an easy spark.

But there was a leather container, not quite a pouch, not quite a box, and old enough to have been machine-tooled. There was wording on the lid, a looping example of the forgotten text that had survived on so many relics of the old country and that for some reason always begged to be touched. Both Margaret and Franklin ran their forefingers over it as tradition required, feeling its embossment but sensing no new wisdom. Inside, and almost bonded to the damp leather, was a useful spy appliance that the fishermen must have used for generations, watching boats or looking out for shoals. It had two eyeholes, protected by circles of degraded rubber, and a pair of glass disks set into each end. Its twin barrels, like two black bottles, were connected by a wheel that would not turn and a stiff hinge fashioned out of some material too unnatural and perfect for anybody to make or find anymore.

Franklin had seen something similar before. His uncle Meredith had owned an appliance like it. He used to claim it was a thousand years old already, older than America. His appliance was longer and had just a single barrel. A spy pipe, it was called. It was meant for only one eye at a time. Hold it properly—if Meredith would let you—and it could rush the world closer, make it bigger but fitfully distorted, like an amberwing reflected in a pond. Franklin could remember looking through it at his brother, Jackson, working in the top field of their land and having no idea, when he stopped to piss and shake himself, that he was being seen and snickered at.

Franklin took the apparatus to the water trough and cleaned the windows of the spy pipes with the dampened edge of his shirt. He greased the stiff wheel and the hinge with a little smoky fish oil. It took a bit of forcing, but soon the parts were moving, and Franklin could widen the barrels to fit his eyes. Now, despite the scratching on one of the glass disks, he could make the reed grass as far as sixty paces from the cabins seem like a forest of thick, tall trees. The chickadees among the branches were like turkeys. He could see the intimate detail of the ground more than a stone's throw away, each pebble, each twig, each snail shell. He merged the twin images into one circle and, fixing the wheels so that the far approaches to the cabins were clear to see, he checked for men transformed into giants and horses enlarged into monsters. He tried but could not put Jackson in the circle. Jackson relieving himself. Jackson in his goatskin coat. No Captain Chief. He tried but could not put his mother there, sitting on the homestead stoop, her old hand raised. He held his own hand up in front of the barrels. His fingers seemed both huge and far away.

"It fools your thinking," Franklin said, handing over the new toy to Margaret.

At first she could see nothing, but soon she discovered that she could revolve the wheel to its farthest, tightest point and view the distance sharply. The horizon had a bulk she'd never known before and a clarity that she had lost in childhood and had thought was irretrievable. "It's strange to think how many eyes have looked through this," she said. "Imagine everything that's happened at the fat end." She tapped the glass as if it were the top of a container. "Dead people would've been in there. And sky-high buildings from the history. All sorts of ships and strangers." She put the spy pipes to her face again and focused on a single bird, black-winged and rafting on the wind. Her eyesight was as good as new. "That hawk's seen something on the ground," she said. "It might be carrion."

"I'll go and look," offered Franklin, but he returned scratched and empty-handed. Not even a morsel of gull-picked rabbit meat for supper.

It was their second day without a proper meal. The novelty of the spy pipes and the pleasures of each other's company could not drive away their constant nagging hunger and their tiredness. As time passed, their fear of horsemen diminished somewhat, but they felt nervous of the open air. The rustlers might still flush them out. Other strangers might bother them. All Franklin and Margaret could do about that was to be watchful and careful, keeping the horses out of sight and the noise down. It was a pity that Jackie chose that day to show her irritation and the power of her lungs. What was the point of their nervous vigilance if the girl was declaring their whereabouts so loudly and with hardly a break? Margaret and Franklin did their best to silence her, but songs and games and fingertips to suck were not enough for her. She was implacable. She seemed to have thinned and darkened, losing volume in body but gaining it in voice. Her lips were sore and dry. She showed little interest in anything but wailing.

After his months at the encampment, Franklin was almost re-signed to being underfed and having what is called a salamander stomach, with folds of loose skin and no fat, but Margaret had gotten used to free meals at the Ark and was soon complaining of hunger pains. Together, the two of them could last for a few more days on their meager provisions, but they could not expect Jackie to survive on smoked fish, stale water, orange salt, and pressed oil. They searched the ground around the cabins for edible plants, but there were no wild greens even at the end of winter. All they found among the worts, the spurges, and the sedges were some immature cattails, with shoots al-most tender enough to eat raw, and a pink bed of early-flowering spring beauty with sweet, starchy roots. Mashed together with oil and water, the paste was edible enough but hard on the stomach. Jackie would take only a fingerful. But finally she slept, exhausted by herself.

Margaret was exhausted, too, and impatient. What kind of free-dom had she found since she had left the Ark? The freedom to be cold, tired, hungry, anxious? She felt more trapped than she had done for months. But even so, much of the euphoria of rediscovering Franklin and seeing the ocean for the first time remained. They spent the afternoon placating Jackie and discussing their options. Stay safe and starve? Push on and take the risks? Wait for a sign?

In those brief periods when the girl slept, they looked out through the spy pipes from a half-open cabin door. Keeping watch. They had good views across the ocean as well as clear sight of all the land around them. Anybody coming to their hideaway could not avoid showing himself; then the pipes would allow for close inspection.

It was not through the pipes, though, that Franklin caught sight of his first oceangoing ship, full-rigged and shirty in the wind. It was heading between the outer banks, which appeared when, inexplicably and once or twice a day, that great expanse of water drew back on itself, as if it had been inclined as easily as slops are tilted in a bowl. Where earlier there had been nothing but waves, bars and pebble banks appeared, and narrow islands of sand. The ship was rising and falling in the sea, uncertain of its own weight, now light enough to hardly break the surface, now so heavy that it sank deeply into the water and all that showed above the ocean were its upper masts and sails. Franklin and Margaret held their pipes to it, picking out the details. There were huts on board, and flags and men among the riggings, and the carving of a huge eagle's head at the prow. Here was their salvation, then, their means of escape. They hugged each other, and when they parted, Franklin danced, despite his unexpected apprehension at this first sight of a sailboat.

"That's the call that we've been waiting for. Deliverance," he said, embarrassed more by their embrace than by his dance. "Tomorrow morning, Mags, I'm going for that ship. It must be putting ashore close by. I'll see if we can get aboard." She shook her head. He took her hand. "I'll come back with some food for Jackie. It'll be okay. I'll be wary for myself. You just keep low and out of sight."

"You'll not go anywhere," she said. "I'll go. It's better if I go. No one's hunting for me. I don't stand out like you, not since my hair grew out a bit."

"It'll be okay . . ."

"No, Franklin. You're to let me have my way. I couldn't bear it if you went and we never saw a hair of you again. Anyway, I'm used to begging for a bit of food. And women make a better hand of getting information out of sailors. That's well known."

They laughed at that, then argued briefly, but Franklin saw the sense of what she proposed. He was relieved, in fact, and a bit ashamed to be so uncourageous yet again. "Take this, Mags." He gave her the spy pipes. "You can trade it for some bacon and our passage fees. I'm sure it's worth a lot, especially to sailors."

Margaret took the pipes. "Good meal ticket," she agreed, but knew at once that she could part with them only if they were prized from her fingers. She needed them to see the distant world. They were of more value to her than to any sailor.

That night they slept with Jackie at their feet and not between them. When he could, when her breathing said that she was dozing, Franklin found that he had taken hold of Margaret's hand. He fell asleep with one of her fingers wrapped inside his palm. He felt her tug it free at sunrise and heard her washing at the water trough. But he kept quiet and still when she slipped outside into the cold and started on her explorations. It wasn't prudent to tempt fate by exchanging goodbyes, not when the task ahead was dangerous. He tried to sleep.

Franklin could not expect a restful day. He was not used to children, so having sole care of Jackie would be a test, not all of it welcome. Over winter he had learned to be less of an optimist. Whereas the old Franklin might have happily envisaged Margaret's journey to the ship as being safe and easy and bound to succeed, the new one needed no encouragement to imagine her in trouble. Margaret robbed or raped, kidnapped or lost at sea, Margaret deciding to abandon him and the girl, Margaret attacked by gulls or tumbling down a cliff into the waves, Margaret losing her way back to the cabins and having to spend the night outside. A landscape full of Margarets undone.

Once he was up and washed, though, and had seen the egg-blue, cloudless sky, Franklin determined to be high-spirited. He would keep his hands and his imagination busy with domestic matters. He'd be a useful rather than a moping husband for the day. He muttered a list to himself, counting off his tasks. He'd take good care of Jackie, but when she allowed it he would see what improvements he could make to their quarters, which for some reason and despite his hunger he already felt reluctant to abandon. He'd make a more comfortable family bed with some fresh-cut grasses. Even though it might be difficult, he'd start a fire in the afternoon, as soon as it was safe to make a little smoke. He'd started fires without a spark stone when he was a boy. Why not now? He'd gather shoots and roots and find a way of sieving clean the drinking water in the trough. He'd find some way of preparing a meal as well. A feast, with meat. Surely he could trap a rabbit or a bird. Surely these salt marshes should boast some prairie chickens or quail. There was no shortage of netting to drape between bushes. He had all day. Even Margaret had caught a quail, that first frosty morning out of Ferrytown.

What Franklin did not have was bait. Although he visited his bush nets every so often during the morning, they remained empty, apart from a few hollow plant stems brought in by the breeze and some sticky yellow spume sent up from the ocean. He tried laying out some of the smoked fish, but not even the spring flies or the gulls seemed tempted by this leathery treat. Why would they be tempted when only a short flight away the sea and the shore were tumbling with food?

He walked with Jackie down to the beach and, once he had washed her, kicked about in the shallow water, much to her amusement, but there was nothing there that he could trust as edible. It all smelled bad: the weeds, the water and the sand, the shells, the battered lengths of drift, the pink-gray armored parts of animals that were not spiders exactly. He did not like the shore. It seemed ungenerous. Its music was funereal. It was a mystery.

He was glad to turn his back on it and return to the dune top and its fringe of slanting thickets, wedged by the wind. As a farmer, he could judge what kind of living such land could provide if—just if— he and Margaret and the girl were forced to make their futures there. He knew it was a foolish fantasy. But somehow he was more comforted by it, by this ill-sited version of the life he knew and understood, than by the growing prospect of the new world overseas and, more immediately, by the thought of swapping solid ground for a tossing deck.

He had heard too many tales about the treacheries of ocean travel for all of them to be as false as his hope that it would only take "all day" to cross: ships becalmed on windless plains of water with great birds circling, waiting for the passengers to die; ships swept forward by such determined winds that water slammed and crashed against the hulls until their timbers split and the ocean's tongues had reached across the decks and snacked on all the voyagers; ships where captains, maddened by the noise and stench of life aboard, relinquished their command to rats the size of mules; ships where travelers who didn't want to starve would have to dine on weeviled bread, share meat with maggots, and drink bilge wine. Then there were pirates, mutinies, and lightning storms to survive.

Even if he could persuade himself that paradise was at the far end of the sea, Franklin was no longer convinced that it was worth the journey. He looked more fondly on the land than he had done for months. Yes, land was something he could deal with. Even this brackish neighborhood. Remove the skin of sand and he'd find fertile earth. He was certain that he could coax a little corn from it, despite the salt and wind. He had the horses. He could make a plow. In time he'd have some chickens and a cow, a pair of goats. Milk, eggs, and meat to feed the family. He'd build a kitchen garden, protected from the wind by logs and fences, for pumpkins, turnips, sugar peas perhaps, some salad greens. And what they couldn't eat, they'd sell or trade or butcher and smoke for winter. There was the little matter of the rustlers, but in this version of his life Franklin was like Jackson, victorious and strong. His captors came to take him and their horses back to their encampment. Franklin sent them packing with nothing but his fists, though not before he'd pulled Captain Chief from his saddle and stripped him of his clothes. Now Franklin stood among his fields and animals, his goatskin coat restored—his brother's and his mother's goatskin coat.

Something in this version of his future nagged at Franklin. Some words, some action. He went through it all again: the clearing of the land, his planting, the harvest, his confrontation with the riders. Now he had it. He'd been a fool not to think of it before! *Butcher and smoke!* That was the simple way—an all too obvious way, in fact; what had he been thinking of?—to provision some food both for the next few days and for their ocean journey if they had to make one. He almost laughed out loud. Margaret had promised that whatever happened, she would be back by nightfall; well, then, now Franklin could almost guarantee that she would come home to a proper welcome and a warm household, lit by flames from a grate and with fresh meat in the skillet. He could not start at once. He had to spend an age rocking Jackie on his shoulder, but just when his patience was almost at an end, she settled down, despite her hunger and her fear that Ma had disappeared for good.

Franklin went out to the horses and renewed their water and their hay. Margaret's mare was a spare horse and not young. The fetlocks and the pasterns on her legs were worn. Her haunches were angular and unpromising. The bigger horse was younger, though. A three- or four-year-old gelding and almost plump around the girth. Its eyes and teeth were clear. And it seemed docile. It'd not prove difficult. Franklin led it to the lee end of the smokeshop and reined it to a high, protruding joist, so that its head was raised. It tried to drag away. It didn't like the awkward and unnatural angle of its head, but tugging on the rein was even more uncomfortable, so it compensated by scuffing the ground with its hind legs.

Franklin left the horse to its devices for a while, not wanting to rush the animal and not wanting to rush himself either. He stood at the smokeshop door, looking up the coast in the direction in which the sailboat and Margaret had disappeared. He had to plan his work carefully. He felt immensely happy suddenly, certain that Margaret would return safely, certain that he would delight her with his welcome. This was something he was good at—tending a homestead, using tools, providing food for the table. It was the life that he'd been born to, and surely one that could not be bettered anywhere. The ocean did not seem truly promising to him, despite its grandeur and its relentless noise, which in many ways was more wearying for him than Jackie's crying. He recognized it now for what it was, an obstacle and not a route to liberty. That was a shock, to realize that he did not truly want to leave America. His dream was not the future but the past. Some land, a cabin, and a family. A mother waiting on the stoop.

The horse had entirely settled now. It had turned sideways against the stone wall of the smokeshop by the time Franklin arrived with the fisherman's toolbox, some rope, and a handful of springbeauty roots. The horse took the roots from his palm almost before they were offered.

Franklin did not need to hobble the horse too tightly, just close enough to stop it kicking or moving away. The animal had been badly treated for most of its life and so had learned to be long-suffering. It did not struggle against the ropes, not even when its hind fetlocks were secured to the building so that it could not move away from the wall. It only nudged Franklin—successfully—for more roots.

Franklin removed the gutting knife from the toolbox and tested its sharpness on some reed grass. The knife was blunt and rusty, but it would have to do. He'd butchered animals before with blunter implements, though nothing quite as large and heavy as this poor creature. Jackson had always taken care of the family cattle. Franklin had been put in charge of goats and pigs and chickens. It was not a job he had relished, but he had enjoyed the meat that it produced and so had never made a fuss. He presumed there was some intimate procedure that was best for felling horses, but he had never been taught it.

He would simply have to use the same method that he had employed for pigs, one determined cut to the jugular and then patience. At least it was easier to comfort and to quiet a horse. Pigs and goats were beyond comfort. They always recognized the smell of butchery. They always ran away from blades.

Franklin took off his shirt and, bare-chested, held the horse's head in his arms and whispered to it, blowing in its ears, "There's a boy. There's a good, good boy. It's not long now." But he was hardly thinking of the horse. There was another animal that bothered him. Captain Chief would have a fit if he could see what was happening. One of his precious horses had been stolen and then slaughtered by a slave. Franklin could abandon any hope of mercy if he was ever caught and returned to the rustlers' encampment. He could imagine Captain Chief swirling around him in Jackson's overlong coat, ludicrous and dangerous. "You cooked our horse? You cut its throat and cooked our horse?" Franklin could not imagine what his punishment might be, though cooking seemed a possibility.

The horse's skin was even tougher than he'd expected. The knife went in easily enough, but it was hard to drag the blade across the throat and find the busy vein. But luckily the horse threw back its head in shock and helped the progress of the knife. A stream of blood welled up and then a gush. Franklin stepped back at once, leaving the gutting knife protruding from the wound. His hands and forearms and the top of his chest were sticky with blood, but otherwise he had done his job quite cleanly. Now he only had to wait. And not for long, he hoped. The horse was suffering.

Franklin did not stay to watch the animal pumping its blood onto the wall of the smokeshop until, shocked and weakened, it fell against the stonework and slipped heavily to the ground. Instead he busied himself indoors, first making Jackie comfortable and then assembling whatever he could find to help with the cutting and the preparation of the meat. He had to leave no trace of any horse. Once he had stored the best meat, the carcass would need to be removed, no easy task.

The horse was just a little warm when Franklin cut into its flanks and upper thighs for the leanest meat. It was a laborious and messy task, and he returned often to the water trough to wash his face and clean the blood from his hands and arms. The horse's smell was overpowering, but the rewards were plentiful. Soon he'd filled one fish basket with steaks and chops and cuts and a second with thin strips of rib meat and red sinew, suitable for making jerky. With some help, more time, and better tools, he could strip the whole horse down, bones and all. Back home, on the family stead, a butchered horse could provide everything from glue to a cudgel, but Franklin was in too great a hurry. There was much to do before Margaret's return.

He tried to pull the carcass away from the smokeshop himself. Within a day or two it would smell and fill with maggots, flies, and rats. It would attract the foxes, wolves, and bears and draw attention to the cabins. But the horse's carcass was too heavy still, despite the butchery. So, although it seemed in Franklin's mind to offend the rules of good husbandry, he harnessed up the little mare and led her over to help drag her mate away with ropes passed through the exposed rib cage.

Together they labored over rising ground until they found a path into the thickest salt scrub in a shallow dip. Franklin did his best to hide the carcass, kicking sand over it and pulling dead leaves and wood onto it, but by the time he and the mare had returned to the row of cabins and Jackie's cries, the gulls had arrived in their hundreds. They could be seen and heard from afar.

❧ fifteen ❧

Margaret spotted the frenzy of the gulls as soon as she reached the dunes above the cabins on her late-afternoon return to Franklin and Jackie. She studied the birds for a few moments through the spy pipes—still in her possession—but their quarrelsome frolics did not disturb her. Gulls were a mystery anyway, she had decided after just two days of their constant, nagging company. They were like the crows of Ferrytown in everything but color, always busy and complaining, always in a mob. White crows. Her day had been disastrous and depressing, but she was in no hurry to be back at the cabins. She was the bearer of shocking news, and she was fearful.

It had been easy walking out that morning—exciting, even. Leaving Franklin and Jackie asleep in their shared bed had made her parting from them especially tender. And somehow her hunger and the early start had made her feel vigorous and purposeful. Certainly the route along the marsh tops and the high dunes was eyecatching, though somewhat baffling for a woman who was not yet used to the ocean. She could not make any sense of how the shore retracted and advanced, and how the sea could express itself in such variety, now blushing blue, now gray as ash, now green. Its moodiness made no sense. What could be the purpose of so much restlessness and indecision? But Margaret was in high spirits nevertheless. The sun was on her side, and what little wind there was was at her back, lending its hand.

By midmorning she had reached a cluster of seven or eight cottages gathered around a cobbled slipway that led through flattened sand ridges onto a beach. Fishing boats were pulled up and full of water, their wooden hulls silvered by the winter and the salt. Plumes of heavy smoke, always a pleasing sight, curled from the buildings and hung across the clearing. Margaret hid her spy pipes under her clothes and walked as quietly as she could. It was not possible to tiptoe through, however. There were too many dutiful dogs for anyone to pass without alerting the inhabitants. But only women and a few young children came to greet and question her, women with faces as weathered and as brown as bark, a couple of them clothed in gaudy dresses more suitable for a town. They wanted to know where she was staying, where she was coming from. They did not touch, but still she felt that they were picking at her, like hens, inquisitive and hungry. Visitors arriving from that side of the coast were rare, they said. "There's nothing up there, girl, excepting wind." But Margaret managed to avoid their questions, saying only that she was lost—a subtle plea for help, she'd found—and that her family was waiting for her. "I hope to find out everything I can about the ships," she said.

"You're hardly dressed for it," they told her, pointing at her yard sandals and tattered patch skirt. "Show your knees to our fire for a little while. There's something spare for you to eat, if you can manage it."

Indeed she could manage it, even though the *it* was fish and bread. At first the low, smoky room, the greasy food, the fug of burning driftwood and animal chips, and the press of bodies all around her made her tired and a little nauseous. The bread sat in her stomach like a weight, but still she was glad of it and the sociable warmth provided by the fire. Very soon, though, she was wide awake and shivering. These women were not the wives of busy fishermen, as she'd supposed, left alone for the day while their sons and husbands went out among the furrows of the sea to plow the water for its crops. They were instead abandoned wives.

"You'd best be warned, sweetheart," one of the older women, Joanie, explained. "Or you'll be sorely disappointed when you reach the anchorage. Best turn around right now and go back to your husband and your kid. Save yourself the misery."

Like Margaret herself, Joanie explained, these women had been emigrants. Two seasons before, they all had made the journey eastward, "full of hope," to the coast and the ocean passage. Several had been through Ferrytown and had mixed memories of their short and costly stay there. They shook their heads at Margaret's news of Ferrytown's destruction but did not seem surprised. Misfortune was universal, and therefore sympathy was hard to rouse.

"There's not a road in this whole land that isn't crowded with dangers," one of them said. "We all started out with husbands. And now we're castaways and jetsam. We haven't got one single man to share between the nine of us. We only share our beds with dogs and kids nowadays. Except when someone's paying us, of course." So that explains the dresses, Margaret thought, and how these women earn their keep. The younger ones and the best kept of the older ones are whores.

"What happened to your husbands, then?" she asked, not really wanting to be delayed by the answers but keen to be polite. Now all the women were speaking at once. Three of their men had been lost on the journey, one to fever, one to drowning, and the other crushed by a collapsing cart. One of their men had, like Franklin, been taken as a slave by a gang of rustlers. Again that phrase, "He could be anywhere by now. Or dead." But the other five men had made it all the way to the coast and, as far as their wives could tell, continued all the way across the ocean to the Far Shores.

"Then why are you still here?" asked Margaret.

"Because about that time the boats decided they wouldn't take us, dear. New rules."

"Wouldn't take you? Why?" Margaret was instantly alarmed.

"Because we're neither men nor girls."

"Nor rich," added Joanie, her voice a little louder and more insistent than those of her neighbors. "That's all they're taking on the boats and has been for more than a year . . ." She held her fingers up and tallied off the types of travelers who might still find a welcome at the anchorage. "That's pretty girls, for one, girls who haven't got a husband or a child, girls that they can marry on the other side, or sell. Families that have the valuables to bribe themselves some berths, is two. Men that are fit enough to put to laboring, or men with skills. That's three and that's all, as far as I could tell. Everybody else can go hang. They'll never get a berth." She shook her head gravely, to allow her sisters to chorus *Never, never, not a chance.*

"You ask me where my family is?" Joanie continued, squatting at Margaret's side and gripping her wrist. "My husband was a carpenter. He could turn his hand to anything from a coffin to a wheel. My son was his apprentice and clever at it, too. Better than his pa, to tell the truth of it. Our daughter was as pretty as a dove and fifteen years of age. No way they'd leave her behind. But me—what am I? What use am I, a married woman?" She spread her hands, displayed herself in the firelight, a weary mother, plump and pockmarked. "And what about my little boy? Step forward, Suff, and show your face to our friend. He was only nine years old at the time. No place on board for him, either."

"Why not?" Again, a question that Margaret understood she had to ask.

"Because they wouldn't be able to slave him in a field or use him in a workshop, that's why. Not yet, anyway. Too young and small. 'Try again when you're a man,' they said. They could have said the same to me, except I'll never be a man. And so I'll always have to be American." She spoke the last word as if it were a burden that would take her to her grave.

"We're all Americans now," one of the gaudier women said. "No ship'll take us, not one of us."

"I told my husband that I wouldn't hold him back," Joanie continued, raising her voice again, "but he said he'd rather stay with me. Keep the family together. I could've cried. But my son and daughter had already set their hearts on it. You know, the 'dreams of leaving.' Young people have a right to want the best. There'd be nothing here for them. They couldn't stay. It wasn't safe . . ."

"There's nowhere safe."

"I told my husband, 'Don't let them go alone. They're not old enough to lose both parents. You go with them, and then I'll follow on sometime, when I'm rich enough—or when I'm man enough.' It bust our hearts, it snapped our family in two, but that's what happened, that's what happens down there every day. You'll see. Me and my small boy waved them off and saw their boat shrink before our eyes and then it disappeared for good. We judged ourselves the most unwanted people in the world. That's our story. And . . . Margaret, is it? If you're not lucky, that'll be your story, too. That's the cold truth. This coast is blighted by bad luck. It's no coincidence. Why does seawater taste the way it does?"

Margaret shook her head.

"There's salt in tears, that's why. The ocean's one great weeping eye. On clear days, we can see the curve of it."

Two women from the cottages joined Margaret for the last part of her walk. She was embarrassed by their presence at first, although there was no one else to witness the company she was keeping or to blush with her when both women linked their arms with hers, taking it in turns to be the windbreak. They were dressed not for walking but for attracting men. They were bare-legged, and even though they wrapped themselves in shawls against the bitter edge of the breeze, their skirts and blouses were flimsy and revealing and their hair was elaborately dressed. The plumper, quieter of the two was probably a little younger than Margaret, but the skinny one was thirty-five at least, flat-chested, spotty, and pallid, though forlornly beautiful in a way that eludes women who have not been toughened by misfortune.

Unlike Joanie, she'd not lost any children to the boats, she said, but her husband, when given the choice of keeping his wife or following his dreams, had chosen the more abstract of the pair. "Life before wife," he'd said. That was two summers ago. She'd had to spend a month or so living rough at the anchorage, learning the crafts of begging, stealing, whoring, and sleeping in hollows. But toward the end of that summer, her fortunes had sweetened a little. She met another abandoned wife, a woman married for just a year but already with a child at her breast and desperately hungry, cold, and heartbroken to find herself so quickly "widowed." Two women now. They were a sisterhood, and though their futures were hardly rosy, their lives seemed a little less bleak. That afternoon, buoyed up by each other's company and impelled by the demands of the child, they explored along the coast above the river mouth, hunting for a safer place to sleep, somewhere free of men. They found the fishermen's abandoned cottages and boats. Within the month, by summer's end, with the stream of migrants slowing for the winter and the sail ships no longer crossing, the sisterhood had grown to nine, plus seven children and the wild dogs that they'd tamed with food and kept as guards.

"We always go down to the anchorage when ships are in," the skinny woman said. "There's pickings to be had. There's sailors—pink as hogs, they are—looking for a woman, and quick to pay. Can't understand a word they say, but when it comes to it, the noises that they make are all the same." The plump one laughed. And Margaret laughed as well, though these were noises that she'd only ever heard from other people's rooms. "Anyway, I call the tunes," the woman continued. "When men are set on that, they're meek as lambs—most of them, anyway. I take control. I do them with my hands if I can get away with it. Easy earnings. Quick to rinse off. No risk of pregnancy or catching Mrs. Phylis. I'm not ashamed. I'm not *happy*, but I'm not ashamed. We have to eat. It's no more than you do with your husband once in a while, I bet." She squeezed Margaret's arm to share the intimacy and laughed. Margaret smiled and nodded, but—this was strange and unexpected—she felt ashamed to be so innocent. Mrs. Phylis. Who was she?

Fairly quickly, however, despite her embarrassment, Margaret was glad of the women's company. Their chatter ate the journey up. Their manner was warm and irreverent. There's safety in numbers. Besides, they knew the quickest route.

The path from the women's cottages soon abandoned the flats and dunes and rose a bit to crest a narrow wind-torn bluff, alluvial and stony, and Margaret, still with a woman hanging on each arm, was looking down on a sight that was cluttered and entirely baffling. The boats, she understood. There were already three sail ships anchored midstream in the quieter, browner waters of the river mouth. Their sails were rolled up and tied back to the masts and rigging. From that distance, they seemed too small to take more than a dozen passengers. A fourth vessel, much larger than the others, its three masts still hung with twelve individual square-cut sails and with further triangles of canvas at the prow and stern, was negotiating the banks and channels, looking for shelter.

A traffic of cargo skiffs and rafts worked between the moorings and the shore. It was only when a man began to climb the rope ladder of one of the smaller ships' sides that Margaret could tell how huge the ships actually were. Even their seemingly tiny flags must be the size of blankets. It was a peaceful, hopeful sight, however. Ships and water. Nothing sinister.

On shore was chaos of a kind Margaret had not witnessed before. There was a wide fringe of mud and weed all along the edges of the estuary, deeply cluttered, on both sides of the river, with great, abandoned slabs of rusting metal red in the sunlight, some of them the

height of twenty men and chilling in their rawness; other pieces were
intricate and inexplicable but no less unsettling. Here were rotting
hulks and carcasses greater even and more foreboding than the junkle on the journey east had been. Nature could not—would not want
to—shape so many squares and rectangles or perfect spheres, so
many ducts and cylinders, so much massive symmetry. This was the
craziest work of men, or of something worse than men. Even the
mud itself seemed unearthly; what earth could boast such oily blues,
such vivid greens, such silvers or such reds? The unstinting details of
antiquities were always baffling. Margaret raised both eyebrows at
the sight, and blew out her breath. She whistled, even. She was
shaken by the discovery of so much debris, especially on this dream-
making coast where surely all the worst of all the past could be forgotten by the emigrants.

"They say it's old-style ships," the thin woman said, "though I'd
have thought you'd have as much chance taking ships like that to sea
as you'd have floating a stone." She shrugged. "Well, as you see, they
didn't get them very far. Stuck in the mud and left to rot." She
laughed again. Always laughing. "Is that stupid?" Sometimes she
wondered if America had once been populated by a race of fools. So
many old things from that time had lost their grip on the world and
dropped away, it seemed to her.

It was not until they had descended from the bluff, walked a further hundred paces inland, and removed themselves from the gape of
the ocean and the nagging of the wind that Margaret's two companions stopped to tidy and prepare themselves for work and Margaret
herself was able to look down and inspect, though only fleetingly—
she did not want to reveal her spy pipes to strangers—the makeshift
town of tents and sheds and wagons that had grown up on the dry
terraces on her side of the estuary. Even from that distance she could
hear the noise of shouting. Anger and impatience were in the air.
Then, on top of that, came the din of tools, the beating of metal, the
snapping of wood, the explosive cracking of fires, the protest of ani-

mals, and the bass note of a population with nothing much to do but sit, wait, hope, and talk.

Somehow the two women from the cottages had enhanced themselves. They'd stowed their shawls between two rocks, reddened their cheeks and lips, tidied their wind-torn hair, unfastened the top part of their blouses, scraped the mud off their shoes. They seemed both younger and older, both somber and comical. And when they embraced Margaret, she could smell some perfume. Kitchen smells. Honey mixed with spice, she thought. Nutmeg. "You'll want to go ahead of us," they said to her. "Unless you're looking for a sailor."

Margaret shook her head and smiled. How thoughtful they had been with her. She could not imagine working at their side, but still she could picture being friends with them. She blew them kisses and went ahead, lighthearted and light-footed. She had not expected such a pleasing jaunt. But now that she was on her own again, the words that Joanie had spoken came back to trouble her: "Because the boats wouldn't take us, dear." *Never, never, not a chance.*

It was not until Margaret had descended through the oak and hemlock woods and reached flatter ground once again that she could see the mayhem of the dockside in any detail. Her spy pipes bothered her. She wanted to avoid any temptation to trade them. But they also made her feel vulnerable, a target for anyone, any thief, practiced at telling when a woman was concealing something of value underneath her clothes. She checked the path behind her—no sign of the two women, whose progress in their finery was bound to be slow if they were to keep their ankles clean—and hastily pushed her spy pipes into the piles of driftwood that had somehow, despite its bulk, been washed up during the winter. She marked the pipes' hiding place in her mind's eye and walked on, feeling less encumbered, more secure, but still nervous about what the day might have in store for her.

Margaret had never known such crowds before, such order and disorder. Ferrytown had often been a thriving, busy place, especially in recent summers, when the emigrants had started passing through. But she could not remember ever seeing more than a hundred people in one place at the same time. Certainly she had never encountered such a press of bodies as this. There was no avoiding it.

First she had to make her way through the village of hastily erected huts and the tarp tents that she had spotted from above. She took her time, observing the formalities with the women and the few elderly men who were guarding their possessions, though hardly anybody responded to her nods and greetings with much warmth. Their focus was the anchorage. Would their husbands and their sons return to say that they'd secured passage on a ship? Would there be more ships? They had no time to talk. Worry was a full-time job.

Then Margaret had to negotiate the acreage of tethered animals and stationed carts that would no longer be of any use, everybody hoped. Hoofs and wheels didn't work at sea, where—wonders of the world—all you needed was the muscle of the wind. What had been of value was now only an encumbrance. Beyond the carts, a pack of dogs, newly homeless, had achieved what most people only dream of and were masterless. They barked, bared their teeth, and snapped at passersby without much fear of punishment. Margaret's whistling did not placate them. She had to keep her distance and walk through muddy garbage dumps rather than over the drier ground that the dogs had claimed. Only then did she find her way barred by the herd of would-be emigrants, their backs all turned to her and many straining on their toes to see how far off they were from what Margaret presumed was access to the boats.

She skirted the crowds, not wanting to pass too closely to their heels, in the same way that she would sensibly, like any town girl, avoid the rears of cattle or horses. Once the throng thinned, she was able to get closer to the riverbank, where she might gain a clearer view. Here there was a market of a sort. Women from Tidewater were selling dishes of hash and hunks of corn bread. Small boys were offering hands of fresh fish—alewives, weakfish, croakers, kings—

none of which she recognized by appearance or by name. Exasperated emigrants were bartering with hard-faced men, hoping to sell their carts and horses and any heavy goods they still possessed before they put to sea but being offered only pittances—a reed hat for an oak table, a bit of bacon for a wagon, a bag of taffies for a mare. The salt air seemed to have robbed the world of value. Already a corral of newly purchased horses was closely packed with animals. An elderly emigrant who evidently, from his loud complaints, had wanted to buy back his own horse with the sack of flour that he'd been paid for it had been refused, laughed off. The purchase price for such a good mount, he had been told, was five sacks of flour. He was damping his sorrows at a row of clay-lined casks where ladles of beer and shots of shrub or hard liquor were being sold. Still, despite his evident anger, he was being pestered, as was Margaret herself, by hucksters offering good-luck charms, ship supplies, weatherproofs, potions to ward off ocean sickness. A good strong mule was not worth anything, but a finger length of pizzle hair, they said, could make you rich and keep you well.

Margaret hurried through them all, trying to seem purposeful and located despite the fingers pulling at her smock and skirt and the feet that tried to trip her, the voices in her face demanding trade and commerce beyond her means and offering goods outside her experience, new friends only from the teeth outward.

Once she reached the riverbank, she jumped down out of the multitude onto the muddy shore with its ballast of wood and metal drift. Now, if she was careful not to sink too deeply and if she kept low enough not to draw attention to herself, she could reach a rusty platform where she could stand and inspect from a distance the faces in the crowd and learn what it was these emigrants were straining for.

All she could see at first was a line of tables, separated from the emigrants by a rope fence, but gradually the procedures became clearer. One by one, each individual or family was being called forward, questioned, and searched by a group of men in black uniforms, looking like no one Margaret had ever seen before, unusually light-skinned, and old-fashioned somehow, in factory-made jackets and tooled shoes. Their beards and hair were trimmed short, like those of teenage boys. They carried heavy polished sticks that they used freely to organize the crowds as if they were cattle. And, so far as she could tell from such a distance, they were speaking in a tongue that made no sense at all to her, no matter how loud the words were shouted or how fiercely they emphasized their spoken commands with the blunt end of their sticks.

Margaret would not join the crowd of supplicants. She kept her distance and she watched, first checking for sign of any rustlers and then, when there was none, scanning the faces of the women for any of her friends from the Ark. Again, no sign. What she witnessed, though, was exactly what the women in the cottages had warned about. The few families that were visibly wealthy or could prove themselves to be secretly rich were being tick-marked on their fore-arms with a blue dye and then allowed to take their possessions through the metal wrecks and walk across the colored mud among the hard straight shadows of the hulks down to the shoreline and the cargo skiffs. Young men and men with bags of tools were being of-fered papers on which to thumb their signatures of agreement: travel for free across one ocean, work for free for one year. That was the deal, no arguments. Show your thumb or show your heels. Pretty girls were being flirted with and told how much richer, cleaner, and hand-somer the men were on the far side of the ocean. A good-looking woman could have three husbands over there if she wanted to.

Almost everybody else was being marked in red—a large cross on both arms—and turned away. They went back to the body of the crowd, crestfallen but ready to try again (once they'd scratched away all evidence of red), though next time with a different story or a dif-ferent hat or more convincing tears.

Margaret did not see the guard approaching. He was almost in-visible against the mud in his dark uniform. He had hold of her wrist—checking for a blue tick, perhaps—before she noticed him, and for a moment her cry of alarm made her the center of attention for the front rows of the crowd. They saw her being pulled down from her metal perch and heard his gibberish commands that she should move away and put an end to her mopery. They saw her being roughly sent back to the riverbank, though she was more prodded than kicked by the guard's boot. When finally, out of reach, she threw a scoop of mud at him, the unsuccessful emigrants cheered for her. It didn't matter that her missile had fallen short by a dozen paces. They were just glad that someone other than themselves had shown a little reckless fortitude. Throwing mud was not the most persuasive application for a berth.

At least now, during this brief celebrity, strangers were returning Margaret's greetings with a smile of recognition. "Good work, sister," they called out, especially the ones whose failure was already marked in red. And, "Step a little closer next time." So she was able to get replies to her questions from those rejected families who were peeling off the back of the crowd, despondent, bewildered, and angry. "They say we have to wait until the summer for the family ships," one woman told Margaret, rubbing at her arm with spittle but seeming to make no impact on the dye. "These sailings are for workers only. They'll take my sons at once, but won't touch me." It was the same story that Margaret had heard from Joanie: mother and son, wife and husband, divided. Another said that she had heard that there were already family sailings farther down the coast, in a much larger port with thirty boats a month for emigrants—"Only a three- or four-day walk, if you can afford the services of a pathfinder to show the best route. They'll take everybody there. Women. Kids. Dogs, they say. We're packing up and moving on today, if we can get our horses back."

Margaret listened to their plans but recognized the bleakness in their voices. They were exhausted by their disappointment. Now they had to split their families or move on to another place or stay here for the season, living on salt and wind. She turned around and walked back toward the woods and the coastal path. She wouldn't waste a moment standing in that line, just to have her hopes and patience crossed out in red. A woman with a child and nothing to her name except a set of spy pipes would never be accepted on those boats. There had to be another dream.

No sooner had she made up her mind to return at once to Jackie and Franklin than she found an even better reason to hasten away from the anchorage. There, among the abandoned carts, just a few paces off, sitting on a crate and wearing the green-and-orange woven top that Margaret's sister had made, was Melody Bose, looking very cross indeed.

Margaret only just remembered to retrieve the spy pipes as she hurried up the path. She used them when she reached the spot where the two women from the fishing cottages had enhanced themselves for work. She focused the pipes on the carts and then the crowd and then the market area and then the encampments, but she could not see her stolen top or any further sign of Melody. She spotted the two women, though, standing by the horse corral, dwarfed by three mounted men in quarrelsome dress, their beards tied with ribbons. One had what looked like a severed hand dangling from his saddle as a trophy. Behind them, turning his horse impatiently and calling to his comrades to hurry up, was Captain Chief, unmissable and unmistakable—as Melody had been—in his stolen clothes, a flag to the eyes in goatskin.

"Back already? Quick work. No tick or cross, I see," said Joanie when the dogs barked Margaret's return to the cottages. "I'll walk with you a little way. I like the company of someone new." So the two of them continued up the rise into the higher dunes above the shore, with four or five of the dogs running ahead of them. "We understand each other now," Joanie said. "You've seen how it is down at the anchorage. There's no way out of here for women like us. Now you know how truthful I've been with you."

"There are other ships and other ports. Ships for families. Farther down . . ."

Joanie chuckled. "Ha, so they claim. That's what they want you to believe. They don't want you hanging around this anchorage, causing trouble, spreading discontent. They'll say, 'That's it, my darling jetsams, we'll take care of your husband and your strapping sons. Leave them here in our good hands. Now off you go, down south. Good girls. There's boats with fur-lined cabins waiting for the married women there, and all the old folks and the kids.' And when you arrive at the next port, well, it's all the same old dance. No moms and kids. No grandparents. 'Try even farther south for better luck.' You swallow that? Well, more fool you. You'll be chasing south until you run out of south and start coming up the other side until there's no north left, and still you won't have found a ship that'll let you board. At this rate, in a season or two there'll be more turn-me-downs on the shores and beaches of this country than there are gulls, I promise you. There'll be no standing room. They'll all be scrapping over bits of kelp and sleeping on one leg. No, listen to me, Margaret. Margaret, isn't it? Your husband, is he fit and strong?"

Margaret nodded, smiled, held her hand above her head. "He's this tall, as strong as a bear. He's big and beautiful."

"What kind of man is he?"

"He's shy, I think, and not uncaring, and—"

Margaret could have made a better list, but Joanie quickly interrupted her. "Well, then, you are unfortunate," she said. She took Margaret by the upper arm. Too fierce a grip, tighter even than the black-uniformed guard's. "Listen to me, sweet. If you're sensible, you'll go back to your shy and not uncaring man and you'll lie to him. Tell him that there are no ships, or that the berths are full, or that men have got to have their balls cut off before they're let on board. Say anything except the truth. Because as soon as he knows that they're looking for anyone with muscles and hardly anyone with breasts, he won't be shy of leaving you behind. Your man will take the ship and leave you here, leave you with your little girl. Trust me. And you'll encourage him, because you love the man, you want him to be free. Women are such knuckleheads."

"I do love him," Margaret said, her voice unexpectedly small.

"Will you love him when he's gone? Will you love him when there is no loving to be had?"

Margaret did not know the answer. She only felt tight-chested and angry. She tried to shake the woman off, but Joanie pressed her face close to Margaret's and said, "Let him go, then. Come to us. We'll find a place for you. You're a handsome woman, in your way. Now just suppose, when you get back to him, your husband wants to take the ships. No one wishes that on you, but just suppose that he's gone and you're alone. Then come back here and we can find a place for you, a bed for you, so long as you're prepared to work with us and do your share. We'd have to dye your hair, of course. Some men are fearful of the red. We'd have to find you better clothes. You understand? Come to us. Come to us."

Finally the woman let her go, although the dogs stayed with Margaret for a little while before returning to their owners and their suppers and their fires. Margaret hurried on, running almost. She was soon breathless from exertion and anxiety. But she slowed her steps when she could see the cabins and the flock of frenzied gulls. She needed time to think. She speeded up again only when she could smell the meat.

In that gap between seeing the cabins and reaching them, Margaret made up her mind. She could not lie to Franklin, no matter how persuasive Joanie's advice had been. He was not hers to lie to. He was not her husband, not her lover, not the father of the child. She had no hold on him. He had set out all those months ago with his brother, Jackson, with little else in mind, like most men of his age, except to reach the coast and sail toward a better life. The fact that for . . . what, three or four days? they had traveled together in the fall and then escaped together for a couple more in the spring was hardly reason to imagine she had some call on him. No, she would explain the situation to him frankly and openly, and offer no opinion or advice. She would not mention Melody Bose, though, if she could help it. The shame, the sin, the cowardice, the selfishness of not having gone up to the woman with news of Jackie, *Bella*—the girl's birth name seemed hard to use . . . Well, such an offense against nature was too great to disclose to anyone. That surely was a heavy sin, to have been so casual with the heartache of a grandmother. For an uncomfortable moment, and not for the first time, Jackie seemed to Margaret to be not so much a child who had been rescued as a child who had been stolen. Such theft, such wickedness, could not be confirmed to Franklin—not for the time being, anyway.

She would, though, have to mention to him that glimpse through the spy pipes of Captain Chief and the presence, on that day at least, of so many armed horsemen. She'd have to tell him, too, about the severed, flapping hand and how she'd felt instinctively that it had once belonged to one of Franklin's escaped comrades from the labor gang.

Most important, what could she say about their chances of ever going offshore together, other than the callous truth? Yes, there were several large oceangoing boats at the anchorage taking emigrants, and fit young men like Franklin were welcome on them. He could trade free passage for work at journey's end. She herself—unmarried, young, a virgin still, and not entirely without appeal, she hoped—could travel, too, probably, "Though you'll think me vain for saying so." Free passage in exchange for making herself available as a bride and housewife to some stranger speaking gibberish (and kicking her).

But there was Jackie to consider. And Jackie was her main concern now. A woman with a child of that age would not be welcome on the ship. That was certain. She'd seen it with her own eyes. Mothers had to stay on shore.

These were their choices, then. No choices, actually. She rehearsed exactly what she'd say: "We'll have to bid farewell to you, Franklin. I know you owe it to yourself and to your brother to take this chance of escaping from America, of getting out to sea." She understood entirely, she would say. She could not blame him for being a strong, tall man. She wished him well in his travels and endeavors. But she would stay behind with Jackie. That was her duty and that was her desire. "But you . . ." No, she would not dare to call him Pigeon. "But *you* should cross that ocean with an easy heart, because there's some good news to go along with the bad. I've already found a home for myself and Jackie. I've found some sisters just along the coast. They'll not take men, but I can live and work with them. They promised it." She would not explain what that work might be. She could hardly admit it to herself, although she was so inexperienced in that regard that the prospect of being intimate with strangers and paid for it was only a little less alien and unimaginable, and probably more likely, than that she would ever be intimate with a man—the man—she loved.

Now, in that final approach to the cabins, Margaret considered Franklin's possible responses: that he would not feel easy abandoning her and Jackie, that they should travel south just in case there really were some family ships ready to take them all, that maybe they should wait until later in the season of migration, by which time passage requirements might have loosened. She would say, "It isn't safe for you to stay. You're already a hunted man. If you care for me and Jackie at all, you'll go. Disguise yourself and go. Our lives will be safer once you've gone." She might then step forward, throw her arms around him, lift her face toward his. "Do what you know you must," she'd say, and close her eyes.

In her toughest and most rational recesses, she expected and she feared that he would simply blush and protest unconvincingly before announcing a bit too readily that yes, her advice was sensible. He would have to take the ship. And Margaret, to tell the truth, was already angry with him, for his good fortune and for his selfishness.

In fact, when at dusk she eventually pushed back the door of the cabin, she was too startled by Franklin's bloodstained hands and sleeves to wonder at the kitchen smells, the newly set fire, the lantern light, let alone speak her well-rehearsed arguments and lines. Maybe it would be sensible to observe the best traditions by waiting for the water to boil on the grate before voicing her difficult news or speaking ill of anyone at the anchorage.

It was as if she had returned as an adult to some untroubled place from her childhood. All was well. Jackie was sitting up happily on their makeshift bed, playing with some brightly painted fishing floats. She raised her hands to Margaret when she recognized her and cried out the sweetest greeting. And Franklin seemed too excited by his domestic achievements of the day and too pleased to see her for Margaret to destroy his boyish pleasure yet with her heavy news and her *no choices*. So she let him show her how he'd fashioned a firestick from the snapped end of a fishing rod and a bowstring and coaxed a flame in a handful of dried grass, how he'd slaughtered and butchered the larger of the horses, how he would use the smokeshop to produce jerky that evening, as soon as it was safe to make that amount of smoke, how he'd settled Jackie and her stomach with horsemeat grilled and made into a broth, how he'd made lamp fuel from fish oil and animal fat, how he'd prepared a feast of meat for Margaret to welcome her back from her journey. He even kissed her on her hand and pulled her to the fireside. "You see?" He was so happy with himself.

Once they had eaten and Jackie had been rocked to sleep, Margaret told him everything by lantern light, watching his face for any sign, any hint, that this would be their final night. But oddly, he seemed almost relieved to hear her news. "We'll have to stay," he said. "If they won't have us, we have to stay."

"They will take you. You've dreamed of it."

"They won't take me unless they let me keep whatever company I want. I won't leave you and Jackie. What kind of person do you think I am? We'll stay. That's it. We'll stay right here. I like it here. I'll be a fisherman. I'll plow some fields. We've still got one horse left."

"You know we can't stay here. It's dangerous. You can't hide all the time, and one day you'll be recognized. The tall man with the funny laugh." She looked at him and grinned, despite the warnings she was offering. "And then you won't have any choice about keeping whatever company you want. You'll be back in the labor gang again. Or else they'll make you dig a hole in the ground for yourself."

"Or feed me to the gulls."

What she said was true, of course. "We can't stay here," she summarized. "We can't go onward. And we can't go back."

"Now that's what my ma used to call a box without a lid," Franklin said. "There's no way in, there's no way out." And then, after a long silence, "Why not?"

"Why not what?"

"We can't stay here. We can't go forward, you say. But why can't we go back? You'll think me crazy, though, if I even mention it. I think I'm crazy myself." He straightened up, took a deep breath, and then reached over and took Margaret's hand. "I can't explain what's happening inside my head. It's full of bees. I can't think straight."

"Go on, Pigeon. Try to say." She wrapped her fingers in his.

"My mother's calling me," he said. "That's what I've thought about. Laying that fire. Keeping this little cabin in good heart. Waiting to hear you pulling back the door so we could eat. Everything I've done for you today, I used to do for her. But I'll not abandon you and Jackie like I turned my back on Ma. So long as I draw breath, I'll never forget her staying in the house so she wouldn't have to wave us goodbye. I shouldn't have left her there. I shouldn't have. I should've had more strength. It's right, what you say. I have dreamed of getting on the sailboat and making a new life for myself. But ever since Jackson died or disappeared, I've had two taller dreams. I've dreamed of finding him again. I've dreamed of walking back onto our land, poor though it is, and taking care of Ma. Those are my biggest dreams. They're bigger dreams than getting on a ship, I'll tell you that."

That night, well fed and warm for once, a little bilious, smoky-eyed, but somehow calm, they thought through Jackson's madcap dream more carefully. Good sense demanded that they move away, out of the orbit of the rustlers, far from Captain Chief (and far from Melody Bose). Franklin's life might depend on it (and so might Jackie's). Good sense demanded that they at least should check out other anchorages farther down the coast. They'd traveled such a distance already. What difference could a few more days make? Good sense demanded that they keep away from those badlands they'd already escaped from, the lawless highway and the debris fields, the junkle and the plains of scrap, the deadly lanes of Ferrytown, the treacherous mountain paths unsuited to anything but goats, the acid earth of Franklin's family farm, the taints and perils of America. But there was no excitement in good sense, and no romance. Sometimes it was wiser to be unwise. Only the crazy make it to the coast, and only the crazy make it back again. That was the wisdom of the road: you had to be crazy enough to take the risks, because the risks were unavoidable. So they came to talking hungrily of heading west, of being less than sensible, of turning their backs against the sunrise and the ocean, of being homeward bound.

But during the night, when Margaret, woken by a wet-legged Jackie, was cleaning up and drying the girl by candlelight, she felt less sure. All she could imagine was Franklin lost again, punished for his loyalty to her. Franklin being led away by Captain Chief. Franklin being set upon by bandits. Franklin being taken as a slave. Whatever happened, she decided, they would not make the same mistake as on the journey eastward, by following the highway. They'd stay on the back ways, living off the countryside, not begging from the few remaining homesteaders unless they had no other choice. Perhaps it would be best to travel at night. That would be possible if the skies were clear, especially as they still had one horse to help with Jackie

and their few possessions. At least by night her tall man would be almost invisible and not vulnerable to any gang master who wanted
some free labor. Yes, that would be their biggest problem, making
Franklin almost invisible. She dreamed of it. She dreamed of
Franklin being what he couldn't be, short and unexceptional.

Margaret woke earlier than Jackie and Franklin, as usual, and
rather than disturbing them just lay on her back watching the inside
of the cabin take shape and listening a little nervously to the ocean,
the wind, the sunup birds, the breathing at her side. She stretched her
legs and flexed her muscles, feeling well, if just a little stiff. She
cleaned her teeth with her nails and wiped her eyes clear of sleep. She
pushed her hands through her hair and wondered if it would be possible, now that they had fire, to heat a little water. She hadn't washed
or even combed her lengthening hair for several days. She was
ashamed of it. What must she look like to her faithful Franklin?

Then she had it. An idea.

The best protection for their journey west. The answer to the
biggest problem that they faced. Now nobody would bother them.
Franklin would be safe, for all his size and strength.

Margaret rolled out from under their saddle blanket and found
the toolbox. There was hardly enough light yet to see each item
clearly, but she could feel them. The gutting knife, still sticky from
the horse's blood. The implements they could not recognize. The
mallet and the skillet. Some loops of string. She felt what she was
hunting for, caught in the corner of the box. The fillet blade. She
pulled it out by its bone handle. The metal cutting edge was sharp.
After the attentions of a decent whetstone or a leather strop—and she
was certain she could find something suitable—the edge of this blade
would soon be dangerous. She'd always been the one at home in Ferrytown to sharpen tools, so she was confident. Yes, this would do. As
soon as Franklin was awake and she had warmed some water, she'd
shave her man, from head to toe. She'd make him look truly dangerous for once. He would become an outcast with the flux.

It was a strange experience, painstaking and embarrassing. Margaret's hands were shaking at first, possibly because she had gripped the fillet blade so tightly and for so long when she was stropping it on one of the horse leathers, but also because Franklin was lying on their bed with his hands behind his head, like a lover. Satisfied. He had started out standing, and she had kneeled at his feet, first softening the hairs on his legs with water and then shaving them with upward movements of the blade, against the nap. But almost at once she nicked him. Just two tiny cuts. The blood spread alarmingly on his damp skin and her hands began to shake even more. So she started again, with better light. "Lie on your back," she said. "Then I can reach you more easily."

Margaret shaved both lower legs first, holding on to Franklin's feet with one hand and cutting with the other. His hair was black but wispy there, on his calves and ankles, and only became more unruly and patternless toward his thighs. She did not shave far above his knees, just the full span of her fingers and no further. These lower parts of his long legs seemed common property and safe. Out of harm's way. A man could show his legs this high to strangers and seem openhearted rather than immodest. But any higher and the intimacy would be too great for strangers.

Margaret kept her movements prim and did not speak. She wanted to appear dispassionate and concentrated on her task. There was, though, ardor in her heart. Just touching him in all his public places was such an unexpected pleasure. The hollows and the mounds, the muscles and the sinews, the rough male skin. Her fingers followed the blade.

Her thoroughness would have to recognize its limits, though. Franklin let her shave his back and chest and every last part of his arms, from the wiry hairs on the back of his knuckles to the tangled, wet, and gingery hairs in his armpits. But he became less comfortable when Margaret started on the mass of hairs around his nipples. He had to hold her leg to steady himself. His breathing became restless.

His eyeballs rolled. His eyelids dropped. "Are you okay?" she asked. He nodded, couldn't speak. He cried out only once and let out a deep sigh, when Margaret was tugging up the hairs below his belly button to cut them as short as she could. She thought she'd cut him, though there was no blood so far as she could see. But she could soon tell what was troubling him. Indeed, it now was just a finger span away from her cutting hand. Franklin was excited by her touch. That was something new—alarming and interesting. So her impulses were both to stare and to look away. "Margaret," he said. And then a little later, "Margaret," again. And then, "Mags, Mags."

Margaret said nothing. She just busied herself, making sure that all the visible parts of his body were as clean and smooth as her tools would allow. It was up to him, not her, if this resulted in anything other than shaving. If Franklin had reached out his hand and pulled her to him, she would have fallen on him happily. If he had taken her hand and pushed it farther down his body under his clothes and into the hair that modesty had said she should not touch or cut, she would have allowed it, for surely it was time for her to take that risk. She would have welcomed taking such a risk.

When Franklin had said so forcefully the day before that he would stay with her and Jackie no matter what, Margaret had known for sure that, given time but as undoubtedly as water runs downhill, they must be man and wife. So even though he was once again too shy and hesitant—too cowardly, perhaps—to take advantage of her shaving him by making love to her, Margaret did not really mind. What was the hurry, after all? They'd not be parting. She could let him take his time, no matter how curious she was about the shadows of his body, no matter how great her desire to kiss him had become, no matter that she herself felt both breathless and light-headed to be so close to all of him. Her bladder seemed to press on her. Her skin felt red and prickly. Her tongue was active in her mouth.

But for all that intimacy, it was the shaving of Franklin's head and face that was for Margaret the most disturbing and surprising. She cut away to find a double crown. A bad-luck sign, as much as red hair was. She loved him all the more. By shaving it, she made it disappear.

At last she stepped back to find she had revealed a teenage face and a boy's head. The gap between their ages, already a caution for her, widened into a chasm. Not six years now but twenty. It was so unusual to see the bare face of a man and his cropped skull that for a moment she was frightened. Franklin's features seemed so large, his expression so undisguised, his skin so shockingly pale and vulnerable, so convincingly sickly, as if the ruse of shaving had actually delivered him the flux. He seemed more natural as well. In a way, this was more like Franklin. It explained his nervousness, his blushing bashfulness, that womanly laugh, those indecisive hands, his fear of taking risks, his failure—yet—to kiss her. He had not quite grown out of being young.

"If only you could see yourself," she said, and laughed finally. A laugh of disappointment and understanding. This "boy" could be her son.

"I can feel it." Franklin ran his hand around his face and head and in a circle around his lips. "My mouth feels strange. Huge ears."

"You look like a boy. A giant boy. A giant pink boy, with flux. The worst case of the flux I've ever seen. No one will want you now." Her two-crowned beauty boy.

Margaret and Franklin were not sorry to wave the ocean goodbye. They'd laid their eyes on it, witnessed its implacable size, its anger, its serenity, and that was enough for the time being. For a lifetime, probably. The ocean was best as a memory or as a prospect. They could not imagine living with it as a neighbor. The noise would send them crazy. Besides, they'd have to watch the sail ships coming in and going out, packed with dreaming emigrants, and be reminded all the time of the distance they had traveled and the dangers they had met, and all without purpose. The ocean, unending to the eye, would serve only to tell again how lost they were, how desolate and damned they might become if they stayed put.

They started out before sunup, to be sure of getting into and beyond the environs of Tidewater before many people were around. Certainly before any horsemen from the rustlers' encampment had begun their day. The panniers of the little mare were not quite large enough to provide a riding basket for Jackie, so Franklin had cut the sides of one pannier and let it out, enlarging it with trawl netting and securing it with ropes. He'd cut two holes for Jackie's feet and legs, and Margaret had made a pillow out of net. The girl would travel like a queen. The other half of the pannier was filled to the same weight as the girl with strips of fumed horseflesh, the best of the fisherman's tools, the spy pipes, a good supply of water, some tinder, fish oil, and the firestick and fire bow that Franklin had made.

They headed north for a short distance and then set their route and their hopes toward the west, taking it in turns to lead. They were too cold and concentrated to talk, though not too cold to smile. Soon the wind and sun would come up at their backs and press them onward, deep into America.

❖ sixteen ❖

Franklin had not forgotten the damage he'd inflicted on the concealed wooden bridge at Ferrytown, or the exhilaration he had felt at cutting through its greasy mooring ropes and seeing it slump and slither down the river's high banks to break up in the water. But he had put it to the back of his mind as important only to the past. He'd not expected to reencounter it or to be so embarrassed and inconvenienced by his handiwork. He'd meant only to prevent the flames of Ferrytown skipping across the bridge like imps.

"Some idiot has cut it," Margaret said, holding up the docked end of the tethering, which was still hanging loose from its tree trunk, each strand and ligament too cleanly cut to be the work of nature. "Now what?"

Franklin shook his head. He did not want to lie to her, but even so he did not see the point in identifying the idiot. He might admit to it once they had crossed the river. If that were ever possible. He had persuaded himself on their journey back to Ferrytown that somehow the wooden debris of the bridge would still be scattered at the bottom of the gulch and that all he'd have to do was clamber down the coulee and use the remaining timber to pull himself through the rapids or, if fortune was entirely on his side, as a set of steps. Apart from that severed end of rope in Margaret's hand, though, the only evidence that there had ever been a bridge was a dangling trail of greening rope and timber on the far and western side of the river. No help to them. But easy to see, because the fires in Ferrytown had done exactly what Franklin had feared. The imps had climbed the river bluffs between the houses and the lake and consumed what once had been thick undergrowth but now looked like a forest of smoke-black antlers with just the first green signs of spring showing on the ground.

There was no easy path down from the bridge to the point where the ferry used to put ashore. No one had ever worn a passage. So Margaret carried Jackie on her back while Franklin went ahead with the mare, crashing through the dry waste and bushes and beating back the more resistant undergrowth with a stick. It took all afternoon, and Franklin's arms and face were raw with blood and scratches by the time they stopped to set up camp for the night. They had reached the low bluffs at the river's farthest limits. Below them were the marshes, vapory and gray, and beyond them, though hardly visible in the afternoon's retreating light, the last remains of the log boardwalk that had led up from the gravel landing beach through levees of sediment and saved the ferry passengers from a drenching first foot contact with the east.

Margaret and Franklin's journey from the coast had been slower but more comfortable than either of them had had the right to hope. It had seemed as natural and inevitable as swimming upstream does for a salmon. They no longer felt defeated by America, as most emigrants had on the journey out, driven eastward by their failings. The mare had proven to be a sturdy companion, eager and accommodating, especially when persuaded by Franklin's switch to brisk up her pace a bit rather than indulge her weaknesses for browsing and flagging. She repaid him with a session of nickering and some petulant shaking of her tail, but beyond that she was mostly, tooth and hoof, a neat, high-bred, dignified horse. However, she was used to being a riding mount, not a pack animal. Now she was required to tolerate bulky burdens—not only the increasingly fretful and impatient Jackie in her pannier and the second, balancing pannier stuffed full of fumed horsemeat but also a long net bag thrown over her haunches and containing anything useful—the toolbox, pieces of leather—that Margaret and Franklin could find. They'd come equipped as well with good materials for a tent. The cabins had not been short of canvas, fishing poles, rope, and netting.

Each morning Franklin strapped these cargoes as tightly as he could onto the mare, correcting any tendency to overtip or slew to one side with stone weights. But she was not used to carrying so inert a load and did her best, if not watched closely, to scrape against a tree trunk and bring the net bag off her haunches and even, occasionally, to buffet Jackie and the panniers.

Still, life for her was better with this family than it had ever been with the rustlers, so she had few excuses for complaint. The mare might have had greater cause to protest had either of the adults chosen to saddle her, but they had not. They had walked at her side, tugging at her lead only when the way ahead was narrow or they were fording water. Except for one tough day, when they had had no choice but to pick their way across the collapsed, bothersome, and puzzlingly extensive remains of an antique town, a sterile basin of cracked concrete, rubble, and building slabs from the old country, the land provisioned them. There was no lack of fresh water at that time of the year, and it was not necessary to beg for food or shelter. They had everything (except variety). There was no reason to seek out strangers. On those few occasions when they passed through farmland or a hardscrabble outpost where a few stalwarts had yet to emigrate, or when they chanced on bands of travelers, all Franklin had to do was show his shaven chin and head, and everyone would keep

a distance. The worst that people would do was shout or, occasionally, throw a stone or a fistful of earth, not to cause any lasting harm
but more to urge the flux to hurry out of sight.

Margaret and Franklin had cause to be genuinely alarmed just
once. A gang of men on foot, trappers or landlopers by the looks of
them, approached their camp one night, after dark, attracted by the
smell of meat and the firelight and the opportunity to steal a decent
horse. Franklin challenged them while they were a few paces off, but
still they came forward. Margaret took Jackie out of sight, under canvas, and shushed her. But no sooner had the leading man seen
Franklin's head and noted his size than he and his companions lost
any appetite they had for supper and theft. They disappeared into the
night a little more swiftly than they had approached. You wouldn't
even want to murder someone with the flux. A splash of blood and
you were dead. Even bruising your fists on such a sick man's chin was
dangerous.

Margaret and Franklin took more care from then on to pitch their
camp somewhere concealed, and they learned to sleep with one eye
working. Otherwise, the journey back proved kinder than their journey out had been. It was as if the country that had once been hostile
to them was regretful for it and was now providing recompense—
fewer dangers, warmer nights, softer going in a season that was
opening up rather than closing down. It even decorated the way with
early flowers. Margaret picked the largest and the prettiest, making
a chain for Jackie and lacing the horse's bridle.

"You'd better smell them when you pick them, Mags, town girl,"
Franklin said. He'd been taught by his mother to hold any picked
flower to his nose.

"So as not to waste the smell?" Margaret could see the sense in
that.

"No, it's because by smelling it you add a day to your life. Don't
smell it, and you throw a day away." So for an afternoon they enter-
tained themselves and kept Jackie amused by picking all the flowers
they could find, sniffing fragrances, amassing extra days.

Franklin and Margaret had grown accustomed to setting up a net-and-canvas home for the night and making fire. But they were tired of it. The journey had been wearying. Jackie had proved to be less accommodating and dignified than the mare. She was by now fourteen or fifteen months old and, like all normal children of that age, preferred freedom to discomfort and play to travel. She had enjoyed the pannier for half a day at most, but after that she kicked against it when they tried to load her in. Once confined, she wailed and screamed in protest on and off throughout the day. As soon as the mare's distressed breathing signified that they should stop for the night and Jackie was unloaded from her pannier, she became a toddling scamp, interfering with the tasks, getting too close to the fire or the mare's hoofs, tasting anything she had not encountered before, be it a beetle or a pinecone. She saw the erection of the tent as an opportunity to roll among the nets and canvases, despite the irritation of her adults, who wanted only supper and sleep.

But Jackie loved it when Franklin sang to her. His antics did not quiet her. On the contrary, they made her laugh and yell, but they did keep her in one place. It didn't matter that Franklin's voice was flat and tuneless and that he knew only three songs, one of them a little bawdy and the other two burial hymns. She clapped her hands and wrists with pleasure. His volume delighted her. She adored the way he matched the words with hand movements, drawing out or pinching off the notes with his fingers. Best of all were the moments when Margaret, exhausted by the travel and up till then too tired even to smile, let alone play, could not stop herself from bursting out with laughter. "Pigeon, that's terrible," she'd say. And, "Stop, stop, stop! You idiotic boy." He *was* a boy. Or drunk. Just look at him. No gravitas. (It was a pity, though, she thought, how quickly his beard was growing back. She'd never had the chance to kiss his chin and throat before they were masked again by hair.)

If they were lucky, Franklin's singing would wear their daughter out. She'd laugh herself to sleep. And then Margaret and Franklin could wrap around each other, fully dressed, and make the best of nature's mattress before—too soon—the dawn, the damp, and the cold put an end to sleep and any dreams of deeper mattresses and wrapping around each other without clothes, when they were lovers and not pals.

But this would be their last night living rough. Tomorrow, if Franklin could find some way across the river, if they could find a house in Ferrytown that had survived the fire, they would be sleeping under rafters.

It was a comfort to be so close to Ferrytown at last, though what they might find there was frightening. If they had hoped for lights and smoke or any other evidence of habitation, they were disappointed. The only signs of life from the far bank that night were dogs calling out to each other and the thudding of the clouds as, coming east, they bounced their prows across the mountaintops.

It rained without regret from midnight to sunup. It was the kind of rain that farmers love, sweet-tasting, temperate, and long-lasting, heavy enough to soak the earth "down to its boots" but not so heavy as to wash the soil away—a good start to the spring. But for Franklin it was unwelcome, a setback. Margaret had said that the raft often grounded on the crossing, so the water would be relatively shallow. He had planned to cut himself a long stout pole with which to test the river's depth and then wade across to Ferrytown, from one shingle bank to the next. For once his height would be an advantage. And if the waters were too deep and strong at any point, he could lug one of the many pieces of dry timber that had been washed down over the winter, wedge its ends, and use it as a body bridge. Once on the other bank, he'd face the trickier problem of how to rescue Margaret and Jackie from the wrong side of the water.

As soon as the mist lifted and he and Margaret were ready to go across toward the place of her birth, it became clear that wading would not be possible. The river had swollen overnight and spread its near bank as far as the bluffs where they were camping. What had been swampy ground with a boardwalk of logs was now a lake with bays of trapped water. And what had been a river narrow enough for a skilled boy to catapult a nut across was now a wide and bubbling sinew of yellow water, so fast and strong that timber twice the length and weight of Franklin was being tumbled downstream as if it were straw.

"It'll pass," said Margaret.

"How long?"

"A day or two. Unless it rains again." She pushed a hand out of the shelter of their canvas. "It's raining now. A bit."

"I'll see how deep it is."

"We'll wait. We'll wait until it settles down again."

Franklin didn't want to wait. Any moment now and she would start to curse the idiot who'd cut down the bridge: "If it hadn't been for him, we'd all be over on the other side by now." Franklin was in a hurry to put that embarrassment behind him, to leave, in fact, all the errors and hardships of the previous fall and winter on the eastern shore of the river.

"I'll take the horse," he said. "Horses understand rivers."

But the little mare either knew too much or had grown lazy. She allowed Franklin to splash her through the shallow fringes of the river but refused even to try the first wide rapid that they met. She reared and tugged at him to go back to the bank.

He tried again, this time mounted on her back and determined to use his heels on her if she refused. The shingle fell away beneath her hoofs and Franklin found himself thigh deep in water, but the mare did not have the strength to swim against the current. She followed it a little way downstream but could not purchase any footing in shallower water until Franklin dismounted and led her out of the channels, swirling at his armpits, and up to safer ground. Margaret, waiting by the tent with Jackie and watching everything through her spy pipes, waved her arms and yelled at him to come away, but everything she said was drowned out by the din of water.

Franklin was too wet and cold to do much more that morning.

He dried out by a fire and watched the river gaining ground on them, spreading even farther east, as if it too were tired of flowing through America. "I'll go back to the bridge," he said.

"Ha, there is no bridge. You'll never cross it there."

"We've plenty of rope. Maybe I can build a new bridge."

"Who'll take the bridge across and secure it on the other side?" Franklin had to laugh, despite his impatience. "No, we'd be better off climbing up to the lake," she continued. "It's safe enough if you keep away from the cascades. We used to swim there when we were kids. My brother used to swim across and fish. Can you swim, Pigeon?"

"I don't know. I've never had to swim."

"Shall we find out?"

They found out in the afternoon, once they had taken down their tent, loaded the mare with all their possessions and the girl, and retraced the route that they had pioneered the day before, up to the bridging point. The water thundered through the narrow passage there, reaching up to snatch at anything loose. The air was heavy with spray. Again they had to break through undergrowth and snap their way through trees, before they came out onto a rocky promontory and could see a more placid expanse of water ahead of them.

The last time they had looked down on the lake had been the day that they had come down Butter Hill from the Pesthouse and fled from Ferrytown. Not a happy day. A day bursting with death. The lake had not stored any memories; it seemed expressionless and bland. Just heavy with itself. Indifferent to visitors. No sign of movement on its surface. Not a wave and not a bird, not a single ship, not a reflected sparkle. No bouncing light. Predictable. Unlike the ocean, it was not threatening. Its smell was not as salty or as bitter. If anything, it smelled a little sulfurous, the odor of an egg just boiled.

The lake's eastern banks, beyond the cascades where the fresh rainwater crashed into the valley, were swampy and thick with reeds but unavoidable. If this was what lay between them and Ferrytown, the quicker they took it on, the better.

It would have been prudent simply to have bided their time on the east side of the river until the waters dropped. But they were being tugged and pushed to cross. Margaret particularly needed to discover at once what had happened to her town and to her family compound. She needed, too, to find a place to rest. Tenting was hard work. The journey might have been eventless, but it was still exhausting. And more than that, she understood that nothing could progress between herself and Franklin until their travels were allowed to pause. She wanted more than anything to settle on one place, a place where they were neither hungry nor afraid. The heart prefers tranquillity. Besides, they could not let the dangers of the crossing paralyze them and persuade them to defer the challenge. Courage. Onward. Wade.

Their greatest fear was losing Jackie in the water. To drown the mare would not be an impossible setback. She was in principle a stolen mare, after all. They had not dared to love her, despite the services she'd provided without much complaint. They had not even dared to name her yet. Even to lose all of their possessions, swallowed by the lake, would not be such a tragedy. They had become used to making do on very little, and apart from the spy pipes, now tied on a thong around Margaret's neck, everything they had ever truly valued—the goatskin coat, the pot of mint, the green-and-orange woven top, the cedar box of talismans—had been lost or stolen ages ago.

The girl was helpless, though. She could walk boldly now. Her legs and back had straightened. She was strong and hard to frighten. But she had never crossed a lake before. Certainly she could not swim. If anything went wrong—the mare bolted or drowned, say, or the currents split them up, or there was sudden shelving where the water became too deep and icy—the two adults might be able to struggle ashore, but what chance would Jackie stand? They protected her against the cold with as many layers of clothes as they could find and then packed her in the pannier as loosely as they dared. Franklin beat the vegetation in his path with a stick, to flush out any snakes or snappers and warn off any bears. Margaret followed with the mare. The mud around the reeds was black and deep. It released thick bubbles and a stench like rotten potatoes as they pushed through it. It was almost a relief to reach the open water where the vegetation stopped.

This time the horse was not resistant. There was no roar of water and hardly any current to frighten her. She was confident, even eager. She waded in, not shying at the sudden cold.

Margaret and Franklin were less agile in the lake. The night of rain was not sufficient to do much more than skim the bone-aching chill off the season's meltwater. At least the water was not especially deep at first. But all too soon the ground beneath their feet and hoofs began to shelve away, and the water was up to their chins and had filled the horse's panniers, so that even Jackie, who had seemed excited rather than unnerved up to that point, began to shout and scream, shocked by the water and the cold. Luckily the mare could swim well, though slowly. She did not try to turn around and gain the bank that they had just abandoned. Some logic told her that her chin would lead her to the other side, and so she followed it, pushing her lower lip through the lake, her nostrils closing and flaring as she tried to find a way of taking in good lungfuls of air but not shipping too much water.

Margaret and Franklin held on to the horse's lead, one on each side, doing their best to avoid whatever she was doing with her legs beneath the water and trying not to add any extra weight to her efforts. They found a way of lying on their sides in the water, so their mouths and noses were not submerged, and kicking out. Pockets of air trapped in their clothes provided a little buoyancy and some protection against the cold. But their hearts and lungs became increasingly agitated. And they were panicking. They were so low in the water that soon all of the banks had disappeared from view. They could not be sure if they were making progress or merely making circles. Their limbs were aching from the cold, and Jackie had gone quiet inside her pannier, her big eyes open and permanently startled.

Thank goodness for the mare. Thank goodness Franklin hadn't butchered her, back at the fishermen's cabins. She knew the way across the lake. She could feel the tug of water to her left, where it was pulled toward the drop of the cascades, and she simply kept the tug on that side, so that inevitably, if there was any pattern to the universe, she was bound to find the other bank. Again there was a mass of mud and reeds to conquer, but they pushed through fearlessly. The water drained out of the panniers. The worst was at their backs.

Oddly, they felt colder once they came out of the water than they'd felt when they were immersed in it up to their throats. Their clothes weighed heavier than wood. And they all, including the mare, were shivering uncontrollably. They needed to get down to shelter and to fire, or they would catch a fever. Jackie's skin was blue. Her lips were purple. They lifted her out of her pannier and cuddled her, though neither Margaret nor Franklin yet had much warmth to offer. The horse shook herself, sending great loops of water out of the panniers and the sodden net bag on her back.

Once they'd found a way around the lake and reached the cascades, the path down into Ferrytown was familiar, though easier to negotiate now that there was little undergrowth (and no need to transport Margaret in a wheelbarrow). First they passed the bridge point and then they proceeded through the forest of burned antlers that they'd inspected from the eastern bank the day before.

Soon they reached the dry, rocky ledge where Margaret had rested on the day that Franklin went back to her home to collect her few possessions. The fruit trees there were little more than charred stumps. But somehow the wooden bench and fishing platform had survived the fire. Now they had open views across the town. It was wise, despite their aching bones and chattering teeth, to make sure that the place was safe. Margaret pulled up her spy pipes to look for any signs of horses or fires or strangers, or even evidence of someone that she recognized from her community. Lifting the pipes to her eyes had become a joy for her. It clarified the world. It made her young. But now the pipes seemed to cloud the world even further than her unsatisfactory eyes had done. The pipes were full of water. She shook them, but that made little difference. All that distance, she thought to herself, all that agony, and still she couldn't see any better than the day they'd fled from Ferrytown.

Franklin studied what remained of the houses until he was satisfied that all the movements he could see were caused by nothing more sinister than the wind, the wild dogs, and the birds. There was no smoke, no sign of horses in what had been the tetherings. He listened, too. No voices. No tools. No creaking evidence of life. "I think it's safe," he said, though Margaret was disappointed at the news. She'd thought it might be possible that some old neighbor had survived, that there might be miracles.

They cut a lonely sight, the final family on earth, as they started across the flood-smoothed slopes between the river and the town. They'd reached the habitation of the dead. There must be ghosts. Their nervousness was palpable. Their steps were hesitant, especially when a pair of buzzards put up from the burned remains of the loft-houses, where the smaller boats had been stored, and dislodged a piece of black timber from the building's skeleton. Even the mare had toughened ears, twitching at imaginary flies. It was here that on that final day in Ferrytown the few late-coming emigrants had gathered, marooned between the water and the flames, and driven away shorn-headed Margaret and Franklin in his strange coat. It was here that Franklin had been cut by slingshot. Out in midstream, the last bones of the ferry raft, still protruding from the shingle where it had grounded itself, split the speeding waters, marking the flat expanse of the flooded river with chevrons of froth.

At last they reached the first of the buildings. Nothing now stood much higher than Franklin. The brick footings of the palisades had survived, and some of the older timbers had proved too tough for the flames and stood like sentinels. But all the other buildings—the men's dormitory, where Franklin had found his brother's shoes; the women's dormitory, where there had been three lines of beds, each with a pile of bright clothes hung over the end; the guesthouse hall with its dining tables; the barns, the yards, the kitchens, and the workshops of about two hundred families—were almost level with the ground. What little remained was scorched and blackened beyond recognition. Even the earth and the flagstones in the compounds were charred. The town was colorless.

Margaret did not pay much attention to her neighbors' homes. Her mind was fixed on family. She hardly stopped to look at the whitened, picked remains of the baker and his daughter, still lying on the steps of the oven house, their bony knees twisted by their sudden deaths, their sides pulled open by animals. They had been saved from the flames and denied their cremation by being caught in the open street. She hurried on, cradling Jackie in her arms, while Franklin followed with the mare.

Too soon she reached the outline of her own compound. She could have stepped across the destroyed outer fence, but habit and superstition made her keep to the old pattern and enter through the space where a wooden door had been. The last time she had entered it, her hair had been shorter than the nap on a gooseberry, and she had been too exhausted by the flux to walk. Franklin had carried her, piggyback, and then, once he had set her down, had had to find a stick and lend his arm to help her walk. Now she felt just as exhausted, but she was glad that Franklin had allowed her to meet her family alone—alone, that is, except for Jackie. He waited in the road outside with the horse, watching her but saying nothing. He could remember his last visit there as if it were yesterday: the barrow that he'd found, the food he'd salvaged from their larder and the list of clothes she'd given him, the smell of her possessions, his guilty looting of their chests and cupboards, the pot of mint he'd saved (and she had lost), the valuables, her comb and brush with their tangled knots of ginger hair. "Will I ever see her hair this long again?" he'd wondered at the time. He looked at her, and yes, by summer's end her hair was bound to reach her shoulders. He felt his own head and face.

There was stubble. A man's beard should be longer than a man's neck, he'd always been taught as a boy. Never bare your throat to strangers. And Franklin had been glad to have started a beard when he was relatively young, a teenager. It had almost masked his sudden reddeners.

Her courtyard seemed larger than Margaret remembered it. But then it had always been busy with equipment, animals, and family. Now every corner was clear, except for piles of wood ash, and the space had been enlarged at one side by the complete removal of the screened veranda. She found the courage to walk a little closer, although she could look only through half-closed eyes.

She saw what she had hoped for. There had been cremations for the family. Her brother's wooden cot had disappeared entirely, and what remained of him was just a few scorched bones. He'd not provided any meals for animals, and so he could hope to rest in peace. "Your uncle," Margaret said to Jackie. And then she went into the other "rooms," through fallen and blackened lintels, beams, and rafters. "That's your great-grandpa. And that's my ma. You would have loved my ma. That's big sister. That's Carmena's place. That's your other uncle and his dog." She had to think before she could remember its name. "It's Jefferson. You could have played with Jefferson. He was a ratter and a tough old dog, but he liked little girls."

They went across the courtyard, past the spot where their neighbors' dead white dove had tumbled to the ground, to the annex house. That had burned more completely than the other buildings in the compound. It had been the straw and wood room and so had almost volunteered to be destroyed by flames. Margaret waved her hand at it. This was more than she could bear. "In there was where your Auntie Tessie lived, and funny Glendon Fields, and their boy, Matt. You would have had a playmate, see," she said. But already she had turned away and was running back to Franklin and the mare.

Her tears came silently. No sobs. No shoulders heaving with the grief. She didn't want comforting. It was best that Franklin thought she was strong. She only muttered the burial lament to herself again and remembered how her home had been before the fire, even before she had closed her family's eyes and mouths, folded their arms in readiness, and covered their faces in their blankets. Instead she did her best to recall her single lasting memory of the voices and the smells of home when she'd been a child of Jackie's age. She could remember sitting on the floor, playing with a red ball her mother had stitched. A dog was barking. Her father came back from the river with a fish and made her reach to touch and smell the skin.

"You know we can't stay here, not even for the night," Franklin said, and then added, almost in a whisper, "Too many bones. Too many for the girl."

"I know." She didn't want to stay in Ferrytown a moment more. But she wasn't pessimistic. There was tomorrow and next year, there was the path in front of her and steps to take, but still she understood that as far as moving on from the family she'd lost in Ferrytown was concerned, there was no way ahead. Coming back had been a reckless thing to do, perhaps. She'd disturbed memories, ash memories. These were the only lasting survivors of the fire, except for those few scraps of metal implements she'd recognized: a pewter pot, the iron grate, the family kettle, dented and blackened, the sharp ends of a shovel and an ax, almost unmarked and uncompromised by the heat. What had the Baptists said? "Metal has brought death into the world. Rust and fire are God's reply." Well, God had not replied in Ferrytown. Metal was the only thing that God had not reduced to ash.

More unburned bodies were out in the tetherings, and even some stockades had escaped the fire untouched. The living beasts had feasted all the winter on the dead, and here there still were packs of feral dogs and one or two remaining turkey vultures tugging at the parchment skins and stiffened pelts of horses, mules, and donkeys, many with their skeletons still picketed to posts. Somewhere among them were the bones of Nash, the boy whose job it had been to guard the animals. Franklin thought of Jackson and his coat. Any hope he'd nourished that his brother had survived was now abandoned. No one who'd slept in Ferrytown could still be breathing air. But he hurried on toward the first slopes of the mountains, still hopeful in his heart. His mother might be waiting on her stoop. This year, possibly, or next, he would return himself to her. But first he had to find a roof under which he, Jackie, and Margaret could recuperate.

Soon they reached and passed through the thicket of junipers, laurels, and scrub oaks, which smelled sweet with spring. The last time they'd been there, the odors had been fungal and metallic. Now they could begin to climb their old acquaintance, Butter Hill.

The going up was easier than the coming down had been, for Franklin at least. On that fall day, Margaret had just evaded death's damp grip and Franklin had had to carry her, despite his painful knee. Every step had been a punishment. Now he walked ahead with Jackie and the mare, relishing the gradient. Every pace away from Ferrytown, away from the ocean, closer to home, was a reward. He sang his way uphill, inventing words and tunes for Jackie but glad to let the girl justify his sudden happiness so soon after their encounters in the town. But Margaret was silent. She kept her distance, preferring her own company. She was thinking more about the only time she'd been up Butter Hill before. That time she'd been collapsed across a horse's neck, weighed down by her blue scarf. (Whatever happened to that scarf? She'd lost so many things.) She'd been as heavy and inert as the net bag draped across this mare's haunches. She half remembered having to give way to descending travelers, her grandpa's voice excusing her, the midges feeding off the lesions on her face.

It was not until the afternoon, when finally the three of them crested the last rise on the path and looked across the flatter clearings of grass and highland reed toward the black-green woods and the high white peaks beyond, that she truly recognized the place. It hadn't changed, despite the bare branches and the blanched-out colors of the undergrowth. It was still a little warmer than the hillside path, its dips and hollows protected from the worst of the wind. It still appeared the safest acre in America, a place of remedy and recovery where surely they could at least spend the night, or spend the month, or spend eternity

"So this is it?" she called out to her family in front. An exclamation and a question.

Franklin turned around and smiled at her, his oversized, boyish face and his shaven head reddened by the sun, not blushing. He laughed with happiness, his long arms flapping like a girl's. He pointed to the forest. "Margaret," he said.

And there it was, just as it was, the little soddy where she'd first met Franklin, the sun-dried turfs, the chimney stack, the boulder walls—the Pesthouse, where her eyes had almost closed for good.

❧ seventeen ❧

Now good fortune showed its face to these four travelers, the man, the woman, the child, the horse, which had finally earned the name of Swim. The Pesthouse was not exactly as they'd left it. Franklin pulled aside the barricade of planks that served as a door, and after he had struck the lintel a few times with his stick to scare off any snakes, he stooped to look inside. There were no smoke fumes, for a start. The grate had not been used for months, evidently. Some of the hut's turfs had collapsed inward. There was pellet evidence of mice and rats. He looked toward the sleeping bench, half expecting to see the ghostly form of Margaret lying there, the bald round head of someone very sick and beautiful. But what he saw, tucked between the bed and the wall, virtually hidden, was just as thrilling and unnerving. His heart missed several beats. Three lucky things inside a cedar box.

By evening they'd sorted out the place, made fresh bedding, started up a fire, dug in the reeds for water, found a little forage for the mare. There even was a stub of candle they could use, a stub of candle that they had left behind themselves. Margaret could sit with its light spread out across her lap and clean the tarnish from her silver necklace. She could revive the color in her finely woven piece of cloth by rubbing off the green-blue mold. She could acquaint herself again with coins from a past when Abraham sat on his great stone seat and the eagle spread its wings. She could not help thinking, too, about everything that she had lost: a family, a home, a length of hair, a green-and-orange woven top, a heavy scarf, a dream of living on a distant bank, a pot of mint that, if it had survived the Ark, if it had defied the cruelty, could not provide its aromatic leaves for her. Still, there was her Pigeon and her Jackie to take the place of everything. And there was Swim. What greater compensations could there be?

Franklin held on to her feet and watched her face, dancing and expressive in the candlelight. He loved her, yes. He loved her now without constraint. There was no urgency. He pushed his finger in between each toe. He rubbed her ankles and her heels. He felt the ridges of interrupted growth at the end of her toenails, evidence that she'd been ill and that her illness had almost grown out. Tomorrow he would find the gutting knife and pare the ridges off.

Margaret and Franklin spent a month inside the Pesthouse, waiting for their moment to arrive and letting a few of that year's early emigrants pass by unhindered. Dreamers do not want advice. Nothing the pair of them could say would make a difference to determined travelers. Let them go down to the coast and find out for themselves. Let them see how pitiless the ocean was. They watched as emigrants constructed a new raft on rope pulleys, tied to rocks and scorched tree trunks, so they could haul themselves across, into the remnants and the debris. They looked down on the little empty town, knowing that the sight of it was punishing. Mostly, though, they turned their backs against the east. Margaret finally succeeded in drying her spy pipes by the fire. She could see clearly once again—the western woods, the western hills, the distances.

The spring advanced itself. The girl began to walk with sturdy legs and say her first words, *Ma* and *Pa* and *Stop*. The winter cold retreated, holding sway only at night. And thunderclouds came eastward, throwing shade across the lake at Ferrytown and delivering the rain that had been lifted from the plains and prairies, from the hopes and promises, from the thicknesses and substances that used to be America and would be theirs. The couple knew they only had to find their strength. And then—imagine it—they could begin the journey west again. They could. They could imagine striking out to claim a piece of long-abandoned land and making home in some old place, some territory begging to be used. Going westward, they would go free.